Fateful Mornings

"Tom Bouman's tools . . . cut straight and true, in this riveting mystery about a good man caught in the ruined Eden of rural America."
—Julia Keller, Pulitzer Prize–winning author of *Sorrow Road*

"Bouman's tender portrait of a widower remaking his life infuses his crime fiction with a level of intimacy that is both rare and winning. I was happy to ride shotgun with Henry Farrell again."
—Attica Locke

"Everyone should be reading Tom Bouman."   —Nickolas Butler

"[A] haunting dissection of the broken heart of America."
—Val McDermid

"Poetic, pitch-perfect sense of place."   —*Publishers Weekly*

"Evocative."   —*Library Journal*

THE BRAMBLE
AND THE ROSE

THE BRAMBLE AND THE ROSE

A HENRY FARRELL NOVEL

TOM BOUMAN

W. W. NORTON & COMPANY
Independent Publishers Since 1923

Copyright © 2020 by Tom Bouman

All rights reserved
Printed in the United States of America
First Edition

For information about permission to reproduce selections from this book, write to
Permissions, W. W. Norton & Company, Inc., 500 Fifth Avenue, New York, NY 10110

For information about special discounts for bulk purchases, please contact
W. W. Norton Special Sales at specialsales@wwnorton.com or 800-233-4830

Manufacturing by Sheridan
Book design by Brooke Koven
Production manager: Lauren Abbate

Library of Congress Cataloging-in-Publication Data

Names: Bouman, Tom, author.
Title: The bramble and the rose : a Henry Farrell novel / Tom Bouman.
Description: First edition. | New York, NY : W. W. Norton & Company, [2020]
Identifiers: LCCN 2019031004 | ISBN 9780393249668 (hardcover) |
ISBN 9780393249675 (epub)
Subjects: LCSH: Suspense fiction. gsafd | GSAFD: Mystery fiction.
Classification: LCC PS3602.O8923 B73 2020 | DDC 813/.6—dc23
LC record available at https://lccn.loc.gov/2019031004

W. W. Norton & Company, Inc., 500 Fifth Avenue, New York, N.Y. 10110
www.wwnorton.com

W. W. Norton & Company Ltd., 15 Carlisle Street, London W1D 3BS

1 2 3 4 5 6 7 8 9 0

For Dad

The interrupted fern is less a lover of moisture than its kindred, and while it may occasionally be found with the cinnamon fern in some springy spot in the open grove, its preference is for the fence-row and bushy half-wild lands that border so many of our back-country roads. Here it often thrives in the face of the most untoward circumstances, frequently perched upon the top of a half-buried stone pile, through the interstices of which its strong roots ramify to the soil below. It is from some such situation as this that the wise fern cultivator selects his plants for the garden, for the labour of removing the stones from about the prize is much less than is required to dig it up when growing in the soil. It is as firmly anchored as any of its relatives and does not come up whole without a struggle.

WILLARD N. CLUTE,
OUR FERNS IN THEIR HAUNTS, 1901

THE BRAMBLE
AND THE ROSE

WHEN I got to the station, Terry Ceallaigh was waiting for me behind the wheel of his pickup. The engine was running, and the windows were fogged. The sun had yet to rise on a cold early morning between summer and fall. I tapped on his window. Terry startled and, seeing me, turned off the truck and stepped out. I got him into the station and started some coffee brewing. My office was shoehorned into the Wild Thyme Township garage, along with the plows and the grader and the fire station. It was tight quarters, but I was only a one-man police department in a northeast Pennsylvania hamlet, and they tell me I have all I need.

With a mug in his hand, Terry drew himself upright and told me about the dead man. "I don't know how you deal with something like that," he said when he was done. "Never seen anything like it."

"Tell me where," I said. I'd already put in calls to Pennsylvania State Police, the Holebrook County Sheriff's Department, and the conservation officer assigned to our area, Shaun Loughlin. Shaun had called the biologist who works with the Game Commission. All the while Terry Ceallaigh and I were talking, I searched him for signs. Terry was a tall, fit man in his thirties with long hair in two braids like Willie Nelson. He smelled like shampoo. Bronze bracelets clinked on his wrists as he raised his coffee mug, and he had tattoos on his hands, which were battered and seamed with engine grease.

I followed Terry back out to Red Pine Road. He pulled onto the shoulder, creek on one side, slope on the other with a logging switchback cut into it. The creek bent under the road and continued into a wooded ravine. This was not Terry's land, but his neighbor Mark Moore's. In years past, kids went down there to leap from a rock cliff into a deep pool in the creek. I got out and went to Terry's driver-side window.

"I can't go back again," he said, pointing into the woods. "Watch your feet when you get there, I threw up."

I told Terry to stick around, and stepped into the woods. Dry leaves underfoot, a touch of red and gold in the green above me, the wind pushing the trees around to reveal the pure blue sky. Red Pine Road was called that because of the species of tree that covered the ridge, a tree as short as it was tangled. The men who first tamed the area would have been disappointed in the timber; they were seeking the much larger hemlocks for the bark, which they used for tanning hide. Those men were also the ones who almost drove the Pennsylvania deer to extinction in the process of cutting away first growth. Eventually they—the Game Commission or somebody—had transplanted Michigan whitetails to replace the local population, thinking nobody would notice. But some families, mine included, remembered through the years that the Pennsylvania deer had been a smaller, less obvious animal.

I had to push through a thicket of pine, and an acre or so of beech tag, blackberry brambles, and maples turning the color of cherry bubble gum. Then a tromp through the shallow parts of the creek. You won't believe me but I smelled the body before I saw it, almost by a mile. That's because it had been warm and something had eaten out the man's guts, from thighs to rib cage. Where he lay was close to the Freefall, where kids used to jump, but not the exact spot. You could tell the body was a man's—an old hairy chest spattered with black blood. He wore a plain blue short-sleeved shirt. His head was gone, and where it should have been was a ring of dried blood, suggesting impact. But for the missing head, this would've been a job for the commonwealth and their game people, not my problem. His arms were spread wide, as if drawing power from the rippled rock below or the sky above, or both. His legs were white and hairless where his jeans had been torn away, and he still had one black leather boot on. Flies circled above him. I took out a pair of earplugs and put one in each nostril. The hillside rose above me, covered with ferns, trees, and moss. I stood there, shifting from leg to leg, looking away and waiting. A fly bit me. I came out of my brown study, taped the scene off, and waited for the others.

Ordinarily the medical examiner, Wyatt Brophy, would take charge of the scene, and he picked his way down the ravine to join me. But because an animal was likely involved, Wy deferred to Shaun Loughlin, who was trained in attack-scene protocol, as most newer COs had to be. Shaun arrived shortly after Wy and got to work. Anything that looked like a bite mark, Shaun shot with his digital camera, laying his ruler into each photo, one shot with, and one without. He also collected saliva from torn flaps of white skin, which trembled at the delicate touch of his swab. He shooed at flies.

"This it?" said Shaun. "No campsite? Tent?"

"This is it," I said.

"We're going to have to get the bear, then."

"Bear?"

He showed me a paper envelope with strands of heavy black hair he'd collected.

"Huh," I said. Well then, where was the head, I wanted to know.

"The biologist is on her way from Harrisburg," Shaun said. "She should be here in an hour."

I looked above us and down the ravine to where the body lay. "Shaun, is it a problem if I climb up?"

"Go around, not straight up. You'll get dirt on the scene."

So I did, walking past another creek bend and then up a gentler incline, until I caught a glimmer of creek below me. On my stomach I eased down to a shale ledge and peered over it. There was the dead man below me, thud. I took a couple photos. I had braced myself against the trunk of a narrow beech whose roots had forced themselves through the layers of rock to the surrounding earth. Just above where my hand was, in a crook, the faintest scuff in the tree's gray bark. A small disturbance, a freshness. The mark was about an inch wide. I took a photo of that.

Down below, I stood next to Wy Brophy for a moment. "Look for signs he'd been tied," I said. "Rope burns."

Wy raised his eyebrows but showed no real surprise. "Look at this," he said, crouching. Where the head would have met the body, there was the halo of dried blood. The stone's surface was blue-gray and smooth, with wavelets shaped by water and baked from mud to stone some millions of years ago. With a toothbrush, Wy cleared away some rust color from the surface to reveal divots in the stone, new and white. He looked up. "The fall couldn't have been thirty feet. Not enough to knock someone's head clean off."

Shaun stopped what he was doing to listen to Wy, then came to look. "Teeth marks? Claw marks? No."

I looked down at the body, imagined a heavy flat stone in my hands, raised it over my head, and brought it down where the neck should have been.

"Right," said Wy. "Repeated blows with something hard enough to chip the stone beneath. The cervical vertebrae are smashed to hell, you can see in there. What's left of them." He took a flurry of photographs, his camera clicking.

The creek bubbled as we circled and circled the body, waving at flies. At one point I found a dried smear of blood on a face of stone. Then Shaun found another set of drops on the flat rock of the creek bed. We took samples. Shaun got a chirp on his radio, hiked back to the road, and returned with three companions: Holebrook County Sheriff's Deputy Ben Jackson, who held the leash of a beagle named Paycheck, and a short woman with white hair like a dandelion. Shaun introduced the woman as Dr. Mary Weaver, the bear biologist. She was dressed for the outdoors, with broken-in hiking boots and a boonie hat on a string around her neck. She had what looked like a .30-06 rifle on her shoulder, a revolver on her hip, and a hunting knife buckled to her thigh.

"Mary runs a lab down to Harrisburg," Shaun said. "We use her for attacks, poaching investigations, and that. She can ID ground meat from a butcher shop. A little piece of sausage, she can tell us deer, horse, woodchuck."

"Delighted," she said, shaking my hand and Wy's in turn. She glanced at the corpse and said, "What the frick?"

"You work any like this?" I said.

"I work all over the East, through to Ohio. I just got back from one down in Georgia. That's the way it's going for these bears. You don't usually see the head come off, though. That's a new one."

Paycheck got the corpse's scent and into the woods we walked, straight to a hole in the ground where the carpet of leaves had been tossed aside and dirt chucked out in all directions. From there, the dog led us to a nearby oak with three trunks joined together at the roots. One trunk was living, the other two dead, cracked open and hollowed out. Deputy Jackson gave a tug at the leash, but the dog insisted, so we circled the tree looking for signs. At the base of one dead trunk, hairy droppings spilled out of a crack barely big enough to fit a foot inside. The old lady lowered herself to the ground and shone a flashlight in, and said nothing. Again, Jackson tugged at the dog's leash, and again, the dog stayed put. I cast my eye up the tree, found an open bole near a joint about ten feet off the ground. I wedged myself between two trunks and hitched up the tree to where I could grab on to a limb and look into the hollow. My Maglite beam caught white flesh and teeth crusted with black blood, and some human hair. The dead man's head was not exactly looking up at me, nor was it not. One eye was aimed at the sky, the other side of his face had been pulled or pushed down into the hollow.

I got down quick as I could to the forest floor, where I took a break and sat until the afterimage of the face cleared from my sight. Then, with a knife, I climbed up there again, and, gentle as could be, slipped the blade between the head and the rotting wood surrounding it, popped it loose. Flies spiraled out from beneath. At that moment, I felt a scrabbling inside the hollow, and Mary Weaver hopped to one side as two shadows shot out of the ground entrance, then stopped in the midst of some blackberry brambles to stare at us: raccoons. With a gloved hand, I took the head by the ear, lifted it out, and dropped it into a paper grocery sack that Shaun Loughlin held open for me. Parts of it had been gnawed to the bone. Shaun took samples of hair and scat from the raccoons' den, and swabbed the head for saliva. Too late, I pulled the .40 and looked for the animals. They had disappeared.

Would you understand if I said it was actually easier, the worse it got? This man, whoever he had been, was nothing but a thing now. A foul-smelling thing, with very little life left to call out to me. We left the head by the body.

The dog led us to the edge of a swamp, dark and surrounded by hemlock, where the creek splayed out into a dozen smaller channels, then into a great brown bowl of water that beavers had dammed. Paycheck lost whatever scent he had.

Out on the road, just a little past the Moores' driveway, I thought I found something. A wobbling tire track in the road; the track became two crisscrossing each other, then they widened out and stopped. I took pictures. An ambulance had arrived, along with another state vehicle and Sheriff Dally's car. The sheriff and I stepped off to the side and I told him, "It's a homicide. Loughlin and the scientist think a bear's been at him. We know raccoons have."

"It couldn't have been a bear, plain and simple?"

"The head's taken off with, I don't know, a sharp rock. Then buried. Angry work, or desperate." Before the sheriff could ask, I said, "We found the head. Raccoons had it in a hollow tree."

"Jesus."

"The bear could have dragged him down," I said, "but why? We can't rule it out, I guess."

"He could've been camping, hiking, fallen, died a natural death, been taken. In whatever order," said the sheriff hopefully.

"The guy had nothing, no gear, no wallet, even."

Dally looked down the creek, where techs had started their work. "If it's a homicide, we'll keep it quiet for now. Why don't you wait here, talk to any press that shows. Keep it simple. Say it's an animal attack, give some broad strokes about the victim—height, weight, race, age. I'll refer anyone to you, and that'll give us some cover. Make it look ordinary. Happens every day."

"All right," I said.

"You know the landowners?"

"Yes. Terry there"—I pointed to his truck—"found him. Lives next door to Mark Moore and his wife. Them two don't get along great, and neither do their dogs, I guess. But they never gave me any problems other than that. Citizens."

"Well, sound them out, if you can. But we'll mostly work it out of my shop. It's watch and wait with PSP; if we need them, they'll take over. I'll have Jackson or Hanluain look through the missing persons, call around. Keep notes, be in touch."

I don't know that Dally and I ever set this in stone as policy, but our practice was to handle our business, if it was our business. If it was a whodunit from out of town, with branches leading other places, we'd leave it to the state police and their superior resources.

I found Weaver pulling equipment out of a maroon pickup with a white camper in the bed. At my arrival, she looked up at me, smiled slightly, and continued to rummage. She lined up a backpack, a tent, a pair of waders, a motion-activated wildlife camera, and a short-handled shovel on the roadside.

"Where's your gear?" she said. "Let's get out there."

"My gear," I said.

"He'll be back. Probably today, tonight, next few days. I'm going to set up. You should come," she said.

"Ma'am, Doctor, we don't have permission to do that. I'm not sure the landowners even know what's going on down here."

"So, get permission. He'll be back."

"You say 'he.'"

"It's a male."

"You know that already?"

Mary hefted the large backpack onto her shoulders, and it reached a foot over her head. "It's always a male. What's your name again?"

"Henry."

"I'd say he's down in the swamp where nobody can get to him unless they're out to shoot a bear. Which we are, once you get your ass in gear. Shaun's coming. Aren't you, Shaun?"

The CO was leaning at the window of his vehicle. "What? All night? Henry, I got plans with my girl. You can handle this, right?"

The biologist looked from me to Shaun and back again. She shook her head. "I'll go out there alone if I have to. I'm not sure you understand. You ever handle a bear attack?"

"I lived out West."

"Oh. Where?"

"Big Piney, Wyoming. That area."

"*U. a. horribilis,*" she said.

"Pardon?"

"*Ursus arctos horribilis.* Grizzly bears. You've worked with them."

"Yes," I said. Out West we had some grizzlies that disported along the Green River and in the higher meadows, where occasionally a kayaker or a hiker seeking virgin ground would startle them into violence. One time when I was out there, a grizzly took a little nip of an ultra-marathoner as he floated barefoot over the hills, hungry for distance, no distance enough. The grizzly had been faster. Just a piece of calf muscle, and the animal was put off by a faceful of bear spray, but it ended the runner's career. In Wyoming such attacks required a conflict coordinator, a kind of field judge who weighed in on whether the bear lived or died. In this case, the coordinator argued that the grizzly had merely been surprised by the runner, and had reacted normally. The ultra man, the outdoors people, and local ranchers all agreed that the coordinator was wrong, and the bear was tracked down and shot. Not by me, but I was on the hunt.

"Here, we're dealing with an *americanus*," the old lady said. "A different animal entirely. Usually amiable. Not a natural predator like a grizzly. But this one is different. And he'll come back. We know that. He'll come back here."

"Doctor . . ." I began, wondering how much I should say. As to this victim's death, we would not be looking for a black bear, but a *Homo sapiens* or two. "I don't know how you can be so certain yet. This could have been just a bear, wandering along, and, oh, hello. They eat carrion, don't they?"

"They do. And a bear that's had man will seek it out again. Henry, I don't see how any of us knows anything about this attack, not for certain, not yet. You could have a man-killer out there. The sooner we get to it, the sooner we'll know."

I took off my baseball cap and scratched my head. "This is a small town without much local entertainment. If you say anything about man-killing bears to the press, well. I don't know what I'll do."

"What press?" she said. "I'll be out in the field. You don't have to talk to them, either. Come along." The old lady was starting to make good sense. She moved closer. "If you get pushback, you might explain that a man-killer isn't stupid. It stalks its prey in absolute silence. You'd be surprised. Most survivors never hear or see it before it's too late, until it's less than fifty feet away. And if it has a taste for man, harsh words won't stop him."

THE STORY of this dead man—and some other animals into the bargain—began years ago. My part in it began only weeks before we found him. Two neighbors, Mark Moore and Terry Ceallaigh, sat side by side at my desk in the station on a late summer afternoon. They also lived side by side on Red Pine Road, each with a piece of land up there. Mark Moore was in his sixties, a transplant to Holebrook County, while Ceallaigh—pronounced *Kelly*—was a younger man from an old Wild Thyme family.

As I said, my office was small, and crowded even more so by the fume of anger hanging between the two men.

"If she shows up at my place again, I'm going to have to shoot her. That's all," said Mark.

"You shoot my dog . . ." Terry warned. He had a chaw in his lip and an iced-tea bottle for the spit. "It's the kids' dog." He turned to me. "You heard him."

"Okay," I said. "Just—"

"Then train her," Mark said to Terry.

"She is trained."

"A trained killer, sure."

"She loves your fuckin dog," Terry said. "I love your dog. They're dogs, they scrap. Sometimes they run away. Sometimes it's coyotes."

"Coyotes?" Mark turned to me. "She comes home one time

needing stitches on her neck. That's one hell of a scrap. I still don't see him paying her vet bills."

"Here we go."

Mark turned to me. "I'm going to say it. His dog—Goldwing, right?—is a pit from the street. She has no ears. She fought for her life, all her life. And I'm sorry for that. But Puff's been afraid of her. Afraid to come home. Or maybe she's dead."

"Show me the proof. Show me the proof. Show me the proof," Terry said. "Show me the proof."

"Shut—quiet, both of you," I said. "There's coyotes out there. Mark, what's Puffball, ah . . ."

"An Airedale. She's not an idiot. She knows coyotes."

"She spayed?" I said.

Mark said nothing. Then, "She's too old for that to be it."

"We've got a bear," Terry added. He spat quietly into his bottle. "Seen it."

"Great," said Mark. "Great." He stood. "Anything comes on my land, bear, coyote, whatever . . ."

"Mark, you shoot Goldie, we're going to have a problem," I said. "Have some sense."

Mark pointed a finger at me and said, "Then *you* find my dog." He stalked out of my office. Terry waited until he heard Mark drive away, and then stood to leave.

"Wait a minute," I said, removing my glasses and smoothing my beard. "Next time, send your wife."

"Excuse me, Farrell?"

"Send your wife. Say you're working. Next time he calls you down here for whatever, send your wife," I said. "He wants a fight, you don't. Send your wife. He'll behave."

"I hear you. Maybe." Terry left.

Terry was right about the coyotes, and he was right about the bear. I'd responded to a Baptist church where the bear had visited a dumpster that summer. By the time I arrived, it had disappeared, and it was all over but the sweeping up. Since, I'd lain in wait on a ridgetop I knew, and seen the big lonely thing huffing raspberries in the dawn. In my mind I named him Crabapple.

THE NEXT TIME Crabapple appeared to me was on the occasion of my second wedding, as the late summer sun blessed Wild Thyme. At the Meaghers' cottage on Walker Lake, where Julie and I would say our vows in an hour or two, caterers and decorators flitted from the house to the yard tying ribbons and placing bouquets of wildflowers. After the ceremony we would be put to cocktails and dinner with most of Wild Thyme and many more besides, and her family and mine would finally size each other up. Until then, I skulked in the mossy-roofed boathouse with the spiders. The scotch I'd drunk the night before had gone down clean, and the hangover was in the nature of a low fever. My head pulsed out into the world, and the world closed back in on my head. The lake water brought a dead fish into the slip to keep me company. I shooed it away with a canoe paddle but it came back, or was a different one.

I had showered and left my own place early to escape Father and Ma, recently arrived from North Carolina, along with my sister Mag and her family. I had nowhere else to be. The boathouse doors framed a sunlit piece of lake and some busy cottages on it. I leaned in a folding chair, thinking.

I heard Miss Julie before I saw her, talking to somebody

who wasn't talking back. A knock came on the door and she appeared there beneath a hairdo full of fronds and flowers. She carried a towel and wore a loose white robe. "I'm going to get in the lake and float. I found these two outside," she said. "You know them?"

I looked out the door and there stood Brit, age nine, and Ryan, eleven, my niece and nephew from the Christmas cards. Ryan wore a shirt and tie, and Brit, a blue sundress and a straw hat. I wanted to hug them, but I didn't know them well enough. Brit looked from Julie to me, and back to Julie. "Him seeing you is bad luck," she whispered.

I suggested the kids and I take a canoe out, but Brit, eyeing the inch of slosh at the bottom of the boat, preferred to wait with the bride. Ryan pulled off his shoes and socks in a split second, took a paddle, and hopped in, and we two shot free of the boathouse. We paddled around Walker Lake, Ryan up in the prow. I knew enough of boys not to make him talk. Out of place at the wedding of an uncle he didn't really know, in itchy clothes, at a big house far from home. He was uneasy. An unmarried uncle was like him. A married one wasn't. Whenever the boy turned his head sideways I looked for Farrell genes in his face—big teeth, long face, ears like a dog.

"Nice place," he said.

"Yeah."

"Big wedding."

"It's all I've been doing for days. Anybody wants to rob a bank, now's their chance." In fact, there had been a masked gunman hitting the gas stations and convenience stores of northeastern Pennsylvania for some months now. I didn't anticipate ever catching him.

Ryan looked back in the direction of the cottage. "You going to live there now?"

"Julie's going to live with me at my place, where you're staying. Good hunting up there. You know," I said, "the Farrells have lived up here since before the Civil War. You belong here, you and your sister, too."

"That's what Granddad says." With the blade of his paddle he pulled up some lakeweed to look at. "You like her?"

"Julie? Yeah, I like her." I did like her. "You?"

"Sure."

Ryan and I drifted for a while on the lake, looking back at the shore occasionally, where at that distance the wedding guests looked like a painting, moving slowly down the lawn toward the rows of folding chairs. The Meaghers had invited an unthinkable number of people. What was planned this day was not for my benefit. By the boathouse I saw my best man Ed Brennan, dressed in his rental tuxedo and waving mine at me, which was still wrapped in plastic. It flashed in the afternoon sun.

Once we were dressed and our ties reasonably tied, Ed and I gazed at each other mournfully, our stomachs wrapped in cummerbunds the color of raw salmon. I peered out a window of my mossy refuge. The Holebrook Farrells and our poor relations were outnumbered four-to-one by Julie's people. But Sheriff Dally was there, as was Deputy Jackson, as was Lee Hillendale and his nice wife Greta, as were two friends I'd made in the army, there with their wives and kids, different now of course. And I'd seen my boss, the Sovereign Individual, walking the cottage grounds like he owned the place. Him and his wife. According to Julie, there was no way to keep him off the guest list, as the Milgraham family had owned the cottage two plots over longer than her family had been on the lake. I was disappointed to see him. But what did that matter in the end? I was nobody in the grand scheme of this wedding.

They have pills for what happens to me in social situations: tunnel vision, confusion, and a tendency to lock my jaw or let words escape in reels of nonsense. You know when you're talking to someone and you realize there's something not quite right? Allow me to introduce Officer Farrell, given to anxiety and depression. His cousins are homeschooled. Oh, and there they all are.

I took my place at the spot under the huge weeping willow in the yard, whose branches had been trimmed to form an archway. Ed was beside me; the several bridesmaids across from us, waiting in a line. Here came Miss Julie on the arm of her father Willard, who looked a little yellow and tired. Not Julie, though, who gave off life in her simple white dress and her flowers. If you knew her, you could almost see her past trailing behind her like balloons: a wealthy childhood, too much education, drugs, her first serious boyfriend dead too young. A checkered career as an EMT down south.

Then a return home to Wild Thyme, to family and quiet, where she transformed, calmly and without regret, into the beautiful rosy person who walked down the path of sun-warmed flagstones toward me. She touched my cheek and told me I looked handsome. I could not get a word out. I took her hand and almost went to kiss her.

I passed through the ceremony as if in a series of photographs. The Episcopalian priest who married us said every sentence like a question, as if to ask the guests for replies. Many waters cannot quench love, neither can floods drown it, *right*?

If one offered for love all the wealth of one's house, it would be utterly scorned, *huh*? My voice shook as I said my part, then calmed as I focused on Julie: the dots of sweat on her cheeks, the damp strands of hair that clung around her ears, her embarrassed smiles.

If there was one thing getting in the way of this wedding, it was me. If there were two things, it was my other wife Polly, dead some years and two thousand miles away—it was unclear how she would fit into my life now. And three, a dream feeling, a fear that if I let myself fall backwards into this miracle of Julie and her sunny goodness, it might dissolve around me.

After the ceremony the ten thousand guests milled around the lawn with drinks. My sister Mag approached me with one-year-old Carter in her arms, a little girl in a pink dress and diaper, no shoes. She handed the baby to me. I can still feel her weight in my arms from that day to this, and her little hand swatting my face. I talked to her. She gave me a peeved look and helped me take off my glasses and untie my bow tie. I thought she was the best company available, but the feeling wasn't mutual, and Mag had to take her away. With my best wedding guest gone, I was able to consider the many people I didn't know, including Miss Julie's relatives and Willard Meagher's business friends. A great-uncle of Julie's pinned me to the lilac bush with questions to make me admit that, more or less, I had amounted to nothing so far and would continue to do so. I didn't like discussing my plans with strangers, so I hid in the woods and sat with my back against a tree. From there, I witnessed a curious scene: Ma gripping Julie's forearm as she passed, their heads together in whispers, and Ma leaning back and smiling. The world was full of secrets.

It wasn't long before we got a wedding crasher or two—a pontoon full of drunk cottagers dropped anchor nearby and wished the party well. Willard Meagher sent a kid out with a bottle of champagne for them. Then a kayak scraped up to the shore and a man dressed in golf clothes and a white hat climbed out. Even from far away I knew who it was: Joshua Bray, an aeronautics engineer who lived on a horse farm here in Wild Thyme, and had a number of side hustles to make himself richer, some I knew about, some I was only beginning to guess. His ex-wife Shelly and I had made a mistake together, and it had ended with bad feeling in all directions. The affair was no secret to Joshua, but it was to my bride, and the time had long passed to where I could tell Julie about it without consequence. I stood up and brushed myself off.

I quick-walked down to the lawn where Joshua stood, but before I could get to him, Willard swept in, clapped him on the shoulder, and handed him a drink.

"Jesus, where you been?" Willard asked me. "Quit your lurking for once, it's your own damn wedding. You know Josh Bray? I told him to stop by. Hope the caterers don't hit me with a frying pan."

"We've met," I said, with a smile I hoped was not too thin.

Joshua returned a perfectly civil smile that contained more: his wealth and comfort, my wild upbringing in the hills; his belonging, my lurking; what he knew, what I needed him to keep to himself.

For the past year, Willard had been trying to convert his grocery stores and convenience marts to a small fortune and then disappear to a beach somewhere. Possibly this was why Joshua had been invited—a potential buyer. I didn't care.

"Bray," I said, "let me show you around." I was hoping to pull him aside and, in the nicest possible way, tell him to get lost.

"It's like he already owns the place," said Bray to Willard with a laugh.

Willard narrowed his eyes, then smiled and said, "Henry's at home here. You be welcome too, Bray." Willard took his leave.

"Bray, I hate to ask," I said, "but can you move it along? We're maxed out. Heads counted, seats assigned, you know how it is."

"I do," said Bray. "I do know how it is. Should Willard not have asked me? I have a lot to talk about with these people."

"Another time," I said. "Finish your drink and go."

"In a minute," he said. "Don't worry, I won't eat your dinner." He joined the wedding guests. I walked to the shore and watched him as he moved through the crowd, smiling and gripping shoulders until he reached Julie. He took her hand and went in for a kiss on the cheek. She didn't know Bray well, so it startled her, but she laughed and took it in stride.

I stood there by the lake, newly married to a woman I never deserved, baffled by my future and caught in my past. For a moment, I wasn't at my own wedding, but in the midst of the Brays' divorce again. I couldn't keep it at arm's length, no matter how I tried; Shelly, after disappearing from Wild Thyme, resurfaced months later at the station. Given everything that had happened between us and was known by a few, I was reluctant to help, or even have her seen in my company. According to a devil's bargain visitation order, she was supposed to have the kids every other weekend, but the last couple times she'd made the trip up to collect them, Josh had arranged for them not to be there. I'd told her to take it to court. I couldn't step in unless there was going to be harm to the children. She'd left in a fury and I hadn't seen her since, but I'd heard rumblings from the sheriff's department and friends: an altercation with Josh in the BAE Systems parking lot, Shelly on the horse farm when she should not have been, Shelly haunting her own family.

Eventually Liz Brennan—Ed's wife, you know—found me. "Go meet Julie up on the hill. She said you'd know where. She wants pictures."

Up on the hill among the Queen Anne's lace there was only Julie in the heart of a happiness neither I, nor our families, nor any interloper could destroy. The photographer was a jolly hefty woman with romantical notions. She tried posing me, my hand gently holding Julie's elbow, gazing into the distance, or I don't know. It didn't work and she mostly followed us around as we tried to pretend she wasn't there. Away from the party, I felt my body relax for the first time all day. We let the photographer head down to the wedding alone and gave ourselves a moment.

I asked Julie what Ma had said to her back at the cottage.

"Oh, she asked if I was going to have a baby."

"Really. What did you tell her?"

"I said yeah."

"What?" That spring we had decided to go off the pill. I looked at Julie and understood what she was saying, and burst into foolish tears.

"Don't make it weird," she said, and dabbed at her own eyes.

"Sorry." I looked down the hill at the distant Wild Thymers, Holebrookians, Farrell relations, and Julie's people. I was going to be a father.

"We can't tell anyone yet. You're the only one who knows, you, and now your ma. How'd she even know to ask?"

The farther I am from a crowd, the better I feel. And if I

can see into the woods, into cover, I am close to home, to my world. Up on the hilltop I turned slowly, taking in the timber-frame artist's studio we'd built for Willard, and the perimeter of maple, beech, and white pine. At the edge of the trees, who did I see but the black bear. Was it Crabapple? I thought so. No doubt he was drawn by the scent of roasting meat, but repelled by people and the music thudding into his wild brain. He moved off. Bears almost float atop their long limbs, you ever really see one? Good for you, Crabby. Good choice, I said to myself. Julie looked up too late to see the bear.

We moved down the hill, back to the feast. Julie's mother Tina had politely, staunchly objected to the pig roast, but I'd insisted on it. That morning, Liz Brennan's uncle Derek, an organic farmer up to Broome County, had driven his pickup through the cottage's yard to the pit I'd dug the day before, climbed into the truck's bed, and tossed out a series of heavy iron devices that looked like pieces of a railroad engine. Put together, they were a spit and the rack it rotated on. He'd stuffed newspaper under kindling and set a match to it. When the wood was popping, he got back into the truck's bed and lowered two huge coolers to me. He opened one; curled in it was the gilt I'd ordered. She'd been raised on acorns, no trash. Together we'd stretched the pig out and got it on the spit, a process I will leave to you to imagine. We slathered our hands from a bottle of dish soap and washed them from a jug of water.

In the other cooler: beer and ice. He gave me one, opened one for himself, and said, "Do what you got to do. I'm set." His small eyes twinkled, and I felt I was in the care of an angel.

Several hours later, as Julie and I returned from the hilltop, we passed Tina Meagher gazing wide-eyed into the field as the pig caught fire. Uncle Derek sat bolt upright in his chair. He rubbed his eyes and slapped at the flames with what appeared to be a dirty towel soaked in water from the cooler. From out of nowhere came Ed with the garden hose. He doused the pig and knocked the fire down. Uncle Derek too sank back into his chair. Tina took a long drink from her napkin-wrapped G&T. I raced across the lawn, but by the time I arrived, Ed was crouched by the fire in his tuxedo, slowly turning the spit. "I don't know anymore," he said. Uncle Derek would not be roused from his drunk.

A few sturdy men in work gloves volunteered to remove the gilt from its spit. One of them was Nate Hancock, a high-school-educated military veteran like myself who was a new part-owner of a couple of Willard's gas stations in the area. We'd met because some of the businesses lately robbed were his, Willard's, or both. After thunking the pig down on the carving table, he pulled me aside.

"Women like her don't come along every day. I don't know how you pulled it off. Well done, brother."

"Thanks," I said, put out, looking for escape.

"I hate to talk shop," he said. "Any news?"

"I've had today to deal with," I said.

"No doubt. No doubt." He stood there, waiting for me to say more. "How about Willard, how's that old savings and loan?"

"Willard's fine, far as I know." In fact, it was a poorly kept family secret that he was fighting lymphoma. Willard was a good-natured operator who drew a lot of people into his orbit. It wasn't easy to see him closed off and weary as he'd been. I searched Hancock's face for signs that he knew, and couldn't tell. "Ask him yourself," I said.

We ate. We drank some beer. I pulled out my fiddle. My old-time group was called the Country Slippers, after the tall rubber boots you wore November through April to step outside for a quick chore, or simply to get through the mud to your car. Ed Brennan on guitar, Liz on clawhammer banjo, and we'd added a percussionist named Ralph who mostly played a box called the cajón. We played a short set of tunes, ending with "Going to the Wedding to Get Some Cake."

Father appeared, wearing his good denim shirt, and clapped me on the shoulder. "Haw," he said. "You got good." This was the man who'd ground me down since I first could talk and understand. I told myself not no more, but something in me still wanted to please him. I was taken aback by how he had changed from a tall narrow man into a bent, slower one. Ma, her long white hair in a bun, clasped her hands and said nothing. She was all the time saying nothing but meaning things. When you don't see your folks in years, of course they'll be older.

At my first wedding, there was no pleasing Father and Ma. Polly and I married in Wyoming with guitars and poetry readings. Sneaking looks at my folks, stiff and outraged in folding chairs out in the sagebrush while they realized Jesus had not been invited, had given me something of a thrill. I was free, vengeance was mine. At the party they drank nothing and said less. The folks had never said much about Polly's death, either. They were in North Carolina with my sister Mag's family by then.

This time, with Julie, there had been some religion. Father's Father had not only given up the real spelling of the Farrell name—Fearghail—but the Catholic faith traditional to our family back in Ireland. He turned instead to Northern Bible Presbyterianism, which as far as I can tell was a vestige of plain Bible Presbyterianism, yet again a version of a version, all them Presbyterianisms particular in their beliefs. Northern Bible folks had dug their heels into a belief that Jesus would return very soon, very possibly before the Millennium of Righteousness. Too late now, assuming that's where we are. Anyway, we grew up being told He would show up any day, and that we could encourage Him with behavior.

The sky got dark and the night got late. I had conversations I can't remember now with relatives I never knew I had. Guests began to leave. I'd forgotten about Uncle Derek until I heard his truck cross the yard.

Julie and I rode to a hotel in a town car. The next morning we took airplanes to Key West, where we lay on the beach by day and ate conch fritters and whole snapper at night. During that week away, autumn had settled over Wild Thyme, and Crabapple had eaten a man.

When we arrived back home from the airport, I'd expected everyone to be gone. But soon as we bumped up the driveway to my little farmhouse, I saw a blue and orange tent in my yard. Whoever pitched it had put it in the western shade of the big maple where the sun wouldn't blaze down first thing in the morning. There was a familiar minivan with North Carolina plates.

"What the . . ." I said. I stepped out, circled the tent, zipped it open, and there was my nephew Ryan, propped up on an elbow, reading a comic book. "What're you . . . what are you doing out here, Ry-guy?"

"I volunteered," he said, and shrugged, embarrassed.

I stood up, and on my porch had gathered Ma, Father, and sister Mag, with Carter in her arms. Mag handed the baby over to Ma, walked out to the yard, and took me by the elbow. We headed out toward the field. "Dennis is gone back to North Carolina with Brit. Ryan, take Aunt Julie's bags in," she called over her shoulder. She turned back to me. "We'd like to stay with you awhile."

A T THE scene, Terry Ceallaigh was still idling in his pickup on the side of the road. I got in the passenger side so we could talk.

"Well, that's about as bad as I've ever seen," I said. "Sorry you had to be the one to find him."

"What can you tell me?" he said.

"It's a head-scratcher," I said, hearing the words out loud and wincing. "I can't tell you anything, except it looks like an animal was involved. I assume we're okay to use your land if we go looking? Maybe camp out tonight?"

"Please," he said. "Hunt, whatever. Listen . . . you don't think . . . Goldwing?"

"No," I said. "No, it looks like a bear. You don't have any reason to think . . ."

"She's a lady, I'm telling you. She wouldn't. If it's a bear, please hunt, camp, whatever. I've got kids. I want it gone."

"So," I said, "if I have it straight, you were out early morning looking for Mark's dog, and you came upon the scene. Goldwing with you?"

"No. If it's Goldie keeping Puffball away, I don't want to scare her off."

"What's really puzzling me," I said, "is where did the guy come from? I know he was missing a head, but he look like anybody you know?"

"No," said Terry. "You got me."

"You have people over to your place lately?"

"Not last night, but the night before. We had friends out, had the bikes out, grilling, drinking beers. Lately, since our thing with the Moores, we tend to shut it down by nine, ten. We wouldn't want you bothered."

"So unlikely you'd have heard anything down by the Freefall while your friends were out."

"Unlikely, yes. We tend to make noise."

"So your guests all left around nine, ten, then you, what? Went to bed?"

Terry gave me a suspicious look, but nodded as if he understood. "No, Carrianne and the kids did. I followed some friends out. To the tavern, then to the Blind Tiger up in Endicott. Must've got home around one? Two?"

"You got names? I'll make some calls, check in, make sure everyone's accounted for."

"I'll get you a list," Terry said, annoyed. I got out of the truck and he drove off.

While the bear biologist gathered her gear, I went to see Mark Moore and his wife, Frieda, on whose land the victim was actually found.

The Moores lived on the ridgetop in a white farmhouse with the trim painted black. They had a one-story shed with a rusted metal roof. It leaned, threatening to tumble down the slope. Far as I could tell, it was the only remaining outbuilding from the original dairy farm that the Moores had bought from the Ceallaigh family in the eighties. In a nearby maple was a boxy treehouse made of pressure-treated lumber and particleboard, with no way up to it that I could see. And to my amazement, a huge old elm tree in the yard that was still healthy, just starting to shed its leaves for the season. As I approached the front porch, I stopped to read the plaque that said it was a heritage tree, an *Ulmus americana*. The lawn was neatly mowed and early autumn had certainly arrived up there, on the hilltop where the maple canopy was edged in scarlet. The next lot over, through a thin barrier of woods, I could hear the Ceallaigh kids' high-pitched voices in the yard, oblivious. Mark was already standing out on the lawn where it began to slope down to the Freefall, hands on his hips. The techs worked quietly but their voices bounced around the ravine, their words lost.

Mark was about my dad's age, sixty-odd, and had lived in Wild Thyme for about thirty years, but I doubted they knew each other. I hadn't known Mark until I was grown, back home from my travels, and had begun dealing with him in my job. He was a handsome, sporty man who was often seen riding his bicycle in colorful tights. He had been an investment banker in New York City in the eighties, but had changed his mind and moved to the area for a job teaching economics at SUNY Binghamton, bringing with him, I'd say, a nothing-is-quite-good-enough vibe from the big city. His wife Frieda was a sweet lady with a loud laugh who had volunteered on the rescue squad in years past, and donated a lot of money now. As well-to-do Wild Thymers, they were friends with Miss Julie's parents, and had been guests at our wedding.

Mark met me with a tight smile and led me into a cluttered kitchen with a huge old farm table in the middle of it. He offered me coffee, and when I said yes, he began rattling with a contraption on the counter. From one of the living rooms Frieda came in, her finger keeping place in the pages of a book.

"Such a sweet wedding," she said, as if we'd been talking all the while since and never stopped.

"Thanks."

"Honeymoon?"

"The Keys."

"Do any marlin fishing down there?" said Mark, still rattling.

"No, lazing, mostly. Swimming. We rented a boat some days."

Frieda touched my forearm and asked me what restaurants we went to. I didn't remember names. With a spurt of steam, the espresso machine trickled coffee into a cup. Mark added hot water from a kettle and handed the cup to me. They waited.

"Well," said I, "I don't know what to tell you. You got a man down there dead."

They sat there stunned for a minute, then Frieda said, "What kind of man?"

"What kind?"

"I mean, what happened to him, did he drown?"

"No."

"What, then?" she said.

"We're trying to figure that out."

"He's . . . You don't know?" said Frieda.

"I can't really talk about it. Right now I'm trying to figure out how this guy ended up where he did. You've got the trespassing signs, and he doesn't quite look the type to go stumbling on someone else's property."

"No," said Mark. "And people around here, they get it now. Signs weren't doing the trick, so we had to press charges. People got fines, I think one kid even got sent to juvenile hall, which we'd never have wanted . . . it didn't win us friends. Our kids caught hell for it."

"We had to send them to the Catholic school in Binghamton," put in Frieda.

"We had our reasons, though," said Mark.

"It's the liability," said Frieda.

"Yes," I said. "Liability is everywhere."

"'The Freefall,'" said Mark, quoting with fingers. "Someday some kid was going to break their neck jumping. Still may happen. And we'd have felt responsible. It took some effort, getting them to understand we can't have them down there. They do, now. Which is why this whole thing is . . . what's it got to do with us?"

"Usually, do you hear when someone is down there?"

"We do. We were here all last night, didn't notice a thing," said Mark.

"And the weekend?"

"We were in New York, visiting my son and his girlfriend."

"Ah. What do they do down there?"

"What would you say Miller does, honey?" said Mark.

"He's a brand consultant, don't be snotty."

"Anyway, that's where we were. So imagine, you know, we get back and there's the first sign we had of Puffy in over two weeks. You remember, she was gone."

"Oh, but Mark," said Frieda, suddenly horrified.

"Jesus," said Mark, catching on. "Jesus."

"We had some blood on the door," Frieda said. "On the knob. It was the same place Puffy always scratched to get in."

"Show me," I said. "The front door, was it?"

"Well, we cleaned it," Frieda said. "We scrubbed it, it's gone."

All the same, I walked out to the porch and looked around with new eyes. Their driveway made one switchback down the hill and passed through a narrow strip of trees to the road. Somewhere in their tree line, a logging road led to the creek.

"When you're gone for the weekend, you lock the door?"

"Yes," said Mark.

"And you leave a light on or two?"

"Yes, on a timer."

I turned to the door itself. The white paint had been stripped to wood by the dog scratching to get in. The knob was clean. Still, if I put my eyes right to the surface of the wood around it, I thought I could see pink. "Any blood around here, on the floor?"

"A bit," Frieda said. "Gone now. We thought it was our girl. This is so much worse."

"We don't know anything," I said. "But don't touch the door, don't use the porch until we get back here and make sure. You got a side door, back door?" In my mind, here was the guy we'd found, a ghost of him, going for the closest light he could see from the road. Finding nobody home, moving on. On foot, by car, the shape he had been in was all unclear. "So as far as you know, here's Puffy come home."

"We thought she was dead, by this point," Mark said. "But yeah, what else could it have been? So we called over to the Ceallaighs', tried to mend some fences, see if they'd seen anything. Terry said he'd look."

"Okay. Listen, you have any notion, however small or . . ."

"Of course," said Frieda. "If we think of anything, we'll call."

"One thing I've got to do is figure out who even knew about the Freefall anymore," I said.

"It's well known," said Mark.

"Do you recall, when you were running trespassers off, who they were? Any of them?"

"You could look that up."

"But do you remember? Would your boys?"

"We can ask," Mark said. "It was a long time ago."

"We'll have to be around the place until we get this sorted out," I said. "You'll hear us down in the ravine, mostly."

I stopped at the site and told the techs to work the Moores' door and porch, take the knob itself if they had to, take the whole door.

The Ceallaighs owned about fifteen acres to the Moores' hundred fifty. Originally, Mark and Frieda had bought their place from Terry Ceallaigh's grandma, and then Terry had bought this piece back from the Moores. It would have been an undertaking to clear their hilltop and tame it. In the Ceallaighs' yard stood a Japanese maple sapling, lonely and small. A dirt track wound around their cleared land, past boulders, down to the edge of the ravine, bouncing over short steep knaps. Their house was boxy and green, not too big. There was an octagonal piece built off of the main structure, all windows, where the kids kept their inside toys. Behind the house stood a corrugated metal garage, also green. Beside that, a chicken coop with a fenced-in patch of dirt. The kids had gone running at my approach. As I got out of the car, I could hear them in the woods, whispering and crackling leaves underfoot. Their dog Goldie, an amiable pit bull the size of a hippopotamus, came bounding over to me.

"Kids, you got to head in now," I said. "Nobody's in trouble. I'm just visiting."

Silence. Terry's wife Carrianne stepped out of the front door, took hold of the dog's collar, and called to the kids again. She was slim, pretty, broad-shouldered. Two boys and a girl shot out of the woods and back behind the house, ducking as if under fire.

"They'll be fine," she said. "Come on, he's inside." Carrianne led me to the kitchen, where Terry sat at the table, staring, hands on his knees.

He managed a smile. "You all taking care of it?"

"Yes," I said.

"Don't give her the details," he said, tilting his head toward Carrianne, who stood against a counter with her arms folded. "She knows enough."

So, leaving out the missing head and the torn-open belly, I went through the same questions that I had with the Moores. Pretty much. They had been around all weekend. I put some of the same questions to Carrianne as I had to Terry, and the story didn't change in any important way.

"Like I said, we were doing what we usually do," Terry put in. "Riding, grilling, drinking beers. Kids making a mess, sleeping late. We had everyone clear out by ten on Saturday night. It's better we don't start friction," he said.

"But the Moores weren't home this weekend, so . . ."

"No? I heard a car go up the driveway. I saw a car. I think," Terry said.

"What time?"

"During the day? Midday? Maybe again at night, I can't be sure."

Carrianne stood up and left. She called from another room, "Let me know when he's gone."

Outside, I whispered to Terry, "I do something wrong?"

Terry looked at the ground, then into the distance. "Carrie is close with Shelly Bray. Our kids and them are school friends. We used to take ours over there for horseback riding, they'd come here to use the track and whatnot. Still do, not as much, and not with Shelly, of course."

"How is she doing?"

"Oh. You know."

IT WAS A cold night camping, with condensation rolling down the inside of my tent. Dr. Weaver and I had no fire. We didn't talk. We weren't even near each other. The sound of the creek flattened the sound of the forest. Still, I heard in the water, or maybe in the woods, the stuttering rhythm of footfalls, branches snapping, the spiraling whines of coyotes gathering, the secret freedom of the animal world.

Mary had gone ahead and set her tent up on the same rock where we'd found the body, and left mesh open on all sides around her. She'd hung her motion camera from a nearby tree, up, with a view of the entire creek bend. I'd brought her one of my walkie-talkies, told her to press the button to make it chirp once, lightly, and I'd hear. Me, I'd perched on the other side of the ravine, on a nice piece of earth covered in red pine needles, with a view down to where a bear might come up from the swamp below. I was without bug spray, not wanting to put the animal off with a strange odor if he meant to visit. I didn't plan to sleep. But even I am not immune to the music of a running creek, and as the temperature dropped and sent the last of the mosquitoes back to wherever they go,

I sank down into the vinyl nest of my sleeping bag and my eyes closed.

Time passed, and then dissolved. A great shadow entered my tent and surrounded me. The smell of an animal, overwhelming because there was so much of it: wet dog, roadkill, and blood, pulsing out in heavy breath. I was between dreaming and waking. The shadow became a black tree, dead, dancing upside down in the creek beside me. I'd had the dream before, and knew to wake myself up. But I couldn't, and then with a thud, the tree disappeared. Two more thuds, loud and close enough to rattle my chest bone. I was sliding down the slope, and my bare foot caught a tree root, my eyes took in the trees and the land around me. The .40 was in my hand. From the creek bed, a woman called for me. The sound of my name dispelled an echo that I had only half been aware of, the whine of a bullet's ricochet.

"Down there, drop your weapon," I said, protected by a tree trunk.

"It's me," said Mary Weaver.

"Drop it anyway, I'm coming to you." When I heard the revolver fall, I went to Mary where she stood, turning in the open, peering into the woods above her.

"He's gone," she said, her voice tight. "Down the creek."

I swept my flashlight beam over the rocks and the water's surface, finding no prints. "I don't see any tracks."

"No, no. This was a man."

THERE WAS A slash in the wall of her tent about two feet long. The doctor had heard the tear, and saw the blade coming in.

She'd rolled away, found her sidearm, and shot in warning the first time, a bullet through the tent's fabric. As the attacker fled, splashing down the creek toward the swamp, Mary managed to get out of the tent and send two more shots after him. It took some convincing to get her back to her vehicle and on the road to my station. But once she'd calmed down, she saw reason. When her taillights had rounded the bend I stepped back into the woods.

Night is a good time to practice losing yourself to the living world. Once you are lost, the beasts are likelier to tolerate you, because you are the same as them. It takes a slow step that means no harm, and believing you belong. And you must listen as an animal would. I let the slope lead me along the most ready path, crawling under weirs of pine branches, across and back until I was within sight of my little one-man tent. Once there, I waited with no sense of time passing until I was sure I was alone, then went to it. It had been sliced open, all the way down one side. My humanness came flooding back as I understood that Mary and her handgun had not done anything to frighten the attacker away. He'd waited, watching, and come back. I moved back to the shadows and waited once more.

Time, gravity, curiosity: all brought me down to the creek itself, and the low smooth rock. Putting myself in the attacker's position, then Mary's, I watched in my mind as the figure splashed down the shallow water and back into darkness, away from the gunfire. I followed without hope of picking up a trail, the creek urging me toward the swamp. Down at the edge of the water, the sky opened up. Orion was on the rise from the southeast, taking his place among the late-night stars. The swamp was a great flat of soft earth cut through with channels of water and ringed by hemlock and pine. Really, as much water as land. On a distant hilltop to the south, a cell phone tower stood. It was the beginning of fall, and goldenrod, reeds, and cattails grew six foot high, silver in the starlight.

I can't pretend to find meaning in a line of bent stalks or a scuff in the earth. I just go where the land takes me, and this in-between place could lead me to any number of dead ends, or bury me if I wasn't careful. Someone knew more than I did, and he was out there. A rumpled bit of something lay on the ground; I picked it up. A camo boonie hat, new and stiff.

"JUST A SHADOW," Mary said, taking a seat by my desk. The coffee maker was doing its job, and filling the tiny office with a welcome, sensible smell. "Tall, probably. Gloves on. I remember the hand coming in."

"What kind of gloves?"

"Work gloves, soft, with rubber fingers. The blade was black."

"The knife?"

"Hunting. Long, not folding. It had a guard."

On the desk between us lay Dr. Weaver's motion-detector wildlife camera, which I'd taken from the tree where she'd hung it. I'd also taken our rifles, but left everything else. Dally had already called me, having been roused out of bed by the dispatcher, who'd fielded a couple calls each from the Moore and Ceallaigh households about the gunshots. I had told the sheriff it was under control, don't send anyone, keep it quiet. Now that I had the doctor safe, I called Dally again and arranged to meet him in Fitzmorris in the morning.

"We better get some sleep," I said.

"If we have to," Dr. Weaver said.

"Mary, you're still telling me the bear killed that guy?"

"Yes," said the doctor. "At least I don't *know* he didn't. And here's the thing: Whether he did it or not, the switch is flipped now. He's eaten the apple; he understands we're food."

I took Dr. Weaver to Willard and Tina's cottage, where Julie and I were staying at the time. With my family visiting, room was scarce at my house. I put Dr. Weaver in a guest room, and got a couple hours' sleep without waking up Miss Julie once.

THE HOLEBROOK COUNTY Sheriff's Department was situated in the courthouse basement, beside a grassy square dedicated to the Fiftieth Infantry Division dead of the Civil War. It was about seven in the morning, just getting light. The rear entrance of the courthouse, where Dally let us in, smelled of fox.

In the years I'd known him, the sheriff's hair had gone from black to pure gray, but the way he carried himself was stiff-necked as it had ever been, and his age didn't show on his face. For any sign he was sixty, you had to look to his hands, to a certain pause before speaking, and a slight cocking of his left ear toward you. He had a good computer in his office and we plugged the camera in, repurposing a connector cord from the printer. But the computer told us 'Device Not Recognized,' so we sat there looking at it.

"It needs software, maybe?" Dally said.

Mary picked the camera up and began flipping switches, eventually happening on a tiny button that lit up a view screen on the camera's backside. It was an infrared, no-glow model designed not to spook game with a flash. We found we could run the time-stamped images back on that small screen, from the final close-up of me taking the camera down from its roost, to the field of vision down the creek to the bend.

"Here we go," said Dally. Our heads knocked gently together as we peered into the view screen. There's a splash in the creek, sparkling droplets in midair, the tread of a boot, the back of a running figure. The screen went white. "Gunshot," I said. After that, another, and then the first one, a little less bright because it had been from inside the doctor's tent. With each shot, Dally gave me the briefest of long-suffering looks.

The old lady said, "Sorry about the shooting. I dozed off, and in comes the knife."

We saw the top of a camouflage hat, which backed away as we reversed through the images, the face hidden. This was the attacker approaching Dr. Weaver's tent. Earlier, we got a better look at a figure dressed in dark clothes, a camouflage hat, and what looked like a camouflage bandanna. The camera caught him midstride, bent almost double as he crossed from the darkness of the woods to the open space of the creek bed. From his posture and clothing, it was hard to tell how tall the person was, but I did get the feeling it was a man, tall, and fit. Was it possible that there was long hair under his hat?

"Okay," I said.

"Okay," said Dally. "That tells us very little. What's he wearing?"

We stared a moment. "Camouflage?" I said. "Could be anybody out here."

Dally gave me another look to tell me he was thinking what I was thinking: It could be anybody, but it looked a bit like one of the Stiobhard brothers, survivalist bandits who came to mind quickly in situations like this. Alan Stiobhard, particularly.

"The mask," said Dally. "He went there with a purpose. He knew he could be spotted. Someone was out there, and it panicked him. Made him desperate. Terry catches him in the middle of trying to get rid of this body and he wonders, did I leave something out there?"

"Something that might ID him," I said. "He came back for it."

"Yes, maybe. But he had the knife."

"If he came out there to kill us, a gun would've been more to the point," I said. "So maybe he doesn't have one."

"Or maybe he wanted quiet," Dally said. "Maybe, maybe." He spun through the rest of the file, until an image brought us both up short. "Is that . . ."

"Yeah," I said. At the edge of the trees, one eye glowed in the infrared haze, an eye in a shadow, a form we could only see part of. The shadow was the same as everything that surrounded it, the darkness of the woods and the hill behind. The eye was looking straight toward the camera. A bear. There were no other images of it. Dally came back to the bear's eye and met its gaze for a moment or two. Mary took the camera from him.

"Okay," I said, standing. "I'm going to go find this guy. Dr. Weaver, you might as well head home. There's no way you're going back in the field now."

Mary was put out, but didn't argue. "You can reach me at the lab."

The sheriff stood too, his knees popping. "I'll just be in your way, out in the woods," he said. "I'll follow in my car, stay out on the roads, keep you close."

We drove through the county, me in my truck, Dally in his

patrol car behind. I parked on the shoulder where the creek passed under Red Pine Road, and Dally moved on, not too fast, not too slow, with his windows open to listen. I stood at the edge of the forest, waiting. But there was nothing to hear except the cars passing between distant hills, and the running of the creek.

THE COUNTY had given Wyatt Brophy a new morgue in the new hospital basement with a separate entrance that opened onto the hill around back. Before that, he'd been in a meat locker in the courthouse, along with the sheriff's department and the drunk tank. In our new century it had become clear that we'd need a bigger jail and a bigger morgue. More and more, people got lost wandering, and after stumbling down a path, they ended up in one bleach-soaked room or another.

The morgue had recently been home to the mortal remains of Don Cunningham, sixty-three and stout, a churchgoing husband, father, grandfather, and truck driver for Grace Services who'd nodded off on the highway with a trailer full of logs behind him. Julie had responded to the scene as a paramedic, though there was nothing she could have done. Don had worked all his life and his back was failing him. There was fentanyl in his system. We were at pains to find out where someone like Don would have got it.

Possibly with Don it was another driver, a truck stop somewhere. A lot of people got theirs across the New York border in Binghamton or Elmira. Up in Wild Thyme I'd handcuffed a father and his grown son back-to-back on the side of the road, broad daylight, after pulling their truck over and finding the father passed out in the passenger seat. The son was nodding over the wheel, eyes leaking. Both had a bag of heroin in their boot. But then there was Aimee Glaser, no fixed address, former waitress and cashier, now prostitute—currently over in the jail because we didn't know what else to do with her. Hanluain found her half dead camping in the woods between the river and the Dollar General. Fentanyl there, too. She had no car. Her source would have been right there in Fitzmorris, but she wasn't saying.

Busy as it was, the new morgue was an improvement in size, tech, and cheer—anything would have been. I expected Wy would be there, gathering his thoughts after examining our body, and he was; I caught him in his front office drinking coffee and looking at his computer, waiting for me and the sheriff. He had a little window facing south with the sun slanting in, and a pair of binoculars there to watch birds.

After our early morning out, Dally had managed to go home and wash, where I was still damp to the knees. We stepped into the cool fluorescent light of the lab, pulled on gloves, and pondered the dead man where he lay, with his head placed at the top of his neck.

"Starting with the cause of death," Wy said. "The likeliest is blunt-force trauma to the head." He turned the head over to its more decomposed side and pointed to a great purple stain extending from the side of the crown down to where the raccoons had chewed the face away. Wy had cut into the skin and peeled it back in a Y shape, showing some of the skull beneath. "It is very hard to say for sure, but I think this is an antemortem injury, given the amount of blood that collected here. Before I cut into it, it had been, you know, more of a lump. And the skull is fractured here," he said, pointing with a pencil.

"Somebody hammered him with something," the sheriff said.

"Well," said Wy. He drew our attention to bruising down the man's left shoulder and arm. "The humerus is nearly broken in two. At first I thought a car. He's parked, or maybe driving, I don't know, and somebody hits his passenger side at great speed, his head snaps against the window, his shoulder against the driver's-side door. I don't know why, other than I've seen it before."

Dally said to me, "We'll need to look at MVA reports from the last couple days. Although . . ."

"Right, this probably wouldn't have been reported. Haven't had any up by me," I said. "But we can call down to PSP, too, they may have handled something."

"Up north, to Broome County, Tioga . . ." The sheriff fell silent.

Wy pulled back the sheet covering the abdomen, exposing a nightmare of human meat and bone where the man's center had been. "Henry, you asked about rope abrasions. Right here, under each armpit, could be what you're looking for. About a half-inch wide. Could have been from a rope. This . . ." said Wy, looking farther down the body, "this is consistent with a large animal, feeding. You can see puncture marks in the skin here, here, here." Blue, bruised holes in dead white flesh. "From teeth, large teeth. Here, places where the skin and muscle has been torn away. Much of the small intestine and large intestine have been removed and probably consumed. Genitals too, obviously. Here's something interesting: the bear, I'm assuming—it'd be nice if Shaun were here—tore away significant portions of the rectus abdominis. But up nearer the rib cage, it left some for us." Wy pointed with a pencil. "There is a clean cut through the muscle, almost vertical."

"How?" I said.

"A sharp knife. I'd say we have the tail end of a stabbing motion, down on a prone victim, entering near the sternum, then up through the abdominals and back out."

"Before or after death, I wonder," said the sheriff.

"Hard telling," said Wy. "Anyway, insect life in the cavity tends to show that the victim was out in the air around forty-eight hours. Heart, lungs, other organs in place, all weighed and bagged now. The liver was intact, not in great shape, so this subject was probably a heavy drinker. There was alcohol in his blood, toxicology otherwise normal. I don't want to overlook his legs. Left leg, looks like some kind of impact tore the patella clean away from the knee joint. Fractured tibia and fibula. Right leg, some abrasions dorsal above and below the knee, with dirt ground in. In other words, road rash."

"Thrown from a vehicle?" I said.

"We're thinking about the wrong kind of vehicle," said Dally.

"Yes," said Brophy. "A motorcycle."

"What about the head?" said Dally.

"Yes. You can see that the cervical vertebrae at the top of the neck, here, and by the base of the skull, here, have been pulverized, likely with a heavy, flat rock, as we discussed at the scene. A lot of the soft tissue has been pulped. But there's at least one clean cut from a sharp knife at the back of the neck, through the trapezius, here. Dirt, decayed leaves, significant insect life in and around the ears, eyes, nose, and throat. Much smaller teeth punctures and claw marks here, here, here, here. Consistent with burial and subsequent discovery by scavengers, as we saw." Wy covered the body, wheeled it to a bank of drawers, and stowed it. "They left the teeth and the fingers. I've fingerprinted the body and sent it in; we'll see what we get back."

I HAUNTED THE RAVINE and the swamp that day, but saw no sign of the bear or the man we were looking for. I did chance to see a family of two does and three fawns playing on a grassy bank of the swamp, the does crouching face-to-face with their fawns and then leaping to the side, playing tag. As I was watching them, I forgot to listen, and before I knew it there was Father, easing himself down beside me.

"Any sign of him?" he said.

"What'd you, follow me here?" It took some self-control not to tell him how close I'd come to drawing on him. He was dressed in my gear and carried my .270.

"You got a scanner at home," he said. "I can't help it if I've been listening. By the way, you ought to use code names. Like we used to. Don't put your business out on the street."

"Father, this is a . . . I can't have you out here." We had started out whispering. Not no more.

"Well, you need somebody."

"I got Shaun," I said, lowering my voice again. "The CO."

"Oh." Father considered that a moment. "How many bear the warden ever got?"

"I don't know."

"How many bear you got?" I didn't answer. "I got two," he said.

"You never told me."

"I don't tell you everything."

"Go home. Or away from here, wherever."

Father stood, slowly and with effort. "I go where I please." He disappeared into the woods.

That afternoon I was alone because Shaun Loughlin had taken a trip down to Game Commission headquarters to collect a bear trap. About four o'clock, I met him on the road by the Freefall. He drove his official truck with a narrow trailer hitched behind; welded to the trailer was a black canister of corrugated steel, four feet wide by eight feet long. It had heavy mesh on one end, and on the other a trapdoor that would swing shut when the bear had crawled inside it. It was rusted in places, a there-I-fixed-it-type deal.

"This is what they have," he said.

"How are we going to get this down to the creek?"

"We're not, I guess. We take it as far as we can onto a trail, and hope for the best."

"Well, it ain't going to work," I said.

All the same, we two hauled it into the shadows, down far enough to where it couldn't be seen from the road. I told Shaun what Wy had told us about the body. The CO baited the trap with a couple pounds of ground beef in a bucket, and we called it good. High up on a flat stone overlooking the most likely path from the swamp to the trap, Shaun and I reclined with our rifles and scopes. I was not expecting to see the animal, but now the hunt for man or beast was in my blood. I scanned the woods until quitting time.

As we neared the road once again, we both stopped short and cursed the sight of a white vehicle parked not too far from ours. A news truck. Not much news out here. With bad accidents or fires they sometimes came to make sense of it all.

Occasionally they made it to a crime scene in time to throw a reporter with a microphone in front of a taped-off place that had once been a home. How else were they going to get out and find news? Just one crew this time, a young man in a plaid blazer and a cameraman from a Binghamton channel north of the border. As Shaun and I stepped out of the trees, the cameraman shouldered his camera and got a shot of us. I caught myself sinking a little down under the brim of my hat and trying to disappear behind my glasses. I remembered what Julie always told me, stood up straight, and took a breath.

The anchor set us up with the woods at our backs, and I told him and the camera we had reason to believe there was a dangerous animal loose in the swamp down there. I cautioned the people not to go into the woods alone, and particularly not in the Red Pine Road area, but if you do, make noise and bring spray.

"What makes you think it's dangerous?" said the anchorman, knowing very well why.

"A man has died," I said.

"What man? How? What can you tell us?"

"I can't say at this time," I said.

Shaun leaned in and mentioned the trap we had. "Don't go near it, folks," he said.

"So your plan is to capture the animal?" the anchor asked. "I assume it's a bear. Or a mountain lion?"

"It's not a mountain—we don't have mountain lions," said Shaun patiently. "It's not a mountain lion. We're not going to be specific at this time. We don't want you sportsmen out here. We know you can handle yourselves. But while we're out here, the best help you can give us is to stay away. I'm sure Officer

Farrell agrees. We get people out here trying to be helpful, and somebody gets hurt."

I stopped in the office real quick on the way home to clean and stow the .40 I had out in the field with me. The light on my answering machine was blinking; it was a message from Dr. Weaver. I called her back, and it turned out she just wanted to ask after the bear, and when could she do the work on it. When I told her we hadn't got it, there was silence on the other end of the line.

"You're getting beyond the point where a dead bear is any use, Officer. After a certain time, we'll never know if we got the right animal. Then you'll have to kill them all. I have a mind to get back up there and find him for you. Whoever you've got, get them out in the field."

I called Sheriff Dally about getting at least Deputy Jackson for the evening, but he said no can do, get Shaun to press the Game Commission for men. I had already asked Shaun this; he'd told me it'd be a day or two.

"But we got a match on the guy's prints," Dally said. "An ex-cop from the Harrisburg area. His name is Carl Dentry, he was military, then Harrisburg police for about twenty years, then an investigator for PDE, then for the AG's Criminal Law Division, then retired about six years. He's a licensed PI in Pennsylvania, but far as I can tell, he's not working. Nothing unusual came up online. Black Nissan Pathfinder and a Harley in his name."

"Oh," I said. The AG's office had resources to investigate a range of misdeeds, from Medicaid fraud to drug trafficking to financial and organized crime. I wasn't aware that they were active up our way.

The Pennsylvania Department of Education staffed investigators to look into claims of teacher misconduct. Basically, they rooted out pedophiles and drug users in the school system. Their investigations sometimes ran parallel to law enforcement, sometimes did more, sometimes less, and sometimes they were at odd angles to what we did. We'd only had one since I'd come back to Wild Thyme, and it had come to nothing, a sweet old guidance counselor with an iron-gray perm on the wrong side of a troubled mother. Carl Dentry wasn't the investigator; I'd have remembered his name.

"You hear anything from PDE lately?" said Dally.

"No, sir, the teachers are behaving themselves, far as I know."

"And Dentry's retired. Well. I've got to call PSP and get someone down there to talk to his wife. In fact, I do believe this is one for PSP. What a shame. In the meantime, we'll find connections he may have had to the area. I'll give the wife a day to absorb the news, then maybe we'll call, see about talking to her ourselves."

Dally faxed me a headshot of Carl Dentry—yes, we still used faxes—and I had a look. He was a tough old barnacle. Unsmiling, narrow, and craggy, with a biker's long mustache. In my mind, I tried to match up the photograph with the head we'd found, which hadn't any beard, and just about could do it.

Mark and Frieda Moore were no help. I stopped by there in the evening, bringing with me the photo of Carl.

Mark took the paper from me and peered into the image. "Is this him?"

"Do you know him?"

Mark shook his head. "Never seen him before. Frieda?"

"No, I haven't."

"How about your house sitter?" I said, thinking of the car Terry said he saw or heard that weekend.

Mark shook his head, perplexed. "We don't have one."

"Oh. Never mind. Anybody else have keys to your place?"

"No. Well," said Frieda, "the boys do."

"The boys," I said. "One's in New York, the other in . . ."

"Portland, Oregon. He owns a bicycle store there. We called; they don't remember anything about the trespassing, who got caught, the boys don't know."

I said goodbye, drove not half a mile, parked on the side of the road, and walked up the Ceallaighs' driveway. I first found Carrianne around the side of the house, where tomato plants spilled out of cages, drooping with the last of the season. Many of them were half eaten already.

"Chipmunks," Carrianne said, disgusted.

"I hear you." I decided to risk it. "How's Shelly Bray these days?"

Carrianne looked at me a long moment. "How's your wife? Terry's in the garage."

I nodded. "My wife is well. Listen, I heard she's been in town. If you see her . . ."

"I haven't."

"If you do see her, tell her, I don't know. Tell her don't go to strangers." Carianne simply looked at me without saying a word. From my pocket, I pulled the folded piece of paper with Carl Dentry's photo on it. "Seen this guy, ever?"

She looked at the face. "No. Is he the guy?"

"I can't say," I told her.

"Terry's in the garage," she repeated.

I passed a firepit circled with fieldstone, a few cords of wood stacked on pallets, and came to the green garage. Inside was a spotless concrete floor, steel tables, a wonderland of power tools, presses and the like, wrench sets, a woodshop with racks of lumber, and the machines. Three Yamaha bikes, fluorescent green, red, and pink. They also had a camouflage ATV, a Gator, a couple snowmobiles, and a small black trailer. Terry's hands were black and greasy, and there were several mechanical parts arrayed on a nearby table, but he was just drinking a beer and staring into space when I walked in. There was a whiff of weed smoke on the air. He handed me a beer.

"Quite a setup in here," I said.

"It never ends," said Terry. "More, more, more."

"Remind me what you do for a day job?"

"You mean, how do I afford this?" he said. "I'm in IT." He named a health services provider that operated several hospitals north of the border. "The day job of all day jobs, though my hours are all over the place. When I started racing, it was just me sleeping on couches, not a care in the world. My first bike was secondhand and I built it up. Got a few sponsorships in the early 2000s, got a better bike, better gear."

"I didn't know you raced."

"Placed a few times. In Pennsylvania and up to Unadilla, mostly. Did an enduro once. We'd go all through the region, west through Pennsylvania to West Virginia."

" 'We.' That where you met Carrianne?"

"Eventually. She was in the WMX Championship." Terry looked around him. "Seems like a lot, maybe. Most of this shit is years old now. We're selling some. I just try to maintain it, give it to the kids one day. What else you going to do? You don't have forever. Get yours, pass it on. This is me," he said, pointing to a framed shot of a biker skidding through a turn, throwing a fan of dirt at the camera. An ad for gear, with his name signed small in the corner as "Ty Kelly."

"You anglicized too," I said. "My name used to be 'Fearghaill.' Where's 'Ty' from?"

"Thought it'd be easier on the sponsors," he said. "Not that they were beating down my door. People know me here as Terry Ceallaigh, spelled the old way, so, anyway."

"The kids must like living here," I said. ATVs and dirt bikes, snowmobiles, hunting, target practice, chickens, light recreational explosives. All the things his neighbors complained to me about. A dream. Yet most kids grew up and left Wild Thyme soon as they could. "You think they'll take it on?"

"I don't know. I do know it's the next best thing to Mark's place," Terry said. "That's home to me, that place. I grew up there as if it was my own. Then Grandma and Grandpa died, one right after the other, and Mark came in out of nowhere and bought it. My people wanted the money. At least he never tore it down, built some McMansion. I always wanted to get it back, looked for it to go on sale. Carrianne's people are from Hazleton, so that's where we settled first, not having any place else to go." He shook his head. "Hazleton is," Terry said, with some discomfort, "overrun. With illegals. This plot came on the market, and we moved up the country."

I pulled out the photo. "Down to business. Ever seen this guy?"

"Can't say I have. But you know the shape he was in when I found him."

Terry gave me a list of names of people who had been out that weekend. Nate Hancock's was the only name I knew. I placed some calls as a matter of habit, but we already knew it wasn't a friend of the Ceallaighs we'd found in the Freefall.

I showed Carl Dentry's photo at the High-Thyme Tavern and at the Loyal Sons of Hibernia. No, brother.

I left the .40 in the locker at the station, but the rifle was mine, and I took it back to the Meagher cottage on Walker Lake. Miss Julie eyed it as I set it in a hall closet, but said nothing, only raised her eyebrows and shrugged. I was later than usual. She had some water just about to boil for pasta, and we had that and the last of the marinara from her plum tomatoes, and red wine for me. It was a one-sided dinner; she had morning sickness all times of day or night. She ate when she felt like it, which was at odd hours. Also, her breasts were swollen and sore, and she couldn't get comfortable with them, and often mentioned it. I knew it and there was nothing I could do for her. But she sat and we talked, and eventually she pulled over her space-age computer and showed me where the local news channel had posted a story about the hunt. "Killer Bear Sought in Holebrook County" was the headline, and to drive the point home, they threw in a stock photo of a grizzly.

THE MAID SERVICE that had cleaned the cottage after the wedding left almost no trace of the party, except for a stink that lingered where we couldn't find what was making it, until one day we did: several shrimp tails wrapped in a napkin, stuffed in a plastic lowball glass, and placed high on top of a medicine cabinet in one of the bathrooms. There were still burned-black pig bones in the yard. I flung the biggest of them into the lake, and the smaller pieces I swept into a garbage bag and put out with the trash.

Almost a full bar's worth of liquor remained, some unopened bottles, some down to a finger. Miss Julie and I spent a moment with our hands on our hips, looking at the little skyline of vodka and bourbon and the cases of wine. Not as if she could drink in her condition, but she had a history anyway—booze and pills. As for me, I knew if I wasn't careful I'd enjoy more of the hard stuff than I could stand. We'd boxed some up and I brought bottles in to work here and there. One to the township mechanic John Kozlowski, a peace offering to the Sovereign Individual, something for Shaun Loughlin.

With the dead man and everything running wild at work, I'd had very little time to check in with my sister Mag. All I really knew was that her husband Dennis had split back south, taking their daughter Brit, leaving Mag and the other two kids. Father nor Ma would talk to me about what had happened between them. Miss Julie's idea was that weddings can expose things going wrong in other lives—can make you see that you will never get to the altar, or show you a chill in your marriage of ten years, things like that. Maybe so. Mag was like me, just quiet, not wanting to bother people. One evening we brought over some wine, a case of beer, and a bottle of gin. Ma looked sideways but I saw Father's eyes light up at the beer, a bright local ale that he'd drank too much of at the reception.

He took one and found a chair on the porch and sat, wheezing like an accordion. Father had never drank much when we were growing up, so it was unusual. And I have to tell you how strange it was for me to see Father even sitting in the first place, when it wasn't at the dinner table, and then only long enough to square his dinner away with stony efficiency. Father had been a stander, a doer, a walker, a worker. He was over sixty now. Up until the day he and Ma moved south, he could still claim title as the wiliest hunter Holebrook County had known in fifty years. He had been king of whitetail deer, wild turkey, grouse, and various critters you could trap for fur. Coyotes, when they reappeared in our hills in the late eighties, Father had shot like a chore, like taking out the trash. We hadn't had bears again until the dawn of the twenty-first century, or at least they were rare, as I understood it.

I took a bagful of things to the kitchen and saw that Ma had gathered clumps of the last bee balm, some different tree barks, and plant roots, and hung them from the beams in the kitchen ceiling to dry. She had been giving us herbal remedies and things since before they were popular. Strawberry leaf tea for fever, a cold heavy nickel on a bee-sting. My grandfather on Ma's side had epilepsy, and took pills for a range of afflictions, but I also remember spying on him as he drank the blood of a freshly beheaded dove, straight from the neck, and later Ma explaining to me why. He died when I must've been six.

Ma gave me a hug. In it, I felt her happiness for me and the baby on the way. I was happy and then quickly sad, as tends to happen to me. I said something I had been thinking since the wedding, but had not said to anyone else: "It isn't fair."

I didn't need to explain it. Ma usually would have said something like, "God has other plans." Not this time. She turned to stow the things I'd brought in cupboards, then, just as I was about to leave the kitchen without an answer, she spoke.

"No, it isn't fair. She was taken so quick. She took you away from us so quick. We never really knew her. So . . . you're right, it isn't fair." Polly. There was an old hurt nesting in her words.

"I wish you had known her." I said it, but I didn't mean it.

Polly was mine. I tried to understand how Ma must have felt, with me gone so far away in Wyoming and her and Father with no money to visit. I might have been dead myself, almost. Almost, though. Ma stood there wringing her empty hands. Then she reached out and put one on my arm.

"What is fair," said Ma, "is to accept what comes your way, good and bad. So be thankful. And don't let any woman, dead or alive, interfere in your marriage."

That evening while Miss Julie packed some of our things to take over to the cottage and entertained Carter, I cornered sister Mag and dragged her out the kitchen door by her ear. I had a bottle of red wine with me, and we took it out to the firepit, not bothering with cups. We passed it back and forth in silence for a bit.

"I hope you know what you're getting into," she told me, and handed me the bottle.

I shrugged. "People been having kids since the dawn of time."

"And getting their hearts broken," Mag said. "I know you. You'll be wrapped around this kid's finger."

"Come on, now," I said.

"I don't know anymore. You try to turn them into good people. And they are so damn happy and proud to give you a necklace of beads they made at school, or tell you the same knock-knock joke wrong for the hundredth time, and it's not long before you get to thinking about the world making them unhappy. When they know what you know. It's going to happen. And you can't stand it."

"That's easy," I said. "I won't let it happen."

She laughed. "You won't let them see things as they are?"

"No, I won't."

"Just like Father and Ma, raising us wild."

"If you think Father ever had his heart broken over us, think again."

She looked at me like I was stupid. "Henry, you think because he doesn't say a thing, he doesn't feel it."

As we talked, I considered her view on Father, so different from my own. But mostly I was thinking about another man in the family. I would tell you it's not that I didn't like my brother-in-law Dennis Conkins. But it wouldn't fool anyone to say that. The fact was I disliked him. It wasn't outright hatred, but kind of what the hell, what is this guy doing here, he's not one of us. Loud opinions, chest sticking out, leather bracelets, and a five-string electric bass for playing three-chord hot country in a bar band. In fairness to him, nobody ever could be us *but* us, growing up so spare and close to the hills out here. So when I started hearing from Mag about their problems, it was with a selfish spark of hope that Dennis might disappear for good. But then of course I thought about Mag, and that there must be something that she loved about him, or maybe once there was. Even more I thought about Ryan and Brit, hopeful about the world like a lot of young kids are, not knowing any better, wanting a dad like everyone else has. Carter was too young to hope about anything other than food.

Mag knew the questions I had, but she waited, listening to the surroundings. "He could be anywhere," she said, meaning Ryan. "He's like a fox. I let him run. He goes out scouting at night, tells Father what he sees." When enough silence had passed, she began, "One of the things I feel bad about is that it was your guys' wedding. I don't want you to feel . . ."

"Cursed? I don't. You are you, and I am me."

"Sure, okay. You couldn't see it unless you lived with him. All that day, it's building. Started even before the wedding. He's got a comment for everything, and he's trying me, he's snapping at the kids. But not until the dancing did I understand. He was truly, truly drunk by then. Out in the dark on the edge of the tent, he . . . he's ready for a fight. So I give him one. I tell him if he's not happy, leave. He stops talking, and something clicks up there, and he says, 'We ain't friends.' Next thing I knew, Father's car's gone, Brit's gone, and they're nearly to Maryland. I wasn't sober either. But you don't expect that. And poor Ryguy, I mean, your father leaves, and he doesn't take you . . ."

"Yeah, why did Brit go with him? Or did he haul her off?"

"I don't know, maybe a bit of both. She probably went with him because she remembers him," Mag said. "There was a time we didn't have any money because he didn't have any work. But he was around. I have to think she's hanging on to that. How could she even know him? He's never there. But he can charm a girl. So there I am, do I call the cops, what do I do? I try and try his phone, get him to agree to go to a motel, don't drive any more until morning, think it over. Which he does. And takes their asses all the way back home in the morning and I'm saying, fuck him. Fuck him. I'm staying here."

Mag was cold, tired, and angry. Sad beyond words, with no life in her. I'd have preferred some tears. It would have meant something was left. Maybe there had been, the week Miss Julie and I were away in Florida, maybe Mag had got it out of her system, maybe she cried her eyes out, I don't know. There was hardly anything that could have turned me against Dennis more than Mag's silence then.

"Ryan will have to go back to school," I said.

"School isn't everything," she said, sounding like Father.

"Have you thought about where to live?"

Then, she did cry. "It's your place, your beautiful place, you want a home, this is the last thing you want."

"Never mind that."

"I know," she said. "We have to go back down there and sort through this shit, one way or another. After I catch my breath, okay?"

"Just make sure you take Father and Ma with you," I said, joking.

"Uh-huh," she said.

IT WAS THE middle of the night, and the Meaghers' cottage clicked and creaked. I moved from room to room, but knew I'd have to get out into the night again before long.

Since Miss Julie and I had been staying there, I'd had the habit of drifting around from room to room at night, cataloging things, staring at the books on the shelves, trying to make sense of my wife and her family. They were readers, they liked classical music and jazz, they had an entire pantry covered with the three daughters' art projects from school, the papers now yellow and curling away from the walls. They had a shelf full of field guides—birds, amphibians, trees, mammals, tropical marine fishes, the night sky—but damned if they knew a real thing about the wild. They had guidebooks to European cities that were years out of date. Nowhere a Bible to be seen. They had glass boxes full of light pink seashells. It wasn't so much the money, but the sheer amount of time they had had to do whatever they wanted. I didn't hold it against Willard, as I knew he'd been grinding for decades on his businesses and other investments he had. He'd made a magical life for his girls where things just appeared. I'd poached my first deer when I was ten and we needed meat. I shot it in the neck and, with Father's help, field-dressed it: cut around its asshole and tied it off, cracked ribs and its pelvis bone, slipped my knife under its skin from sternum to crotch, pulled its guts out. I cried the whole time, and tried to give Father the knife back. Anyways.

I'd gone to bed early. Miss Julie's newly sharp sense of smell demanded clean sheets every day—the Meaghers had a closet-ful of smooth, cloudy sheets—and she'd collapsed into sleep around nine-thirty. I'd lain with her, with my hand on her thigh. An electric fan hummed on the dresser. I'd fallen asleep with the thought that if we didn't lose the baby in the first tri-mester, we'd almost certainly have the baby, and if we had the baby, I could die having done mostly everything I'd wanted to.

A few hours later I woke from a dream where I heard chil-dren's voices in the outdoors, which resolved into a memory of the Ceallaigh kids playing in their yard, which turned into a waking nightmare of my nephew Ryan running for his life from something in the woods. My heart felt like it had stopped and I knew that I had not done enough about the bear or anything else.

As I moved from room to room, I convinced myself not to call over to my own house, get Mag on the phone, make sure Ryan was in his bed. Ryan was fine. He was five miles away from that swamp. The Ceallaigh kids were fine. They were inside. I was the one who was not. I knew my mind was not right, and still I knew I had not done enough.

By the time I was in uniform, Miss Julie was also awake, eating a late-night bowl of cereal. "Can't sleep, baby?"

"Nah. You?"

"Not when you're ghosting around the place," she said. "You going to have any help out there?"

"I'll call Shaun."

"Isn't he all the way in Sayre?" she said. "Oh, your father called. Just before you got home. Sorry, I forgot."

"I'll check in with them in the morning."

"If you live that long," she said. "You could ask your father for help."

"No. I'm just going driving. I won't get out of the truck."

"Bullshit," she said kindly. "It's just a bear, right? A black bear."

"The bear is just a bear," I told her. She didn't have details of the dead man.

"Famous last words. Be careful. We have to be careful."

"I know it."

I took the .30-06 and a buck knife. I didn't call Shaun. I parked on Red Pine Road and followed the driveway up to where it met the cleared acres below the Ceallaighs' house. From there, I followed the dirt track they ran their machines on, looking for something in the starlight: a disturbance, a smear where it shouldn't be, something quickly covered over. Always my eyes were drawn to the house. It was shut up tight, with no signs of anyone trying to get in. I shouldn't have been inside the curtilage without a warrant, but I had to be close enough to the house to touch it, to settle myself.

Up beyond the house, yellow light poured out of the garage door, which stood open. That time of night, I figured that someone had just left it that way by mistake. A silhouette crossed the lit doorway and I stopped dead. Terry was pacing back and forth, a bottle of bourbon in his hand, muttering. I heard curses, not out of anger, but something else. He slapped himself on the side of the head. He took a long last drink, left the bottle on a table, and walked out of the garage door into the night. I let myself sink into the tall grass. He was not twenty feet from me. He looked around him, then up to the sky, slapped himself on the chest twice, and made his way inside.

I crept to the edge of the woods until I heard the creek below. Without letting myself think about it much, I ducked onto a deer trail that led into shadow. Humans had made the path their own; its surface was hard-packed earth. I walked it as if I belonged, slowly and with no purpose, in the direction of the swamp.

Rocks wobbled under my feet as I crossed the creek at a shallow place. I moved out of the trees and into swamp that was not solid, not liquid or air, but all of those things at once. I was thigh-deep in water, then hopping from island to island of tough green grass, always with mist rising between me and the path forward. I stepped around dried reeds clattering quietly. The Milky Way stretched across the sky, beyond time.

There was no scat, no animal noise, and the most I could do was startle a pair of south-traveling loons from their beds. Even they didn't complain, just flew away into the night sky. I came upon the remains of a Canada goose—just the wings with feathers intact and a scattering of down. And then another set, and another. The rib cage of a beaver. In a small meadow farthest from the houses and machines, I found a lump of shit. Something within it glinted in the low light, and I nudged it with my boot and found a rivet from a pair of jeans, still attached to a scrap of denim. I risked my Maglite and found the scat was seamed with fine, short hair. I clicked the flashlight off. Even with my rifle, I was not top of the chain here.

Nearby was a stand of dried cattails. I slipped into the midst of them, crouched, and waited. The place had a black smell.

As a film of light crept from the east, the quiet suddenly broke open in a scream. Or a howl, I couldn't tell animal or human at that distance. I launched myself back into the world, in the direction of the road. I hit the mouth of the creek and ran up the ravine.

Next to the bear trap, the white bait bucket lay on its side. The trap's door had shut. The closer I got, I understood that it was not a bear or a person in there, but a smaller animal, with room to move back and forth from the end of the trap to the rebar cage that formed the door. I shone my flashlight in: a terrier, light brown, with pink in its muzzle and wild, rolling eyes. Seeing me, it backed up. I called to it but it didn't come.

I laid the .30-06 on the ground, sprang the trap, and crawled halfway inside. It smelled of old ground beef in there. The dog had taken a shit. Its yelps drilled into my ears. I got ahold of a forepaw and dragged it to me. It bit me on my hand and wrist. At the trap's opening, I gathered the dog in my arms, stood, and began walking uphill toward the Moores' house.

The terrier squirmed and bit, but I held on, cursing it. She craned her head over my shoulder and let out a string of furious yaps. I turned, and the dog spilled out of my arms and squared off against a massive black shadow not fifteen feet behind us. The bear pounded toward us, swatting the dog aside and into the brush. The black smell from the swamp surrounded me. He took two strides and was on me, his weight pinning my shoulder. His paw spread. I found the handle of my knife with my fingertips. I hit him three or four times with my other hand, but he didn't care. He turned his head to the side and opened his jaws, and I looked into his pink mouth and breathed in his heavy breath.

Gunshots echoed into the ravine. The bear shuddered, shuddered again, and with a look of surprise, he fell partly off me. I kicked at him and pushed myself backward. He rose and came at me again. I drew the knife. At that moment, Father came running. He fired again, point-blank into the bear's neck, where neck met skull. The animal deflated right there in front of me. Father stepped on the bear's neck, aimed, and sent a final round into its brain.

As my breathing slowed and adrenaline seeped away, I heard myself repeating a terrible, obscene curse. Father said, "It's all right." He held out a hand and pulled me up. The bear was a male, could have been Crabapple. Father went to get the rifle I'd left by the trap. We found the dog whining in the brush, limping away from the fight. She tried to take off, but I caught her. Her name tag read PUFFBALL.

THAT'S HOW I came to be driving both Crabapple and Carl Dentry down to Harrisburg at the same time, in the same van.

As Shaun Loughlin and I wrapped the bear up that morning, Father tried to lay claim to some meat, and was floored when I told him no.

"We need to look inside of him," I'd said.

"I don't want his innards," said Father.

"He's eaten a man," I said.

"You have a point. Listen," he said, "you ought to take care of yourself. And if you need help and I'm around, just call me. Don't make the wife do it."

"Julie called you?"

"Middle of the night, yes, and I don't mind." Father had saved my life and reminded Wild Thyme who he was. In fairness, he was not one to boast. Miss Julie, she came from a world where you asked for help and got it, no questions asked. Somewhere in a small, dirty cupboard of my soul full of mouse droppings and broken toys, I grudged them both.

We loaded the bear in the back of my truck and I hied him to the morgue, where we put him in cold storage. From there, I checked in with the sheriff, and he agreed we had a chance for me to dig into Carl Dentry's life—to visit with his family, to check in with his old department at the Harrisburg PD, with the Department of Education folks, the

AG, and whatever else I could find in a couple days. I took a nap while Dally contacted the Dentry family. Then I woke up and kissed Julie goodbye. Now that Crabapple was dead, she seemed glad for me to have this time on the road. I borrowed a van from the sheriff's department and started my journey midday. Carl was in a heavy-duty box. We had the bear wrapped tight in clear plastic.

Around this time in the season, a lot of skunks had been killed in the county. Their tails rose like surrender flags as cars passed. Some got trapped near peoples' houses and businesses, killed with .22s and dumped in the woods. There had been so many that it seemed they were in the middle of some kind of mass flight, one step ahead of doom, and we were the ones standing around with no clue. No other animals would eat skunk roadkill, and the township was fogged with it. I ran over a dead one in the van on the way to 81, and the smell followed me halfway to Harrisburg.

North of Harrisburg is a sturdy village named Linglestown, with a little hotel, a café, a bar, and an antique store. Also a funeral home and crematorium. That's where I was taking Carl. Carl's wife had arranged that the home would keep his remains on ice for a week before they cremated him.

In the parking lot, a heavyset man in his twenties stood by a blue pickup truck. As I backed the van into the delivery entrance, he walked over, and when I got out to open the van's rear doors, he stuck out a hand. It was Ray Dentry, Carl's son.

"Sorry about it," I said.

"Yeah. You don't expect this. A heart attack, maybe."

Two funeral home employees wheeled a gurney out of the

door and slid Carl's box onto it. I heard his head roll and hit the side of the box. So did Ray.

"So he died fighting a bear," Ray said.

"Not exactly. I was hoping to speak to your mom?"

"She's not ready today. She'll see you tomorrow."

"All right, that's better for me anyway." I gave him my cell phone number. "If you want to talk . . ."

"I better go in and see him while I can."

"Don't," I said.

"I appreciate that, but I'm going."

"Please don't. What are you going to get out of seeing him now?"

"I don't know yet," Ray said.

"Look, I've got somewhere to be before the end of the day, but I can wait awhile. I can meet you at the bar, the hotel bar up the street when you're done?"

"Maybe."

Ray disappeared inside the funeral home, and I got in the van and drove to the bar. I ordered a beer and didn't drink it. The place smelled like most bars do midafternoon when nobody's in them—beer, bleach, leftover cigarette smoke. In front of me I had a book of poems that Julie had bought for me, *The Collected Poems of Theodore Roethke*. Ray came in, sat down a stool away from me, took off his hat and placed it on the bar. His face was white. He ordered a beer and sucked it down in three great swallows. He ordered another.

"Jesus Christ," he said. "Jesus Christ."

"Some of what you saw, we had to do for the autopsy."

"Did he suffer?"

"They think he died from a blow to the head. Maybe in a motor vehicle accident? I can't say. Keep that between us for now."

"I made them promise to wire his head back on. I know they're going to cremate him, I just . . ."

"I get it."

"Them tossing his head in the oven like a football."

"I told you not to look," I said.

"Yeah, well, I did so Mom doesn't have to." His color returned somewhat. "Tell me what you know."

While Crabapple waited in the van, Ray Dentry and I talked it over. I told him about where Carl was found, and in what state, and where the head was, and about the raccoons. I told him that the bear had been killed, but not how, and not that I had him with me.

"Well, if all that's true, how the fuck did he get down in the creek?" Ray said.

"That's what I want to know."

"Someone dumped him?"

I shook my head as if to say, *Who knows?*

We each had a couple beers, and Ray expanded on the subject of his father. "I had no beef with Dad," Ray said. "He knew how to do things, and he told us. Engines, camping, fishing, fighting. He was not a man to fight with. He didn't seek it out, but he could handle himself. What kid wouldn't want him for a father?" There was a long silence. "He kicked us out, one after the other, once we graduated. Four of us. I was last to go. He didn't have to kick me out. I didn't want to be sucking around the house. I'm a Marine, like him. One tour in Iraq. Now I sell cars, man, I sell the shit out of cars, Subarus. That's easy. Easiest thing I've ever done. Everybody wants a Subaru. Love is what makes them. I do fine."

"Where are your brothers and sisters, they coming in?"

"Of course. Two sisters and a brother. Denver, Orlando, Atlanta. They got far away from this little nowhere town." The bartender was an older man with long white hair and fading tattoos. He had begun listening to the conversation, and rolled his eyes. "I'm youngest, I was last to go, so I knew Dad best," Ray continued. "They all have their problems with him. He did whatever he wanted, Mom didn't have much of a life for herself, whatever. He was a good dad. A good dad."

"He talk about his work?"

"Back when he was a cop, yeah. Stories from the street. After that, no. He seemed less happy, but maybe that was him getting older, I don't know."

"Anything stand out now?"

Ray shook his head.

"No problems with the estate? No debts?"

"Not that I know. Truck, Harley cruiser, trailer goes with it, camping gear, all that shit. Mom won't want it. Maybe we ought to sell it."

At this, the bartender approached. "Who's your old man?"

"Carl Dentry," said Ray.

"He was a customer. Sorry about it." The bartender took a bottle of whiskey from under the counter and poured us each a shot. "I'd buy his cruiser from you."

Ray and the older man traded stories and names for a while. The bartender asked, "How'd he die?"

"A bear ate him."

At this, the bartender burst out laughing. "That's one way to go. I'm sorry."

I left Ray at the bar and stepped into the sunlight. The future is coming fast: no meat, no guns, no hate, no violence, no want, no mistakes. One big community of ourselves, respecting each other and moving forward. Strong, brave, happy, beautiful, free. Just turn on the TV. We need these lies. We need these things. But we'll never have new selves, no matter how many things we buy, no matter how many ones and zeros we absorb from our computers. We don't even have old selves. What we do have is what all animals have: life. In the light of the future it's easy to forget that the animal world is all around us, and we human beings are in it—we *are* it—until we die. I'm not trying to preach. I'm just trying to say that if you've got to go, why not feed a bear while you're at it.

The Mid-Atlantic Wildlife Research Center was headquartered in a black glass box on the eastern bank of the Susquehanna River, south of town. I parked by the lobby doors and went in to let them know who I was, and that I had Crabapple with me. The center was on the ground floor of the building, through another set of glass doors. A girl in a white lab coat sat at a reception desk in a smaller lobby full of stuffed animals, including a coyote and two yearling black bears. I asked for Dr. Weaver and the young lady went to get her. Mary appeared, almost unrecognizable in nice slacks and a pink shirt, with the girl pushing a stainless steel dolly cart behind.

"You meet Becca?" Mary said. The young lady and I shook hands. "She's stuck with me for a semester, getting a microbiology degree at Penn State."

Becca pulled on a pair of blue rubber gloves and handed me some. We went out to the van. As Mary watched, Becca and I dragged Crabapple out of the back of the rear doors and lowered him gently as we could onto the dolly.

"When'd you get him?" Mary asked.

"Dawn."

"You get him yourself?"

"My father, actually."

"Sounds like a story there."

"Bear's been on ice at the morgue all morning."

"Okay, not bad. Whatever he's got to tell us, we'll find out today."

"Today." I felt suddenly tired.

"Yes, today. Time is money. All you have to do is watch. Or don't; I don't mind what you do, but we're cutting him open today."

In a cold, small room with no windows, Becca followed Mary's instructions, beginning by cutting away the plastic containing Crabapple's body. That released bear scent into the room, along with a rush of roadkill. Out in the open, the bear flattened even further. Seeing him again didn't give me a flashback or any fear. Under all his fur, he was slim, not much extra on him, like all wild things that live right up against it.

Mary noticed this. "He hadn't bulked up that much for winter," she said. "That could be why."

"At least it wasn't personal," I said.

Much like dressing game, Becca slipped a sharp blade and two fingers through the bear's fur and unzipped his skin from his rib cage to the tuft of his dick. She cut around his genitals and anus and pulled that section free of the pelvis, tying off the small intestine. She cut into the bear's throat and separated the top of his esophagus, tying that off as well. Then out came Crabapple's whole guts from throat to intestine, sliding free of the body in a bloody pile. The idea was, if they could find anything human in the bear, then they could be reasonably sure we'd removed the right animal from the population. And the farther down those human contents were in Crabapple's system, the more likely he'd had a hand in Carl Dentry's death, and hadn't just stumbled upon him. But by my count, as many as seventy-two hours had passed since this bear would have had access to Carl's body, so it was hard to imagine what there was to learn from digging around in him. Anyway, they did, and got some samples from the slurry in Crabapple's stomach, which included whole berries, feathers, scraps of skin and bone, hair, and a lot of other treasures from lower down in the intestines, all removed and separated in small hexagonal dishes.

We left Becca to run these samples through her computer system, which identified strands of DNA by species, and could match specific animals, too. Becca would also take dental tools to Crabapple's mouth in search of scraps. It would take a while, but she said she'd call if she found something.

"Where are you staying?" Mary asked me.

"I'll give you my cell number," I said. "I'm going to find a motel somewhere and sleep."

"A motel, nonsense. Stay with me and my husband. We're right over in Camp Hill. Your own bedroom, clean sheets, no bugs."

"Thanks, no." I didn't feel like eating. Plus I wanted the freedom to pass out, or to wander in a place that was totally gray and dominated by man. Night was falling.

Yet somehow I ended up following Mary's car over a bridge, across the Susquehanna, and into a neighborhood where all the streets were named for old colleges. Mary and her husband Alex lived in a white-painted brick house with a neat, weedfree lawn. I parked in the driveway and we went in, leaving our boots in a tiny mudroom off the kitchen. I had my duffel bag with me. Alex stood at a counter with a knife, slicing green onions. He kissed Mary on the forehead, raised an eyebrow at me and my bag, and offered us both some of the wine he was drinking. Jazz floated from a stereo in another room.

"Good, now go clean yourselves up," Alex said. "Out, damned spot."

Mary led me upstairs to a clean guest room with maroon bedding. "There's a bathroom, towels, what have you, you're good."

I sat on the bed, in a safe old house, behind a closed door and a drawn curtain, with a trumpet insisting on the stereo downstairs, and breathed the dry wine in and out of my mouth, resisting the bed's pull. After I had taken my shower and got into street clothes, I did lie down for a minute that turned into an hour, and was woken by a knock on the door and Mary's singsong invitation to dinner.

We ate at a battered old table in the kitchen. Alex had made a huge bowl of noodles with crispy tofu and vegetables cooked just barely past raw. The noodles were coated in a red spicy sauce that did not look too good to me after watching Crabapple get cut open, but there was no meat in the dinner, just a bright garlicky spice. We had finished eating and were on our second bottle of wine before Mary asked about the bear's death.

"I thought I was in for more of a fight than I got," I said. As I told the story, I could see Alex getting pulled in.

"What happened to the dog?" he asked.

"She's okay as far as I know. We took her to her owners up the hill. Scared, beat up. But she's a dog."

"She stood up for you," Alex said. "Mary won't let us have a dog."

The wine had puzzled me and loosened my tongue. "I haven't felt like owning a dog in a long time," I said.

"You struck me as a dog person."

"I was. We had beagles. A few of them, growing up. Pearl, Abraham, McGillicutty, who we called Cutty. They—it was good we lived in the country, because when they bay . . . These were good hunting dogs, and—things weren't ever very funny in our house, but these dogs, they were a laugh. Cutty was a problem. He disappeared, then came back, and some months after that, down came a neighbor lady with a basket full of Irish terrier–beagle puppies. Bright red beagle ears, so cute."

"Are you married?" Alex asked.

"Yessir, just."

"Kids?"

"On the way. We're supposed to be taking a class on how to change diapers and all that but . . . that's not what worries me." I realized then how desperate I was to bring this feeling into the light. It felt safe with these people that my wife would never know.

"What worries you?" said Alex.

"Never mind," I said. Mary leaned back in her chair and looked at me.

Later in the evening, as wine and fatigue began to overtake me, she and I sat in a small library wall-to-wall with books and photographs of family, of Mary in her younger days with a different man and a couple kids from infancy to college age. "Me in another life," she said. We had lowballs of gin and ice burning slow in our hands. "It was hard to change. But he's worth it."

"Sure."

Mary said, "You think that bear had any cubs?"

"I don't know."

"When did you start seeing him around?"

"Summer," I said.

"He's a young enough animal," Mary said. "It's possible he was chased off from his territory by an older, tougher bear. And he had to adjust to new territory, and adjusted the wrong way. Or found the wrong territory." She sighed. "I don't know if he had any cubs."

"Does it matter?"

"No, actually. You know, female bears have this thing, I don't know if you'd call it a capability. Delayed implantation. That means they can be impregnated by more than one male at a time, and the embryos wait to develop until Mom bulks up enough to support the pregnancy. Cubs from one litter can have different fathers. But the fathers aren't about raising the cubs. They're about eating, sleeping, and getting their rocks off." She swirled the icy gin around in her glass and drank. "Humans are different."

"We sure are," I said. I thought of Crabapple, free to follow his ways of the world. If he'd had cubs, they'd never know their father, and they'd never miss a thing.

I slept in a comfortable, clean bed without a dream or a care. I slept for what felt like an instant and then the smell of good coffee and the clatter of a morning routine woke me.

"THEY TOLD ME not to talk to you, but I had to know." Carl Dentry's wife June was young, with short blond hair and a pleasant round face. You think "widow" and a certain picture comes to mind, but June was only about sixty years old, sixty like forty. She sat across from me at a booth in a Linglestown diner.

"They told you not to talk," I said.

"People . . . from his work. They said to wait, that it was important . . ." She searched for words and hit a dead end.

"I thought Carl was retired."

"Well, he is now. Sorry. Yes, he retired. He worked for PDE, that's the Pennsylvania Department of Education? Then for the AG's office for a short time. He was an investigator. Before that, a cop in Harrisburg. He liked being a cop least. He got out of that and did other things."

I'd seen his employment history, the broad strokes. He'd left the force just a few years before full pension. He must have really hated it. "So who told you not to talk to the police?"

"Not any police, just . . . Carl had a friend, Allie. She works for the attorney general. She said she'd look into things, that she couldn't say more yet. Talk to the state police if they come, but . . . not anyone local. I guess that's you, but what could I possibly tell you that you don't know?"

"When was this?"

"Oh, yesterday. I called her after you called me."

"And when was the last time you saw Carl?"

"Days ago. At least four. Four days ago was the last I heard from him on the phone, I think. He had his bike, camping, fishing. When it all comes down to it, I want to sleep in a bed. And he always wanted an outdoor life. He's a rambler in his old age. He loved the road."

"On his motorcycle, or in his truck?"

"Motorcycle, of course. You don't have it up there? Anyway, he had gear with him to camp. There were times he'd meet old buddies."

"Was that what he was doing this trip, meeting someone?"

"He didn't mention it." But she gave me the names of a few men who had gotten together in the past.

"And it was nothing to do with any investigation, far as you knew?"

"Investigation? No. He was licensed, he took on a local job here or there for a friend, but not for some time."

"So what was the trip for?"

"For fun, as far as I knew."

I didn't like her answer, but I let it go, partly because of her shift in tone. I waited and said, "Any particular connection to Holebrook County you know of?"

"No. None."

"He ever race motorcycles, motocross?"

"Uh, no. He cruised at the speed limit."

"Enemies?"

"He had people he didn't like, but not enemies, no." She leaned back in the booth. "I thought . . . Ray said a bear?"

"Yes," I said. "But that may not be how he died. And nobody can figure out why he was in the county in the first place. I was hoping you'd have that answer."

June shook her head. "As we got older, we were happy to grow apart. Not separate, just apart a little. We had different interests. He had friends I never knew. He probably got drunk and slept around a bit when we were kids." I must have looked uncomfortable at this. "It's okay," she said. "We loved each other. He grew out of it, and I look at the big picture. But I can't understand this."

As we parted, I asked her for someone to call or see in the departments where he worked. The only name she had for me was Allie DeCosta, who had started out working for Harrisburg

PD, like Carl. She had gotten him his job at the Department of Education.

I placed a couple calls to the AG's office, and was told each time that DeCosta was unavailable. I left my name, said it was important. Once, I got through to her voice mail, mentioned Carl Dentry's name, and said I'd be around all day. I parked on Market Street and walked up and down the couple blocks there, exploring, looking up at the high buildings covered in Harrisburg soot, and decided it would be too much to try to talk my way into an office at that point. Instead I ambled up in the direction of the state capitol with its bright green-and-gold dome.

I took a seat on a bench in the sun and watched the government people walk to and fro in suits. Eventually my cell phone did ring, and it was an unknown number. I picked up and Mary Weaver was on the line.

"You got your bear," she said. "He could have done it."

"Oh?" I said.

"Meat takes about thirteen hours for a bear to digest. But you know what doesn't break down that quick? Hair. We matched hair in the animal's intestine to your victim. We couldn't have done that unless we had a follicle, that's where the genomic DNA is, but Becca found one, and there you go. So he could have killed the victim, but not necessarily. He definitely ate the victim, so in that sense you got the right bear."

"What if there was more than one?"

"What if? But not likely. Bears have territory, the males especially. You can tell the family. That ought to give them some peace."

"What are you going to do with Crabapple?"

"Who?"

"The bear, I mean."

She thought a moment. "We'll do right by the bear."

I wandered the grounds of the commonwealth capitol and the downtown streets, appreciating this concrete place that man had tamed. And I was just thinking how civilized, not a sign of the ceaseless struggle of living things, when of course I happened to see a few scattered homeless people wedged into doorways. I got to the river and my heart reached for the wild, open space. There, I found another bench and my phone rang again. The woman on the line said she was Alexandra DeCosta.

"So you're calling about Carl." DeCosta had a thick mid-Penn accent with the muffled vowels, everything turned to an *o* sound except *o* itself, which became *a*. Questions said like statements, *l*'s dropped from the ends of words. There was a sorrow in her delivery that was real and put-on at the same time. "Poor Carl. How can I help, hon."

"I'm trying to understand what happened to him. I don't even know what he was doing up in our county."

"Well, me neither."

"It couldn't have been work-related?"

"What work? He was retired, finally. And this is what he gets." Her voice caught. I gave her a moment.

"You were close."

"He was like a brother."

"Is there any reason, anything you can think of, where Carl might have . . . taken an interest in someone up my way?"

"Oh . . . sure. There were some matters that never got to the next stage. No evidence, no will to prosecute. Some that bothered Carl, some that bothered me, men who we dug up in PDE investigations that went nowhere, but . . . nothing connected to Holebrook County I can find. I've been looking."

"What about at the AG's office?"

"Can't say."

"Well, can I help? You could give me access to his files, I'll—"

"No, hon. As I understand it, state police is taking the investigation over, so there's not much for you to do. I'm only in this for personal reasons."

"What about these cases that went nowhere, you got any names?"

"I'm not able to give names. If I were, I'd give them to the detectives." Her voice took on a tone of warning. "Officer Farrell, you're a little . . . involved here, aren't you?"

"How do you mean?"

"Just take care of yourself."

"Miss DeCosta—" I said, but she had hung up.

WHILE I was out of town, the HO Mart got robbed again. Masked men had been climbing north from Williamsport or Scranton, we assumed. Or maybe dipping down below the border from New York State, targeting lonely gas stations in the hills. Whoever it was, he always used a handgun and was covered with a hood, bandanna, glasses, and gloves. He never spoke out loud. Some of the victims claimed it was a black guy, others said he was white, maybe Latino. Nobody knew for sure. He used a different vehicle every time, covering up the license plate before pulling in. The HO Mart had already had its turn a couple months back, and I figured it was safe now. But we'd never found the guy, and here he was and gone again.

I got back from Harrisburg around four, and there was still some time left to take statements and look at surveillance footage. I'd had the fond hope that it was the same guy who'd shown up on Mary Weaver's trail camera, but no. Different body type, different clothes, different weapon. An overweight gothic boy named Kyle Mylnarz had been behind the register, and showed up to the store to give his account. He reported a man in a black hoodie with goggles and a bandanna this time, face down-turned, broad shoulders, short. An anarchist type. He communicated only with the handgun he carried and a palm smacked on the counter when the clerk had been slow. This was what was on the video. There was no sound recording. The car had driven away south on 37, and from there the driver could have turned onto any of a dozen roads within five minutes, and after that, two dozen more roads. I left wondering why this didn't happen more often.

Nate Hancock had been to Afghanistan as an army mechanic about eight years earlier, and had got out of that line of work and into franchise management, as it happened, stores my father-in-law Willard Meagher owned. Willard now saw these businesses as stones in his pathway, and was in the process of unloading them. Hancock had ended up with almost half ownership in two Ho Marts, and was saving money to buy them outright. The day following the robbery, he showed up with blurry video stills from several store robberies, his two stations and two others in the area. He watched me go through the photos without saying a word. His point was perfectly clear—the clerk in each photo was Kyle Mylnarz.

"How long has he been working for you?" I said.

"Hired him in June when the school year was up," Nate said. "He needed full-time work, his people are from Hallstead, over in Susquehanna County. The son of a friend of a friend, or I wouldn't have hired his fat ass. He also works at a store near Great Bend, that's these," he said, thumping at the photos with an index finger.

"Nights, mostly?"

"Yes," Nate said.

"He ever work a day shift when the store got robbed?"

"Day shifts don't get robbed. Two employees in the store. And it's daytime."

"Okay, so the time of night could be the factor, not Kyle. But I take your point, I'll keep an eye on him."

"I don't know what I can do at this point. The stores are bleeding. State police ain't done much. I want to handle my business, but Willard's been giving me an earful about this and every other thing, and he wants too much money, and you know how he is, you married into a fuckin lifetime of it." Nate was describing a Willard I didn't know. I let it pass.

"Give Steve Milgraham a call and tell him your troubles," I said, referring to my boss, the township supervisor. "Your business is in trouble, and if we can't cover you with the resources we have ..." I opened my hands in a helpless gesture. "But don't tell him I sent you." I had been asking for at least part-time help since my previous deputy had quit and moved elsewhere, and the answer had always been no. Nate winked.

"Listen, while you're here, can you help me out? You friendly with Terry Ceallaigh?"

"He told me you might ask," Nate said. "Yeah. Terry used to work for me when he moved back from Hazleton, until he found IT work. We're friendly. I ran into him Saturday night with a few of his motocross buddies at the High-Thyme. They moved on from there, and I joined them. The girls with these guys, I'd follow anywhere. Frankly, by the end of the night, Terry was in no shape to drive, so come time to head back south of the border, I followed him home."

There was nothing on Kyle Mylnarz in JNET. I tried looking another way, searching the name "Nathan Hancock," and came up with nothing other than one DUI five years ago. I called down to Dunmore and requested PSP's file on the robberies, plus stops made on the routes in the days leading up to each one. They gave me more than I asked for—every stop made anywhere near the stations for over a year. Nothing jumped out as to the robberies. There were three Schedule I drugged-driving offenses that I hadn't known about. Shelly Bray made two appearances, once for parking on the shoulder at night near the horse farm, no citation issued. Once for speeding, mid-morning, same route as the HO Mart, south of it heading north.

I put the gas station robberies aside and returned to Carl Dentry's murder. I had yet to look into any connections, criminal or otherwise, people may have had to the place where he died. The one area I knew to look into was old trespassing complaints the Moores had brought decades earlier, and any pleas that resulted. That might at least give me the last bunch of hooligans who knew of the Freefall and used it, and lead me somewhere else. That time predated JNET, and the records would be housed, if anywhere, in a dusty courthouse attic in Fitzmorris. I headed down there.

The Holebrook County clerk was a soft, stout man with close-set eyes and a nose like an old tennis ball. He did not share the modern view that information should be made transparent; he was more in the nature of a sorcerer guarding secrets. He sat behind the counter in a high swivel chair, his fingers laced over his belly, not saying a word, as I told him what I was looking for. The clerk then told me that unless I had some kind of case number he couldn't help. More than that, he couldn't let me up into the attic by myself. The system would break down, all human knowledge would be lost, and barbarians would set the woods on fire. So I did what I had done in the past, which was to swear him to secrecy for the purposes of a highly sensitive investigation, and told him I had to pass through the wooden gate that separated him from the mob. Muttering, he let me up the stairs to the attic.

A heavy old light switch. Cluster flies, dead and alive. It looked like the clerk had been through and restacked everything a little more neatly, but in different places. The dust had been swept and reswept, but never quite removed. Once the files had been alphabetical, but not no more. A starting place: Alan Stiobhard, who was a little older than I, had at least one juvenile offense in his file that had gotten him sent to Tiernan's Gap, a detention facility a bit north of Harrisburg. It would have been twenty years ago. Not that I thought he'd ever have let himself get collared for something like trespassing, no profit in that, but maybe I'd get a sense of what happened to Holebrook County juvenile offenders, who in the system would have been involved, anything. I knew where Alan's file was, and I pulled it out. I was looking for his adjudication for theft of car parts from a junkyard business. That's what got him sent down, in the end—something small and ordinary. But the papers weren't there. I went through the file on Alan twice, but there was nothing on him before age eighteen, not even the letter his father had sent to the judge who'd put Alan away. I knew it was possible for people to have their juvenile records expunged; I just hadn't thought that Alan would have bothered with it. I headed down the stairs.

"Hey," I asked the clerk, "who's been up here?"

"What do you mean, sir?"

"Records are missing. Juvenile adjudications."

"It happens."

"Yeah, but who's been doing it?"

"Well," said the clerk, "I can't tell you whose records they might be, or how many. But you might ask the lawyer who's been making requests, or the DA who has to review them. Or the judge who's been signing the orders."

"Can I see the requests?"

"I've been told to destroy the requests along with the records. Time marches on."

I WILL TRY to make a long story short: I asked the Holebrook County district attorney Ross where these requests to expunge were coming from.

"They have to notify me of the requests," Ross said, and shrugged.

"Yes."

"It's Casey Noonan's project, far as I know." Noonan was an old lawyer who'd moved on to other pursuits, including, until recently, landlording. But he'd sold some or all of his real estate to a limited liability company whose members were unknown to me, save a few sleazy opportunists I had yet to tag. At the mention of Noonan's name, my ears pricked up.

"In what way is it a 'project'?"

"Helping the county clear out our files, I don't know. They're decades old, some of them. It gets to where I just fuckin sign them and hand them over to Heyne. Henry, I don't know anything about this. Okay?"

Jeremiah Heyne was an elderly magistrate who clung to the county's legal system like a snapping turtle. I headed over to the magistrate court, in a plain little annex not far from the county courthouse proper, hoping to catch him in his office. He was in session, so I waited in the hall for court to recess, which it did before too long, the door opening and dislodging a collection of petty disputants who had taken things a step too far, and who never did learn to dress for the occasion. The magistrate was still at his bench.

"Judge," I said, "how are you?"

"Dandy. What do you want?"

"I went looking for old juvenile case files," I said, and the old man stiffened. "I gather you've been handling some motions to expunge?"

"Yes, yes, yes, Casey Noonan's project," Heyne said. "You know how old lawyers are. Look, I help out where I can."

"How many are we talking about, Judge?"

"I don't know. A few."

"So this is all coming from Noonan? Some kind of pro bono thing?"

Heyne showed a flash of anger. "I don't know where it comes from. Where does it come from? These are community members, decent people. They want to move on. So let them."

This puzzled me; nobody who knew Alan Stiobhard would have called him a community member. He was decent, in his way, but wild as a bobcat and quiet as a snake. He lived indoors sometimes, but out among the stars just as often. His community participation was that he sometimes sold drugs, burgled houses and businesses and never got caught, and found comfort in the beds of unlikely young women, many of them married or not old enough to drink.

"Can you give me names?" I said. "For an investigation."

"That's the point of expunging the offenses. You let them go. But you can always ask Noonan." Heyne said as I turned to go, "Officer, is there a problem?"

I shook my head and shrugged.

With no papers and no names, I had to fall back on institutional memory. I went to see Sheriff Dally, who I thought would have been a patrolman or a deputy back then. His admin directed me to a repossession at an address in south Fitzmorris.

I drove out there to a suburban hill expecting a scene, but all Dally was doing was looking on as a tow-truck driver winched a sapphire-blue F-150 out of a driveway. The owner never came out of the house. The vehicle was so shiny and new that the guy who'd bought it may not have really needed it anyway.

"You've been thinking," said Dally.

"What do you remember about the Freefall, where we found the guy? Going back twenty, thirty years. Anything?"

"Not a thing."

"The Moores said they pressed charges and got kids sent down to Tiernan's Gap back in the eighties or nineties. Or a kid, anyway. Just trespassing. There would have been some friction over it. Were you around then?"

"Yeah, I probably got called up there a couple times," Dally said, looking wary. "It's hard to remember that far back."

"You might've had to testify or something. I assume these kids wouldn't have pled if they'd known they'd get jail time," I said.

"Yeah, I don't remember. What's the point?"

"The point is . . . I don't know."

I drove over to Casey Noonan's house on a hill, and was told by a neighbor that he was in Vermont.

With nobody talking, I was left with one option. Old Account Road climbed a wooded ridge into the Heights: a nickname for a collection of trailers and small houses scattered onto steep plots, where people who did not like town life settled. As I crawled up the road in the patrol truck, I tried as usual to look into peoples' business, but curtains of green and orange and gold leaves hid homes on either side. Many more huts, pop-up campers, and tents could be found farther in, and I did not know where: follow the four-wheeler trails to deer trails, to rocky dells and firepits scattered with bones and empty cans, and you might find the men who lived as shadows in the woods and who were not at home anywhere else.

I had not had word of Alan Stiobhard in some time. Not since the shooting death of a prisoner last year, out in the hills. He stayed invisible until he wanted to be seen. But I'd grown up around the Stiobhard family, and pulled off Old Account Road and into the yard of Michael and Roberta, the Father and Ma of their family. In their yard I saw not Alan, but his younger brother Danny, splitting firewood. As I got out of my truck, I drew in the fresh air of the Heights, along with a funky scent of ash-wood sawdust and two-stroke exhaust from a chain saw that sat on the ground nearby. Danny was shirtless, and the extra flesh on him shivered as he brought the maul down on a massive piece of ash, which split right in two, first try. I stayed in the driveway, mindful of the dog they kept on a chain, who eyed me over crossed paws from its doghouse door.

The Stiobhards and I had come to an understanding over the years: they might be useful to me in some half-legal ways, and I might give them space to flourish at their enterprises, as long as nobody got carried away or hurt. You can say what you want about that. I had no deputy.

Danny was glad of the excuse to stop work. He pulled on a T-shirt and waved me into the yard. I watched the dog the whole way. Soon as I turned away from him, he ran out, snapped his chain tight, and bellowed at me until Danny shut him up. Danny lit a rollie, pulled off his gloves, and stuck out a hand for me to shake: strong, friendlier than it used to be. His gloves were the cotton-and-rubber kind you get at the gas station.

"The mighty hunter," Danny said. "I'd love to talk, but..." he said, pointing to the wood left to be split.

"I'm looking for your brother," I said.

"Out of town."

"Out of town what for? Where?"

"Out of town I can't say." Danny tapped ash from his cigarette. "Maybe I could help you," he said.

"The reason I need Alan," I said, "is to talk about Tiernan's Gap."

"Oh. That?" Danny said. "Good luck getting a fuckin word out of him about that."

"You remember anything?"

"I do. I almost got sent there myself. Brother Alan kept me out."

"Stealing car parts."

"Couple of masterminds. Listen, if I'm talking, I'm not getting the wood in." He handed me the maul, handle first. Plastic handle, sharp blade, scarred head.

"You want me to split your firewood?"

"Not mine," said Danny. "Mom and Dad's."

In the yard was a mix of ash, maple, and beech, bucked but mostly not split. I made straight for the ash, but Danny redirected me to the maple. As I hammered away, breaking apart years, knots, and trees within trees, Danny's raspy voice sailed over the noise.

"We were trying to get an old Buick running, like in tech

class, but on our own. Except they don't want you to do any-thing yourself in this world. We took a thing or two from the Stokes junkyard. Ollie Stokes couldn't catch us, but he swore he saw Alan, and it wasn't the first time either. So out comes your buddy the sheriff, though he wasn't the sheriff then, and takes Alan away. We think so what, been here before: a fine, we can't pay it, Alan'll come home, and we'll carry on as usual. Brother Alan got a nine-month sentence for larceny. Wasn't no burglary, we didn't go to anybody's house. He never made it home until nine months later."

"What I don't understand," I said, "is why. No kid gets sent down for petty theft. It's summary, it's nothing. Something must have happened, he fought, he ran."

"I don't know why you think that. You think they won't make us pay, one way or another?"

"Maybe he should have pled."

"He did fuckin plea, goddamn it. Just like his free lawyer told him to. And he got nine months. That's why Dad wrote a letter, went down to the courthouse, too late." Danny shook his head. "That was the beginning."

"Of what?"

"Of the same old shit. Feudal times. Anything to make us mobile, like a car? We can't have that, unless we're yoked to it by money. Anything to make us strong, like a firearm, they'll take that away with a law. Anything to make us smarter, like knowledge, we get reeducated at the public school."

"Easy, now." I'd heard Danny on this subject before. He wasn't totally wrong. But I knew to head him off or he'd carom into false-flag theories and black helicopters. I swung the maul into a knotty piece of maple.

"And while I'm on the subject, how come your game commissioner comes sniffing around my place, counting points on our bucks and handing out tickets for not wearing the orange hats, but he won't lift a finger when one of the landed gentry lights up an innocent sow bear with a fuckin semi-auto? Out of season?"

"What?"

"You don't get over to Josh Bray's place much anymore, do you. She's hanging from a tree out there."

"When?"

"Just yesterday."

"I'll look into it," I said. Hearing all this gave me a queasy feeling. I hadn't seen Bray since my wedding, and that was how I liked it. But I couldn't ignore this. He was not one to communicate directly, and the sow may well have been a message.

"I don't care what you do," said Danny. "You got what you need?"

"You spend much time at Red Pine Road as a kid? The Freefall, the ravine there?"

Danny snorted. "Seen you on the news and I thought, he'll be by to talk about this murder. Officer, you stopped splitting. And no, we ain't been there lately."

"Danny, a bear—"

"Come on, now."

"I'm just asking did you go as a kid."

"We had other places."

"There were kids that may have got placed for trespassing up to the Moores'."

"To Tiernan, for trespassing?"

"I believe so, can't find the records now, can't find anything."

"That rings a bell, but I don't know. You could ask my brother's so-called lawyer at the time. Noonan couldn't keep a fuckin newborn baby out of Tiernan's Gap."

By this time Mike and Roberta, known as Bobbie, had appeared on their front porch to lean on the railing and watch me work. Mike was short and squat, with hair growing longer in the back, Bobbie in a sweatshirt that read I JUST WANT TO DRINK WINE AND PET MY DOG. She waved, and I handed Danny the maul and walked over.

"How's your wife?" Bobbie asked. "She needs anything, you call."

"Thanks, we got it covered." We hadn't made news of Miss Julie's pregnancy ourselves; I blamed Ma.

"We're so happy for you. I don't have any grandkids!"

"How's things up here?"

"State your business," said Mike.

"I had some questions for Alan, or maybe someone else can tell me. About Tiernan's Gap."

At that, Bobbie's face fell and she went inside.

"What do you want to upset her for?" said Mike.

"Sorry."

"Anything I had to say about that, I said to whoever would listen at the time. You can ask Dally, or the fuckin lawyer, or the judge. Christ, not even the Stokes brothers wanted Alan to go down. But I said it already. Back then."

"All right."

"Good," Mike said. "Be safe. We see any bears, we'll call your daddy."

"Hey, now," I said. "If I'd had my rifle . . ."

"Let the old man have a win. Shit, I don't know what I'd have done. You pulled your knife. That's all anyone can do. What I don't get is, why'd you lay your rifle down in the first place?"

"To get the dog out of the trap."

"You had no idea a bear was on your ass?"

I CALLED UP Shaun Loughlin and asked him, "What's the highest fine for bagging a bear out of season?"

"Three large," Shaun said. "Where we going with this?"

Joshua Bray had hung the sow from the maple tree of his dooryard. She was dirty black, with a clump of burs on her haunches, streaks of blood through her fur, about a half dozen bullet holes in her, including one to the head. Shaun took photographs of the bear, and we knocked on the door, but nobody was home.

"He works in town," I said. "The kids will be in school. He may have cameras going—watch yourself."

Once I had thought that Shelly Bray, Josh's now-ex-wife, was my last chance. We had our time together. She hated her husband Joshua, and I hated myself. So there was balance, and the stakes were low. Yes, she was married. I hadn't had morals in a hard-and-fast way since I'd stopped going to church in the army, but still, I didn't cast the commandment aside lightly. Once I did, I did it all the way. And I'll tell you that I still remember that time with a warm, illegal feeling. Summer midmornings together in the spare bedroom of the Bray family's house, meeting out in pretty places of the woods to enjoy ourselves and our lives again.

It came with a price. Shelly's marriage exploded and she lost the kids, my boss found out, I nearly lost my job, and I had to keep all this from Miss Julie, because when we first got together, Shelly and I had yet to split apart.

It seemed at first that I could simply creep away from it all. Then came signs from Joshua I could not ignore. One day when their divorce had yet to be finalized, one of Shelly's beloved horses had supposedly lamed himself. Joshua had gone out there and used it as target practice with his assault rifle. It was an ugly act, and one that had felt directed at me as much as at her, a threat. Shelly had asked for my help and I couldn't find a way to hold him to account, and that was the last I'd seen of her for some time until her visit to my station. Now here I was again.

Shaun tacked a citation to Bray's door, and we knelt by the trail of blood and matted grass that led up the hill. "He wouldn't have done this on his own," Shaun said. "It looks like they dragged her out with an ATV."

The Bray farm was no longer home to any horses. In the stables was a Polaris four-wheeler, framed by an open barn door and in plain sight. We found smears of blood on the grips. Shaun took photos and physical evidence. I glanced around the interior of the barn looking for cameras, finding none. Still, I couldn't be sure. Of the crates and tarped-over machinery there, I touched nothing.

The trail led straight through the empty pasture and into the forest. At a certain point the blood drew us off the path and into a rocky pile where generations ago farmers had quarried blue shale, now grown around with beech and maple. Shaun held up a hand, and we lay down quietly behind a log and waited. Squirrels chattered, then ignored us and went about their business. Noise of mankind barely reached us that high on the ridge. A sweep of a car on 189, a machine struggling somewhere. Around us and above us, tree branches scraped, and a black scent got my heart beating faster. Shaun became still, focused through his scope on the old quarry. A bear cub, invisible a moment earlier, swung its sweet face left and right, and scampered up the nearest tree.

"WE'LL KEEP THEM UNTIL JULY," Mary Weaver said. The two of us stood side by side, watching Shaun and another CO each carry a limp cub in their arms, down the hill to a truck in the driveway. "So they have a fighting chance once we set them free. But we can't let them bond with us, so you know what we do? We blast noise at them, spray them, beat them if we have to." The biologist turned her head to gaze unhappily down the hill at Joshua Bray, who had returned home from work with his kids only to find a number of state and local vehicles crowding his driveway. He looked none too happy himself. "We ought to just shoot them. They can't win."

Bray stood in the yard, a cell phone pressed to his ear. You understand this is me talking—he was a little nothing of a man. I don't mean physically, though sure he wasn't too tall or strong; he just never seemed to me to have any kind of presence. Quiet and neat, the guy who'll go along with whatever the bigger, louder guy says. But my experience with him revealed a hidden mean streak that corresponded with what his ex-wife had told me. And he had me in a grimy little trap. He had never said anything about it, but it was clear: do him wrong and Julie Meagher Farrell, great with child, might get emailed movies of me and Shelly in bed, or told something worse, I don't know what.

I had not wanted to be there when he got back, but the cubs had us running around longer than we'd planned. I was standing with Mary Weaver pretending I had something useful to say to her, waiting for Shaun to get done with the four cubs and handle Bray for me. But then Mary marched down the driveway to her truck, saying to Bray as she passed, "Good job, cowboy. Your kids must be so proud."

Bray didn't answer, and I pretended not to have heard, but I could feel him looking at me. Then up he came and stood beside me until I turned to him. He waited a moment before speaking, and then held out the citation that Shaun had pinned to his door and said, "Can you take care of this for me?"

"Not my deal."

"But you could talk to them."

"Well," I said.

Bray shrugged and turned to go. "I'll have my lawyer handle it."

"You shoot that bear all by yourself, Bray?"

"It doesn't take an army," he said. "Why do you ask, Farrell?"

"I never knew you for much of a hunter."

"You don't know me at all."

TWO PSP detectives called the sheriff, and set a meeting to take possession of the Dentry murder investigation. One morning we gathered around a whiteboard in the sheriff's department to share impressions and the files we'd been able to build on our own. The detectives, Collyer and Garcia, were narrow, gym-strong men who exchanged looks and often seemed to know things they didn't share with us. I was more than happy to hand off to them, curious as I was about the dead man.

In the meantime, let nobody accuse me of not doing my job. I spent a couple afternoons and evenings parked in my personal truck in Hallstead, near Kyle Mylnarz's apartment. Hallstead was like Fitzmorris, but smaller, and the next county over. A little river town with farms in the hills and a bright oasis of fast-food joints and gas stations near the highway. Kyle lived in a third-floor apartment on Main Street, above a closed Chinese restaurant. Out behind in a dirt lot was a rusty Dodge Neon registered to his mother. I parked in an alley to watch the lot exit and a set of wooden stairs down the back of the building. I took license plate numbers of visitors. Kyle drove everywhere; the chain restaurants down the way, the vape shop, and a gym called Pure Power, where I couldn't follow him in or see inside. Once at night I saw Mylnarz leaving his home to find a haggard man waiting by the stairs, seeming like he might be asking for money. From a distance I couldn't tell. The man reached out and took Mylnarz's sleeve. Mylnarz shook him off, cocked a fist back, and the stranger crouched into the shadows. I chose to let Kyle drive away that time, got out and looked for the beggar, but he'd disappeared.

And Mylnarz still worked at the HO Marts, of course, second and third shifts. Nate Hancock had given me his schedule. In the darkness, I stayed close to my radio and kept one eye on the bright squares of gas station interiors with my scope, one eye on the road, waiting for a strange car with no business in the township, or for any vehicle I'd come to associate with Mylnarz. If Kyle knew he was being watched, he gave no sign. He just stood at the counter, drinking a soda big as his head, not a care in the world.

I also haunted the valley between the Moores and the Ceallaighs, not really working the case anymore, mostly waiting and listening to normal life righting itself. Goldie and Puffball carried on long, echoing conversations from their yards, and early evening dirt bike engines scrounged for speed around the Ceallaighs' track. I didn't expect to find anyone out there, not with my truck parked on the shoulder for all to see.

Days passed with no word, and I began to wonder whether the death of Carl Dentry was getting the attention it deserved.

Andy Swales, a lawyer based in Scranton with a lake house up here, one of the slick operators I'd run into before, called me twice and left messages about Joshua Bray's citation. I waited until after work hours, called back, and left a message referring him to Shaun Loughlin. Swales and I had some history, too, and I had no desire to speak to him directly.

We had a dinner at Aunt Medbh's house with my folks— pasta with venison meat sauce. The food was good but of course things felt a bit wrong, with what Mag's family was going through. To end a long silence, I committed the sin of asking Ryan how school was. He froze, shrugged, and said nothing. I didn't know then that he'd already been to the Vice Principal Simms's office twice, and that Simms had been pinning him to the wall with questions about his home life. I also didn't know that Ryan had started playing hooky. At the table, I only sensed the awkward anger of a kid, which I well understood. So I turned my attention to Father, and asked him where he got venison this time of year, anyway. He froze, shrugged, and said nothing.

Later, I caught up with Father on the porch, where he leaned on the railing, looking out across the field.

"Hey," I told him, "I never told you thanks. For the bear. Thank you."

"Oh, sure," Father said. He took a drink of beer. "Let me know when you're going out in the field again. Two of us, like old times."

"What old times?"

"With you, growing up."

" 'This is the only round you're getting. Don't come back without dinner.' And you stayed home with your feet up, those old times?"

"You wound me, boy. You think I stayed home?" He shifted away from me. "What're you so mad about."

On the drive home, Miss Julie was tickled about something.

"What?" I said.

"Henry."

"What?"

"Henry, look."

I took my eyes off the road for a moment and saw my wife's sweater pulled up and her breasts hanging free, each one covered with a bright green cabbage leaf.

"Guess whose idea this was."

"Ma's."

"It's amazing."

I CAME BACK FROM patrol the next day to find a gleaming muscle car in the township lot. I parked and unlocked the station door, and was in the process of putting my .40 in the gun safe when in walked Andy Swales, tall, bald, and tan. A few years ago the lawyer had built a small castle above one of our lakes. A local family had lived as caretakers in a trailer on his land, and had come to terrible grief there. He had been involved with the young lady who died. Because of that, I assumed, I had not seen much of him since. Then came the phone calls about Joshua Bray's citation, but I didn't think he'd have the sand to come see me in person. Yet here he was across my desk, measuring me with unblinking eyes, always looking for angles.

He didn't speak right away, so I said, "What brings you up north?"

"Closing up the lake house for the season."

"I'm surprised you still use it."

He sighed and said, "Yes. It's been hard to enjoy. But try selling a place like that. Who around here could buy it? So I rent it out. People take it for a week or two at a time and it'll probably pay my property taxes."

"Good for you."

"Henry, Josh was out walking the trails. He happens on this bear. Can I get you to see reason?"

"Talk to Shaun Loughlin."

"He sends me right back to you. Says he wouldn't have known a thing about this except for you. And the thing is, he doesn't know how you knew. I told him, and I'll tell you, I think you got a raft of problems with this ticket. My guy's willing to drop it if you are, but he's upset."

"And we all know what happens when Bray gets upset."

"What does that mean?"

"Tell him to keep his fuckin gun in his pants, that's what it means."

Swales cocked an eyebrow at that. "Haven't you taken enough away from this family?" He stood to go. "Listen, if three thousand dollars will do it, here you go." He tossed a manila envelope on my desk. "But I don't want you harassing my guy. There's another two thousand in here, for his next expensive mistake. You just hang on to it."

"I'm not taking this. I'm not touching it. Pick this up," I said.

As Swales walked to the door, he said, "If the citation goes away, we'll take that as a good sign. If it doesn't, we'll take it amiss."

"Swales."

But he was already gone and I was speaking to a closing door. "Jesus Christ," I said, and put the envelope in the safe.

BY OCTOBER, the High-Thyme Tavern had not opened its windows in many weeks, and the smell of grease and spilled beer had taken over. One surly barfly, still shedding dust from the sawmill, sat at the bar and drank Jägermeister, feeding the juke-box dollar after dollar to play Joe Walsh's "Life's Been Good" on repeat. I can't complain, but sometimes I still do. By the tenth repeat and the eightieth minute, I could see that the drunkard, whose name was Colin Yardley, was heading toward an ejection. He could see it too.

The song ended. Another man walked over to the jukebox and pulled out his wallet, but Yardley met him there. He put one hand on the machine, the other on the man's chest, and said, "Life's been good."

Four strong men frog-marched Yardley out of the bar as he screamed curses. In the process, someone wrangled his car keys out of his pocket and gave them to the bartender, a forty-ish man. I heard what sounded like fighting outside, and turned to the bartender, who shrugged. When Yardley tried to reenter, he had a bloody scrape on his cheek.

"You're barred for two weeks. Two this time," the bartender said.

"I give a fuck."

"Come back in two weeks. You see Henry right here. You want to keep at it?"

Yardley glanced at me, then at the floor, and muttered, "I need a ride home."

"Call your wife."

"She's at book club."

Eventually someone steered him back outside, and I ordered myself a Flower Power. I was not at the High-Thyme to keep the peace, but to play a show with my band the Country Slippers. I had been the first to arrive, dressed in one of my thrift-store suits, according to our stage presentation. Dress like an album of old family photos. Our percussionist Ralph was usually late, and Ed and Liz often had trouble getting out the door, with their two kids and babysitter. I couldn't interest Miss Julie in going out to the tavern; the oily smells and loud voices got to her anymore, with the baby the size of a plum, growing daily and causing trouble with her stomach.

And it was a good thing. As I looked up and down the bar I caught unfamiliar faces, and flattered myself that word had spread. There were two unaccompanied women about my age, each seemingly apart from the other. One I didn't know, but her jeans and sweatshirt did nothing to disguise that she was a professional of some kind, an outsider, and I almost thought cop, as she easily deflected a wobbly advance from an older man. The other woman was pretending to look at her phone, but taking in the scene, and glancing at me. She was alone and pretty, with dark hair pulled through the back of a baseball hat in a tight ponytail. Her, I knew well. Though she avoided my eyes, there was a reason she was in the bar that night. It was Shelly Bray, returned to Wild Thyme.

I hadn't heard about Shelly's life other than what Terry Ceallaigh had told me. She'd moved away after the divorce. The most recent home I'd known her to have was a rented apartment in Binghamton. Last I'd seen her was in a car outside the Bray horse farm here in Wild Thyme, the farm her husband got to keep, along with the kids.

I worked up the courage to travel the length of the bar and say hello to Shel, but by then she wasn't to be found, and it was time to start the show.

Over the past couple years, the Country Slippers evolved a way of playing where we'd begin with a wordless tune, say,

"Billy in the Lowground." But if the spirit moved us, we'd stretch it out, or remove one piece and sister it on over here, until, hey, it's not "Billy," but "Whiskey Before Breakfast," which we'd sing not too well, then ease back into "Billy." It kept the sets fluid—pools and rills. And the band had to listen to each other too. We couldn't sit back and think about life's little ironies while playing a tune the same way every time, because there was no same way. This came first from an understanding between fiddle and banjo, and an ear for the unstruck chord. All the while, I looked for Shelly and didn't see her.

After the show was over, and by the time we'd packed up our instruments and hauled the PA back to the closet, business was sparse enough that the bartender had left his post for a minute to smoke his vape out on the porch. He handed me an envelope full of small bills. "How'd it go?"

"Fine," I said. "You?"

"Good. Good crowd tonight. Good."

I walked out to my truck, not drunk, but buzzing from a few beers and unburdened of nervous energy. Footsteps followed me as I walked to my truck.

"Henry," Shelly said, her voice snagging me from behind, unmistakable and urgent.

"I thought I saw you in there."

"Got a minute?"

"Uh, how long of a minute? I've got to get home, my wife . . ."

"I heard. Congratulations. Can we?" she said, gesturing toward my truck. Inside the cab, she tucked one foot underneath a thigh and turned to me. There was vodka and cranberry on her breath, and the cab soon filled with the sweet smell. Shelly was always athletic and that hadn't changed; her jeans fit like a radio country song. When we'd had our thing, I'd mostly known her face brightened by mischief. Now worry seemed to bring her down. Still, I admit my heart raced to be close to her again, and I half thought our conversation would end with a suggestion I'd have a hard time refusing. "Carrianne said you asked after me."

I shrugged and didn't answer.

"I'm fine," she said. "We're fine. I'm here because I know something about the man Terry found."

"Oh?" I began looking for an out.

"I've been trying to get the kids back. Looking into Josh's past. You know he'd been in some trouble when he was a boy. Setting fires, shoplifting, he said. Not to hurt anyone, just a kid acting out. So he claimed. But I got thinking, how much do I really know? So I've been sending out FOIL requests, with nobody telling me anything. Finally I reach a woman in the attorney general's office who'll listen. I talked to her on the phone. She—"

"I can't really talk about this." I could hear people leaving the bar, car doors opening and shutting, engines, laughter. "I can't be out here with you like this. It's a small town."

"Okay, but can I—this lawyer, unofficially she told me, find some dirt, some leverage, improve the situation with the kids outside of the courts. Carl was who she suggested. A private investigator. I was the one who hired him."

I took this information and turned it in the light. The woman in the AG's office must have been Allie DeCosta. Why she hadn't shared this with me on the phone, I could only guess. Eventually I said, "Are you safe?"

"He doesn't know I'm in town. Henry, I've been living with

this and trying to figure out what's right, trying not to ruin my kids' lives. If Josh did it . . ."

"It doesn't look good, but you don't know anything. Not for sure. Why would he want to kill anybody?" I didn't think him above it, but I wanted to hear her answer.

"He has his reasons," she said. There was truth in her eyes, and a plea. "State police have been by to ask me questions. I didn't tell them all I know. If I tell you, can you protect me?"

"I'm not sure," I said.

She leaned back, away from me. "I need to think," she said. She reached for the door handle.

"Shel—"

"Yes?" she said.

"Come see me at the station tomorrow."

"Maybe." She left.

I called Sheriff Dally at home, had to call twice before he'd pick up. I told him that Shelly had hired Carl Dentry to look at her ex.

"Yeah," Dally said, "we knew that. It was at the investigators' request we keep you away from the Bray part of the case," he said. "For obvious reasons. You've got a personal connection; let's not pretend."

"So he fuckin did it. Why hasn't he been hauled in and charged?"

"There's nothing on him," Dally said, tired. "His alibi is good. He'd had the kids down at his parents' place in Wilkes-Barre all weekend."

"Check his phone—"

"Henry—"

"—and his emails. Apps, whatever."

"It's being done. That kind of thing takes time. Henry, think about how we found Carl. That Bray, he's a chilly son of a bitch, but would he have done all that?"

We hung up and I drove away. Home, I rinsed off in the shower and slipped into bed beside Miss Julie, who was snoring. My mind was racing, but an hour or two later, I must have fallen asleep myself.

THE NEXT DAY, Shelly never showed. I could only guess what she had to tell me. I took a deep breath and placed a call to Allie DeCosta's office at the AG; she didn't answer, of course, and I didn't leave a message. I decided I couldn't wait forever, and I went out into the field, which got me nowhere.

Every Thursday night, Miss Julie and I took a class in Binghamton called Mindful Baby. It was in the basement of St. Pat's on the West Side. There were four other couples in there with us, more or less pregnant than we were, but all due in spring. We sat cross-legged on the floor without shoes; three weeks of this and I never remembered to wear good socks. A doula led us through visualizations and breathing exercises, and showed us movies about natural birth and breastfeeding and how to swaddle your baby. We practiced on dolls. At first I hadn't wanted to go; my people had raised babies for generations, resulting in me. I had turned out fine. But it was important to Miss Julie and so it was important to me.

Last week we'd been given homework to come up with a secret list of things you were grateful to your partner for. I had written mine out and brought it folded in my pocket. I was distracted by the Dentry matter, so it was a good thing I had my notes. The room fell a little extra silent as I fished my list out of my shirt pocket. Julie tucked some hair behind her ear and looked amused. "Um," I said, mad that I had to put our business in the street. "You are a great baker. You make me laugh. And that isn't easy," I added. "You put up with my moods. You listen. You are secure in your, um, self. I'm sorry . . ."

"No, keep going," said our teacher.

"You don't let things get you down," I said. I put the list away and looked at my wife. "You are like the sun. To me. Like sun on water. In summertime? Like when we got married. That's how I feel. I don't know how I got so lucky. For our kid to have you as a mom . . . well." I looked around the room, abashed.

For that speech, I got a kiss on the cheek.

"I never knew that you were always what I needed until you came along," she said. Here, she told the story of when she first knew I was interested, when I picked her wild mushrooms, and called her up later that night in a panic to make sure they weren't poisonous. It was funny and sweet the way she told it, but I'd almost had a heart attack over those chickens-of-the-woods. "You'll always do right by me. You are strong, inside and out. I know it was hard for you to take a risk on me, and on fatherhood, and I'm grateful. The world is full of people, but there aren't a lot of guys like you for girls like me. There aren't a lot of fathers like you. You are a total weirdo. I love you."

Miss Julie's appetite had returned, and we picked up a pizza with sausage and spicy peppers on the way home.

Back at the cottage, there were two police cars parked on the shoulder. One was the sheriff's, and the other an unmarked blue sedan I guessed correctly was a PSP vehicle. Miss Julie stiffened and said, "How about a break for once?"

"I'll get rid of them."

Julie had no intention of sharing our dinner, and hustled it inside without saying hello. I met the sheriff and Collyer and Garcia in the yard.

"Sorry to intrude," Dally said.

"The wife says I can't ask you in." We all shook hands.

"We may need to take a look inside," Collyer said.

I stiffened. Dally was smiling but there was tension in it. "I thought you and Julie were living up where Medbh Brennan used to be. We went up there, your whole family was home except you. Sorry. Glad to see your parents again."

"I'm sure they were glad too," I said.

Dally nodded. "Your sister says to call her," he said.

"Okay, thanks for the message. Is that all?"

Garcia cleared his throat and said, "It's about Shelly Bray."

And I knew. "What happened?"

"When did you last see her?"

From that moment on, I measured my responses. "She reached out to me last night."

"Why?"

"You know why," I said. "She had information on Dentry."

"How, by phone, email?"

"She was at the High-Thyme—at the bar." I turned to Dally. "Sheriff, I called you right after—"

"That was about when?" Garcia said.

"I'm a little fuzzy on that. I wasn't on duty. It would've been around midnight? Phone records would tell you."

Collyer took over. "So you'd been drinking. Anyone see you?"

"Everyone saw me. What does that mean?"

"Did anyone see you leave? Easy. You know we've got to do this."

"I don't know that you've got to do anything. People saw me there because I was playing in the band. My wife can tell you I came straight home, if it comes to that. She was home." But I didn't convince myself or the detectives. "What happened?"

Dally said, "Ms. Bray was found dead in her car near the old Ravine exit off 81."

I knew the place. It was a few counties south of Holebrook. The commonwealth had blocked the exit off with a couple concrete dividers, but there was room on the side of the road to get by. The off-ramp was cracked and scattered with rubble. It sloped up, and then dropped straight down and curved into the woods. The exit, and that road, was not supposed to be in use.

"Dead how?"

"That's the question," said Garcia.

"Well, did she crash? What was she doing?"

"Also good questions. A one-car MVA is possible."

"What was her tox?"

"Mr. Farrell, we're getting a little sidetracked—"

"It's 'Henry.' But if you can't say that, it's 'Officer.'" I thought of Miss Julie and the baby the size of a wild peach, waiting, and how easily things could be taken away in our civilized world.

"Just tell us what you know," Collyer said. "Take a deep breath. You're a citizen in this. You said it yourself, you were off-duty when you met her."

"How did you know I talked to her in the first place?"

"You were seen."

"All right," I said. "So why'd you have to ask?" They had either been to the tavern, spoken to someone who had been there the night before, or both. The bartender had been out on the porch.

"And you left about the same time?" said Garcia.

"Yes. Listen, I thought you'd be here on the Dentry murder."

"We are. And now Ms. Bray, unfortunately."

"She said she had information to give me. I told her see me at the station. So . . ."

"Any idea about the nature of that information?"

"No."

"You had been involved with Ms. Bray, though?"

I closed my eyes and began to panic. "Some time back. I hadn't seen her in at least a year. I was surprised when she showed up."

"Why?"

"I don't know why, I just was."

The other men left a silence for the rest of the answer I didn't give.

"All right. Thank you for your cooperation, Officer," said Garcia. He put a hand on my shoulder. "Relax, okay?"

"Right," I said.

Garcia and Collyer got in their sedan and drove away. As Sheriff Dally was about to do the same, he reminded me to call sister Mag. "I think we spooked her," he said.

Inside, I struggled to seem calm. Julie knew not to ask me about work unless I volunteered, so I hoped that I wouldn't have to make up another lie. I needed time to figure out the right thing to say.

I HAVE TO turn now to earlier events. Some of what I learned, I was told not that very moment, but a few weeks after. Some of it I learned years later, on the purest blue winter day of negative five, with hilltop trees frozen white from root to overstory, and snow squeaking under our boots, too cold a day for any game to move. Some of it I know because I've been to the places myself. Some of it, it is fair to say I don't know for a fact, and could be drawing from my own life as a boy very like Ryan Conkins, circling back years to follow this story forward to its end.

Here's what: One morning, Ryan had ridden the bus to school just as he had done since his mother enrolled him at the Theodore Roosevelt Middle School. He had his lunch, a watch, and a map. He was new and it was early in the year, so they hadn't caught on to him yet, and didn't seem to care about calling home or going after him. That was coming. *But*, he thought, *let them catch me first.*

All families fought. All fathers made you feel small, said things like "stupid hurts" and shook you by the back of the neck. Mothers were disappointed and secretly unforgiving. Sisters were embarrassed for living. It hadn't occurred to Ryan to be unhappy about that; that was the way things were, and if he ever thought about it, he was glad to have his family. But he couldn't take it for granted that his father would be around, or Brit, either, the best friend he had. And he thought about that. He thought about what had happened at the wedding and the spot they were all in now. It was like a hole in a pair of jeans. Small at first, but bigger every day. At what point did you say, this hole is too big, can we patch it? Or, I can't wear these anymore, I got to throw them out, can I have a new pair.

Ryan was moving out of one world and into another. His parents were weaker than he'd known and couldn't be trusted. Which meant all so-called adults who had tried to tell him about the world might have been wrong, or they might have been every one of them agreeing to the same lie. A lie that contained ten thousand little lies: The things you learned in school would be useful one day. Anyone can be anything if he tries hard enough.

No, he was on his own. This new world was confusing and he wanted to change the way it felt, but didn't know how. So he got angry, and changed himself instead. He couldn't be angry around his mother or his grandparents, especially not Grandfather, and he couldn't stand to stay at school, which would mean that the new world was real, and what he was hiding under his anger might break out.

The other day in math he'd been lost in thought and hadn't done the work, and the guy teaching the class had asked him a question. Ryan gave a shrug, was met with a glare, and the teacher wrote something down about him in his notes for that class. This morning, in an English class of thirty kids, where they took turns reading passages aloud from busted-up textbooks full of stories—books that the students at Teddy Roosevelt covered in brown paper to keep them alive another year—Ryan began to moo. He didn't know why at first, and when the sweet, large, older woman who taught the class asked him, he merely shrugged and said, "Moo." Seeing the look on her face hurt, but he got what he wanted: a referral to the vice principal's office. Ryan's last time there, the VP had asked him if everything was all right at home. Asked him things about his home. This had made Ryan furious. He'd had to swallow that. Instead of going there again, he simply took his bag from his locker and walked out the door and into the hills.

School was on a hilltop just north of Fitzmorris. Wild Thyme was about eight miles north of that, which if he went quickly and as the crow flew would take him two, two and a half hours. It was a country place with enough cover to get him within sight of his uncle Henry's farmhouse on the hill. At first he'd fretted that he'd get caught, or that he'd get lost. Once he realized that it didn't matter, he enjoyed himself crossing enemy lines, waiting for silence before he crept across roads, slipping beyond the sight of a house into the forest behind, unseen. Sometimes stopping to watch people, or climbing up a silo ladder. When he got back to Aunt Medbh's house, he waited in the woods until he heard the bus drive by, and then appeared on the driveway and refused to talk all afternoon and night. With his baby sister vacuuming up attention, nobody asked much of him.

On his third day playing hooky, he walked along a straight clearing in the woods that was covered in soft new grass and old straw. Sections of a light green pipeline rose out of the ground like a creature. At one point he tried turning a wheel on the pipe, but wasn't quite strong enough. Above him and around him, the trees were mostly still dark green, with a red or orange burst to catch his eye every twenty feet, and a sky the cleanest blue that drew him up on his tiptoes to look into it. At his feet: moss, wintergreen, the femur of a deer, roots. Once, crossing a dirt road, he had to move deeper into the woods to avoid men standing and talking by two white pickup trucks. In the middle of a golden field with no building or road in sight, he lazed, eating his lunch with the crickets all around him. For some time he peered closely at the petals of wildflowers and let beetles and ants crawl onto his hands. These were all things he didn't get to see or do in the courtyard of the development where they lived in North Carolina, where the air was warmer and thicker, and there was no place to go where someone hadn't been before and left trash.

To get to Aunt Medbh's house from the south, Ryan had to cross a creek, and then a road that curled around a few high hills, with the house up top on one of them. The driveway was to the north, so he'd either crawl through the field next to the house or move around the woods at the edge of the clearing, so he could show up coming from the right direction. He climbed the hill on aching legs and took up his post on a dry, flat rock to wait for the right time.

Before long, he heard something moving in the woods behind him. The sound became the steady footsteps of a person. No, two. He slipped behind the rock where he'd been sitting and lay still. The footsteps stopped somewhere to his left, and some rustling and scrabbling followed, and then silence. Ryan waited a minute and then picked his head up to where he could see: Off at the edge of the woods, behind some saplings and brambles, were two men. One held a scope to his eye and was looking straight at Aunt Medbh's house. The other stood beside him on the other side, and Ryan could not get a clear look. For a wild moment he thought, was the one with the scope his dad, back from home to get him? The height was close, the body hidden under baggy camo, the face behind a bandanna. No, it wasn't him, but a stranger. The hands were harder than his father's.

The one stood for some time spying, then turned, took a water bottle or flask from a pocket, pulled his bandanna down, and had a drink. Not his dad, but a puffy, unshaven face of a man about his dad's age. He handed the bottle to the other, also in camo, and squatted, giving Ryan a look at the taller one. As the first man looked around, Ryan eased back. When he rose again to look, the strangers were not where they had been. Slowly, Ryan craned his neck to get a look at the field between him and the house; they were not there. Turning back, he faced the first man, who was now just twenty feet away, looking at him, face still uncovered. When the man took a step, Ryan ran out into the field and toward the house with all the strength and speed he had.

Later, as night fell, if he worried about the men in the woods, it was not much. They'd been dressed for hunting, so probably they'd been scouting. Maybe they shouldn't have been there, and were mad he'd caught them. He didn't know enough to tell someone, and telling someone would raise questions he didn't want to answer.

It had gotten cold enough that Mag had made Ryan move from the tent in the yard to inside the house at night. He'd broken down the tent and stowed it in a downstairs closet. With Grandfather and Grandma in one bedroom and his baby sister out cold in another, his mom's bedroom floor was his best option. That night, he lay awake. His mother finished brushing her teeth and peed in the upstairs bathroom—he could hear it—and came in wearing her night-tee that showed too much of her white legs. Ryan rolled over and faced the wall, angry without knowing why.

"Love you," she said. She read until she fell asleep with the light on.

He'd got away with it. They still didn't know that he'd left school. Not skipped, left. He'd never go back. And what they also didn't know, because they hadn't bothered to notice, was that his backpack was still out there at the edge of the woods, on the wrong side of the house. Slowly he raised himself standing and slipped out the door of the bedroom.

I N THE morning, Ryan was gone, along with his tent, sleeping bag, my .270, my third-best knife, a map, food for a few days, and all of the cash he could scrounge from the house—we guessed about a hundred dollars. I had a few theories, and quickly ruled out the first, that he was heading toward Binghamton, north of the state line to catch a bus somewhere, maybe following his father. If that were so, he'd have to ditch the rifle. He hadn't left a note, and he didn't have much money. Mag didn't think that's what he was doing, and neither did I. My next guess was that he was heading south on foot. If that were true, he'd still need more than a hundred dollars and his two good legs, and I only hoped he wouldn't be so careless as to hitchhike. The third and most likely possibility was that he needed time to himself, and was taking it somewhere nearby in the woods he'd spent the past few weeks exploring. Mag called the school and learned that they didn't have good attendance records for him.

I spiraled out from the house, and in one of the places I'd taken Ryan to in days past, a flat sunny spot in the woods with grass and a scattering of bluestone slabs, I made a troubling find: the tent, disassembled flat and abandoned.

I asked Father what he'd been telling the boy, teaching him.

"Nothing I didn't teach you," he said. "His father sure isn't going to do it. I've been telling the boy things for years; nobody mentioned it until now."

"Hunting?"

"Among other things."

We put out an alert for Ryan. I held my family, told them I'd find the kid, and went in to work, where I hoped I'd be able to think clearly.

Later that morning the sheriff called me in to Fitzmorris, and suggested I wear comfortable clothes instead of my uniform. I protested. I was going looking for Ryan, I didn't have time, it was ridiculous. No good. I wore the uniform but not the .40, drove down to Fitzmorris, and made myself available at the Holebrook County Sheriff's Department in the courthouse basement.

Ben Jackson led me down the hall to one of the interview rooms. "Any sign of the boy yet?"

"No, and I've got to say—"

"I understand. Hanluain's out looking in the meantime."

"Hanluain," I said, frustrated, and stopped myself. "Just watch out he doesn't come upon my father unawares. What about Paycheck? He may be quickest."

"It may come to that. Keep it simple in there."

So there was I, on the wrong side of a heavy wooden table, tapping my foot and looking from Garcia's face to Collyer's as they looked back at mine. In came Sheriff Dally with a coffee for me. I let it sit.

"Can we just," said Collyer, "go over your relationship to Ms. Bray again?"

We did so.

"So you never got into her vehicle with her?"

"No," I said.

"Did she touch you, make physical contact with you, last time you saw her?"

"Not that I'm aware."

"Did you still have any feelings for her?"

"No."

"Were you attracted to her?" Garcia said. "It's all right, no judgment."

"I'm married and my wife's pregnant. Shelly and I were through."

"Congratulations. I'm ... trying not to disrespect you or your wife here."

"Try a little harder."

"Look," said Collyer. "Let's be real for a minute. People have all kinds of lives. You know that." I checked in with the sheriff. His face was blank.

"Henry, did you ever visit Shelly Bray in her motel room in Fitzmorris?" said Sheriff Dally.

"No, Jesus Christ. I didn't know she had a motel room. I never even knew where she lived after the divorce. Sheriff, you tell these guys they got the wrong idea here. I don't know who's saying what, or what you found, or what you think you know. I told you the whole story. I went home to my wife. Talk to Shelly's husband."

"Why do you say that?" said Collyer.

"You know why."

"Henry," said Dally, wincing, "can we reach out to Julie?"

"You don't have to ask me," I said, hoping I was hiding my panic. "You want to talk to her, talk to her. Are we done?" The detectives and the sheriff didn't answer, but exchanged looks. "I have to go find my nephew."

"Take Jackson with you," the sheriff said.

"I don't want him. Let Jackson look someplace I'm not already looking."

The three men shifted eyes at each other. "We'd like to have someone with you for the next little while," said Garcia. "To be safe."

"Jesus Christ, don't waste your time on me."

But as I pulled out of the courthouse parking lot, Deputy Jackson followed in his patrol car.

Miss Julie worked for Franklin Ambulance, the county's only commercial ambulance company. They were located on a side street in Fitzmorris, in what used to be a mechanic's shop. The three garage doors were all open, showing all three vehicles home and in service. As I got out of my truck, Jackson opened his door too—I held up a hand to him, part plea, part warning, and headed into the station alone.

At this point, Miss Julie was showing and I had been hinting that she should stop working soon, or change her job for a little while. Paramedics ride in the back of the ambulance without any seat belt, for one. They do a lot of lifting of bloody, flailing, sick, and dead people. But my hints had annoyed her, and this was not the time to bring it up again.

In the common room, Miss Julie, uniformed in blue with her hair pulled tight into a ponytail, looked up. Her face fell when she saw mine.

"It's not about Ryan," I said. "We haven't found him yet."

"Oh. Okay," she said.

"Can we talk a minute?"

We went out into the cool fall morning outside the station, where her coworkers wouldn't hear. Miss Julie took note of Jackson sitting there in his car, but had the good sense not to wave to him or show much on her face. And I explained to her about me and Shelly Bray. Back when Miss Julie and I were getting together, I didn't know where it was going, and at some point she was in my life, and so was Shelly. And that's no hanging matter. It's the twenty-first century. But Julie once asked me if I'd stepped around with married women, because there were rumors, and I'd point-blank denied them. She had me for the lie, the skulking, dirty secret. If only I hadn't made it a secret. And the whole time I was telling her about it, our baby was between us.

"I'm sorry," I said. "You should have known about it a while back."

She didn't say it was all right. "Why are you telling me now?"

"The other night at the bar, she was there."

"Oh?"

"Julie . . ." I began.

"Go on."

"I'd never."

"You did," she said.

"Before you—mostly—and not behind your back. Not . . . really."

"Behind some other idiot's back."

"The marriage wasn't going good for them."

"Oh, my god, that's what they all say."

"Anyway, I'd never. I love you."

Miss Julie turned her face down the road. "So, Shelly Bray."

"She's dead."

"Jesus."

"She got ahold of me after the show. She said she had some information, something to tell me, but before she could come through with it, she was killed. That night. Two nights ago."

"Henry, let's get out of here. Out of town. I want to deal

with this, I want you to help me understand it, but I need us to be safe."

I stifled a flash of anger. Just go to some new place, some new house, why not. "They're going to want to talk to you. We need to find Ryan..." I looked over at Deputy Jackson in his car. "Listen, the sheriff and two state police detectives had me in an interview room this morning. It's possible their people found a trace of me, a hair, something, in Shelly's car. Maybe in her motel room, I don't know." Miss Julie gave me a look of horror. "I would never go there," I said. "I'm a policeman. There are people who want me gone. Including Shelly's husband, and whoever killed Carl Dentry. I wasn't in her car, and I wasn't in her motel room, not for any reason. But she was killed the same night she talked to me, and we have a history, so they're going to follow me for a while, search our places... and I need to get word out. For the family. To get Ryan found. We can talk when this is over. Until then, will you do something for me?"

A long silence. Then she said, "I'm listening."

WHILE JULIE WAS at work, the PSP searched the cottage at Walker Lake. Deputy Jackson and I stood in the yard and watched. The Sovereign Individual did a slow roll past in his truck. I saw him and Jackson exchange a look I couldn't read. I took five minutes to walk down to the boathouse and open the doors. Jackson followed. No sign of Ryan, and everything looked like it was in place, but hard to tell with their six small boats of different kinds, and jumbled-up stuff there. We took a pass through the woods that bordered the cottage plot and up the hill across the road to the timber-frame studio we'd built last year, full of Willard Meagher's half-done abstract paintings. No sign, but again, I couldn't say what was or wasn't a sign.

Then the circus traveled over to Aunt Medbh's house. While my family stood out in the yard, they searched the place. I kept a wary eye on my father, who stood glowering for a minute, and then disappeared into the woods. Before we left there, Deputy Jackson asked Mag for some clothing of Ryan's. Mag gave him a T-shirt.

In the Wild Thyme Township building's parking lot, they searched my station and my patrol truck. John Koslowski, the township mechanic, tinkered quietly on a dump truck in the garage, watching from the open door. Inside the one-room station, I let Collyer into my gun safe, remembering too late about the money I'd yet to turn over to the Game Commission and otherwise return. Collyer looked inside the envelope and said, "What's this?"

"A fine."

"You in the habit of collecting cash fines from the people here?"

"No."

"You have anything to document this?"

"No."

Collyer looked at me as if in bafflement, set the envelope aside, and continued picking through things. At some point Sheriff Dally showed up. Outside, they turned to my personal vehicle. The forensic techs laid all my junk out on a tarp, piece by piece. Behind the pickup's seat is where they found a red shock cord and a jack handle that wasn't mine. I know my things.

A tech showed the cord and the handle to Collyer and Garcia. It got quiet fast.

"Henry Farrell," Collyer said.

"Hold on a minute," said Dally. "His nephew's missing, his family needs him. This is a plant. It's obvious. It'll wash out."

"Henry Farrell," Collyer said again.

"We'll keep him for you," said Jackson, stepping forward and putting himself between me and the PSP detectives. "Don't worry."

A long silence passed. Garcia said, "No, we insist."

"I'm going to insist right back," said Dally.

"With respect—" began Garcia.

"I thank you, but no. You understand, my department covers all of Holebrook County when we have to."

Garcia smiled. "You called us in. We didn't call you. Do you serve this township?"

"When we have to. But that's beside the point. We serve Fitzmorris, where Ms. Bray's motel room was. We called you about Carl Dentry, not her."

"Officer Farrell isn't sheriff's department. And he's the only local police for this township."

"That's right."

"Our jurisdiction arises automatically when local law enforcement no longer covers its primary jurisdiction. And that's what we have here, because Officer Farrell is under arrest."

"Not yet, he's not. Again, our remit is the entire county."

"Just take him and let's go," said Collyer to his partner.

"Deputy Jackson," said Dally, "will you make Officer Farrell at home with us somewhere? The old lockup would be best; I don't know what kind of space we've got in the jail at the moment. Gentlemen, if you insist on insisting, we'll have to get a judge to sort this out, and I don't want to put on a spectacle."

"Sheriff . . ." began Collyer, and then thought better of it.

My mind raced. I barely followed what they'd been saying. I struggled to slow and center myself. The sheriff had bought me some time and safety, but in the end I could not submit to him or anyone. That decision, I'd already made. I'd seen too many things go wrong in too many ways to trust in my innocence alone. I turned my thoughts to the lockup in the courthouse basement, and how I might get out of it.

"You ready, Henry?" said Jackson. I got in the backseat, in the cage. "We've got to make a stop."

We drove down Route 37 in silence. It was the long way around to Fitzmorris. "Might as well read you your rights," Jackson said.

"Consider them read," I said.

"We know you didn't kill her," Jackson said. "Any ideas?" I didn't answer, but I didn't have to. Jackson said, "The ex-husband was with the kids." Jackson turned onto a dirt road that led down over a creek and then up into the hills that marked the edge of the Heights.

"That doesn't mean he didn't have it done. Where we headed?" I said.

"To get Paycheck. Least I can do while you're our guest is take him out and look for the boy." Another long silence passed. "We need people out there who know how to look."

"Is that what the sheriff thinks?" I leaned forward and took stock of the weapons in the car. One on Jackson's right hip, my guess was a shotgun racked on the other side of the panel separating me from the front seat. In my job, drawing a firearm is not necessarily a show of strength. I don't say this to criticize guns. I have shot people and would again if it was called for.

But every time I've pulled a gun on the job, I've been on my back foot. Anyway, I didn't have the .40. I'd left it in the locker out of my respect for the sheriff and the day, and my gun belt felt oddly light, like I might float. What I did have was everything else, and I wasn't handcuffed.

Paycheck was one of a pack of hounds bred and trained by a husband-and-wife team, Jimmy and Amy Bernard, who lived on about thirty acres up in that area. Their place was surrounded by woods. We came to a stop in the front yard of a log cabin.

"Well, I better see if I can find that dog." Jackson walked around the side of the house, toward the kennels. I could hear the hounds bellowing from somewhere behind the house. He came back around with Paycheck, who was running himself around in circles at the end of his leash and flinging spit. Jackson opened the other rear door.

"I'm not staying back here with him," I said.

"Henry, come on."

"No fuckin way, man. You can't put me back here with the dog."

Jackson sighed, pulled Paycheck back a couple paces, and let me out of the car. I could have run right then. I got in the front seat. Pulled my handcuffs out of my belt. Jackson got in the car, buckled himself, and put a hand on the steering wheel. As he turned his head to talk to the dog where it pawed in the backseat, I handcuffed Jackson to the steering wheel, the right hand. He swung at me with his left, and I leaned out of the way. He swung again and I pressed his arm across his body, then took the keys out of the ignition.

"Henry, goddamn it, what the fuck."

"Hey, man. I'm sorry." I opened the passenger door, flung the shotgun away, and put a foot out into the free world.

Jackson reached his left hand across his body to his right hip, where his pistol was holstered. I took his wrist and felt the anger in him. I helped him remove his gun and put it in his glove box. "Henry, come on. Henry."

"Drive yourself to my station. Get John to find the spare key, it's in the middle drawer of my desk. He'll let you out. I didn't kill anybody and my nephew's gone." With my Maglite, I did the best I could to pulverize his radio where it was bolted on the dash.

"You're making this hard. You can't come back."

"I got to find the kid and then we'll see," I said.

"We're going to find you, you know."

"Yeah." I got out then. An orange jet of pepper spray followed me out of the vehicle, over my shoulder, and past my face. It felt like fire.

"Come on, man," I said, wiping my blazing eyes, coughing, and rocketing snot out of my nose. "Did you have to?"

Jackson too was drawing his sleeve across his eyes and had opened the driver-side door to let air through. He said nothing.

"Okay," I choked out, my throat closing. "See you later." I walked to the woods, ducked under a few branches, and went on my way.

RAN THROUGH the woods with eyes that hardly saw. My uniform was soaked through and my side was twisted in a knot. I couldn't draw enough breath. All my life, out of one trap and into another. A vine dangled over the quicksand to pull myself out, into another mess. From junior high to high school was a blessing, and then a curse; the inmates made all the rules, and changed them every day. From high school to the Tenth Mountain Division, and the army pulled me free of childhood, of fading beliefs, of a house that couldn't afford me and didn't want me. Then, after an adventure overseas, how to shake loose the army and its discipline? I had no ideas and a lot of training. I was tired to death of not being free and I wanted to make the rules. Being nothing and making no money felling trees all day wasn't freedom. A cop, I'd thought: that would put me over top for good. It took more school, more fluorescent lights and waiting around.

There was one shining moment in the Wind River Range, in Wyoming, where I'd met my first wife. Polly was no dream. But she died before we'd had a chance to live the life we imagined. Now Shelly was gone, whoever she'd been to me. I hated to think of what was on the horizon next, and didn't dare call Miss Julie's face to mind, didn't dare think of our baby.

A series of traps, and things ripped from me that I couldn't live without. That was the pattern fate made in my life. I'd have changed it if I could. But a small-town cop has no power over how things are deep down. I always felt that what set us police apart was not power or a badge, but a point of view about fate. The people we serve are tangled in it, the ultimate trap in life. Our understanding of its workings, the way we tried to find patterns in it, the way we could laugh at its jokes—that was something we got to wear like a uniform. The people we collared were surprised. A man pulsing with drugs and drink is marched past his neighbors in restraints, naked but for a look of wonderment on his face. How did this come to be? You, you fucked up. But we, we saw it coming for miles.

As I was slipping around peoples' homes and setting their dogs barking, I wouldn't have put this into words. I'm telling you now. Then, I felt it as a lack of outs, a spike of fear. Fate had closed in on me. With all that I knew, I hadn't seen it in time. I would never feel completely like a policeman again.

I waited in the green shadows beneath the hemlocks that grew behind Mike and Roberta Stiobhard's house, unsure that Julie had brought the message. Out front their dog was restless. At one point, Bobbie came out back and raked some leaves, whistling. No sign of Danny or Jennie Lyn, and of course no trace of Alan. By now, citizens would be searching for my nephew around Aunt Medbh's house and the cottage on Walker Lake, probably doing as good a job as the state police, and getting under their feet into the bargain. When night fell, I'd be able to move more freely. Until then, I could not be seen by the wrong people.

When I looked next, Bobbie had gone back into the house, but she'd left something hanging on a tree by the edge of the woods. I crept up and found a camouflage coat and a small green backpack. The coat had to be twenty years old, soft and faded. In the bag: cans of pineapple juice, sandwiches of pre-cooked bacon, a bunch of bananas, and many apples. A jar of preserved venison. Also, an entire package of cookies. A hunting knife and a black .38 revolver. A handwritten note that gave me the name of a place I knew and could get to on foot.

A couple times, I dropped to the ground to avoid passing cars. Once I took a long way around a field that was being brush-hogged late in the season. Behind a double-wide trailer, a shaggy pony was tethered and had eaten the grass to stubble in a perfect circle.

I blamed Shelly for getting killed—for being the kind of person who that happened to, for getting in the way of my life at every turn. She was dead and I was angry. I didn't have time to be anything else. Later, I would remind myself that anger was nothing but confusion. I watched my feet, followed the deer paths, and kept silent.

The farther down off the ridge I got, the closer together the houses were. I heard the chain saw's roar over the hill, and crept around the edge of a little bog and up the slope to where a lone man had felled about an acre of trees behind a small house. I recognized Danny Stiobhard's flatbed truck, fitted with slats to make a bed, where he'd loaded some firewood. Danny was bent over a tree, chain saw at full roar, bucking the trunk into pieces. Every now and then he straightened up, quickly scanned the woods, and went back to his work. I got close. I was never sure that he saw me, but after some time he switched the saw off, took off his ear protection, and walked to the edge of the trees not far from where I crouched. He stood as if taking a leak, whistled a bit, and said, "There's an old fella in the house. He likes to supervise. We got one chance; you'll see it."

Danny returned to the truck, heaved armloads of firewood into the back, and got in. He backed the truck way up the tree line. I ran low and climbed into the bed as he was pulling forward. Danny had left a narrow channel in the firewood where I was meant to lie. I took off my glasses, pulled some logs over me, and protected my head with my arms. Soon I was pinned on all sides by a pile of sharp, split wood that smelled like the weekend. The truck shook itself awake and moved out of the yard and to the road. As we picked up speed and made a few turns, I tried to get some sense of where we were, but couldn't. There was a heavy bounce as we hit a pothole somewhere and everything in the bed floated for a second and fell; a corner of firewood knocked between my elbows, and busted my upper lip. I felt around my teeth with my tongue, and nothing was missing. Pepper oil residue from Jackson's spray can got in the cut. Soon, though, the fall air rushing through the gaps in the logs cooled me.

The truck turned onto a dirt driveway and swayed up a long winding course, idled for too long, then backed into a structure. Firewood was lifted, and I sat up and saw four silent, curious animal faces craning to look at me: llamas raised by Lee Hillendale and his wife Greta on a farm northeast of Fitzmorris. The animals gathered at the far end of a horse barn that had been refitted to house them.

Lee Hillendale was there in his shirtsleeves. Hillendale was Holebrook County's best criminal defense attorney; he'd crossed me on some cases and made me look a fool, but it wasn't personal. We liked each other, and the more I knew of him and Greta, the more I liked. Contrary to outward appearances they were devoted hippies, living life their way in the Endless

Mountains. Either Lee or Greta was rumored to be wealthy. If not, it was unclear how he could make a living defending DUIs and assaults for degenerate clients who mostly couldn't pay.

"You look terrible," Lee said. "You want some water or something?"

I removed my shirt, found a slop sink in the barn, and washed my face and beard, then dried myself on a blanket that smelled like llama. "What do you hear in town?"

"Nothing. I took a turn past the courthouse and it's quiet. Nothing on the news."

"They'll come after me," I said. "I need you to take a record of what happened." I glanced at Danny.

Lee held up a hand. "Danny, Henry's too polite to tell you to leave. I'll buy this load of wood. Two hundred?" Danny said nothing. "You can pile it out in the woodlot."

Danny turned to me.

"Thank you, brother," I said.

He said, "Oh, you're mighty welcome, sir, I'm just the fuckin . . . field hand around here." He pulled the truck out of the barn.

"If I can help, I will," Lee said. He rolled up his sleeves. "Julie didn't say much, but by the way you got here, you have an issue with the law."

"I do. And I'd pay you to clear me, somehow, even after . . . If I get killed, I want my people to have the story. I wish I knew who to trust." I put on my shirt.

Lee locked eyes with me, and said with absolute kindness, "Hey, I've been doing this a long time. I don't talk to cops, man. No offense to the cop in the room. But whether you did it or you didn't, I'll need three hundred an hour in the end."

"You don't need money now, a what, retainer?" Miss Julie's people would have whatever money Hillendale needed up-front, but I hated to ask.

"No, you're fine. We've got a relationship."

The field was calling me back, but I knew I had to take enough time to give Lee the outlines of what I knew and what I had done. As I said it aloud, an understanding of the worst kind dawned on me: as long as I was alive, they'd have a harder time fitting me into their frame. Once I was dead, they could say what they wanted. If I was dead, I had done it.

When I finished, Lee shook his head and said, "We have seen the best of our time. Machinations, hollowness, treachery. And *you* . . ." he said, standing, thinking. "You're out of your mind. Turn yourself in, babycakes."

"I need someone to keep an eye on Julie," I said. "I asked her to go to her parents' place, but she—"

Across the dooryard, I heard a familiar whistle approximating the tail end of a bobolink's song, sailing across the dooryard, a Stiobhard signal. I took my bag and stepped into the nearest stall in the barn and sank out of sight. The llama in the stall with me shied into the far corner with fear and disgust on its strange face. In that far corner lay a gawky baby llama, its legs tucked up under it. When I didn't move, the mama craned her neck down and bit me, catching mostly my coat, but some of my arm. Then she retreated to the corner and her baby. I'd heard no car coming up the drive, but in a moment Sheriff Dally was in the doorway of the barn, greeting Lee.

"Sheriff," Lee said loudly, "what brings you here?"

"Oh, business. The things I deal with anymore. I've got a headache you wouldn't believe."

"Have you tried working your pressure points? There's one right between your thumb and pointer. Just go like this—"

"Any word from Henry Farrell today?"

"Why do you need him?"

"He's . . . he'd do well to come down to the courthouse and talk." I heard the sheriff take a few steps into the barn, unsettling the llamas. My stall-mate had craned her head out to gawk at the newcomer. "The animals look healthy. But what would I know."

"I'm not sure why you're here."

The sheriff took a few more steps. I heard Lee keep pace with him, slowing him down. The borrowed .38 was in my hand.

"Julie Meagher Farrell was seen going into your office earlier today. And here you are, in the middle of the day, in a shirt and tie. Your animals look fine."

"Sometimes I miss them during the day. That's the beauty of a solo practice. I can do what I want."

"I see you've got Danny Stiobhard out there. He working off some fees?"

"If I see Henry, I'll tell him you'd like to speak with him. What's it about?"

"He'll know." Dally's voice, though quiet, bounced off of the barn walls. "He needs to see me *first*. That's important. He can come to my house if he has to."

"All right. If I see him. I don't know why I would. Now, Sheriff, let me tell you something." The footsteps stopped. "It's none of your business who comes to my office, or why. It's certainly none of your business what I do with my day. And one more thing: leave my fucking llamas out of it."

Both men laughed in the end. As the sheriff left, Mama

craned her head down, gently took my arm in first her weird lips, and then her huge teeth, and clamped down so tight the world went red. I was happy to give her and the baby the run of the stall, and moved into the shadows of the barn away from the door. Lee caressed the animal's neck and puttered around the barn as if I weren't there at all.

Danny Stiobhard came back in. "He may be watching the place," he said.

"I can't ask more than what you've done," I told him.

"I ain't doing it because you asked."

Lee said, "However you get Henry out of here, I don't want to know. I'm heading in for a sandwich, and then over to the courthouse."

"Stay safe," I said.

After the lawyer left, I told Danny to take me to Red Pine Road. He grabbed a couple hay bales and a blue tarp and threw them in front of the barn door. I crept on my belly around the side of the barn and to where the distance to the tree line was shortest. I waited, waited, then slunk low to the woods and made my way to the roadside a few hundred yards north of Lee's driveway. I saw no sign of the sheriff, and neither did Danny, because he slowed down for me where I could swing into the truck's bed and under the tarp.

IF THE SHERIFF's people were out looking for me, then they stood a chance of finding my nephew, too. And they'd be keeping an eye on my family up by Aunt Medbh's. I could have stayed hidden if I wanted. It was a risk, visiting Carrianne Ceallaigh. She didn't like me and had no reason to talk, except that Shelly Bray had been her friend. State police might have people down by the Freefall at any time. I had Danny drop me off at the other side of the swamp down there, and wasted no time getting through the woods to the Ceallaighs' rear property line. Nobody was out there.

I brushed off my clothing and gave myself a sniff—nothing I could do about it. I crept to the front of the house. A mid-sized black car with PA plates was parked in the driveway. A look inside told me it was a personal vehicle, so I risked a knock on the Ceallaighs' front door.

Carrianne appeared and told me it was not a good time. Looking at me, she must have known something was off. For her part, she was harried, and her eyes were red.

"It's important," I said. "It's about Shelly."

"Hold on."

She closed the door and I waited there a moment, down at the dirt track that wound through their land. The door opened once again. "Come on in," she said.

Too late, I caught something wrong in her tone. A stocky woman with dark hair and glasses stood inside, with a hand reaching into her blazer. I put my hands up, and forced my eyes to move slowly around the interior of the house.

"Don't run," the woman said. "You know me. Allie DeCosta, AG's office—"

I turned to the door where I'd just come in, but Carrianne blocked my way. I bolted through the house to the kitchen, where I knew there was a back door. I slammed through that and was free, but looked down to find the Ceallaigh kids looking up at me from the yard in wonderment. Then I felt DeCosta's weapon touch behind my ear, where the kids couldn't see. We went back inside.

"Goddamn it, sit down," DeCosta told me, pointing to a nice-looking sofa in the living room. "What're we going to do with you."

"Nice meeting you, but I can't stay," I said.

"All right, let me just call the detectives, then, let them know where to find you," said DeCosta.

"They can try." I scanned the room again.

"Okay, calm. We're both here to help, you and me," DeCosta said, sending me a message with her eyes.

I stayed on high alert, but stopped my mind racing toward flight. "Yes," I said. I pointed to a chair where I could see out of windows on two sides of the house. "I'm just going to move over there."

"Sure," said DeCosta.

I did so. All this while, Carrianne sat silent across the room, her head in her hands.

"I'm sorry about Shelly," I said carefully. "But I didn't kill her and I don't have time. My nephew's gone missing. Nothing comes before that. I came here in the first place because Shelly told me she had some information I was supposed to know. Carrianne," I said, "you two were friends. I'm wondering if you had any idea what she had to tell me. We could just . . . tell somebody that, and clear this all up, and I can do what I have to do."

Carrianne didn't move or give any sign that she'd heard me.

DeCosta spoke. "What Shelly knew, I knew, pretty much. She'd been FOIA-ing information from state agencies. The AG, state police, PDE, Department of Public Welfare. FBI. Except that last one, all those agencies are currently in a joint investigation and audit of the commonwealth's juvenile adjudications."

This had to have been a response to the Kids for Cash scandal down in Luzerne County, where a judge got together with a few businessmen to populate a for-profit detention center, sending relative innocents down and taking kickbacks. It got some national attention. It turned out I was right.

"Pure cover-your-ass, after Luzerne," DeCosta said. "What are best practices from a justice standpoint. Shelly had been asking about her ex, who had been placed at one point. She never knew what for. And because of this ongoing statewide thing, she was provided some documents, but not enough. She wasn't going to quit. We spoke a bit on the phone, and I could see her point of view. Of course, with so many agencies in play, I couldn't let her know much, so I gave her a name of someone who could keep her busy. Let her believe work was being done, but keep her out of our hair."

"She told me she was the one who hired Carl," I said.

"But the question is," DeCosta said, "where did that lead Carl?"

At this, Carrianne Ceallaigh burst into great, harsh sobs.

"Come on in the kitchen," said DeCosta. Away from Carrianne, DeCosta told me the story of a girl named Lily. That's not her real name. Age ten, Lily lost her father and uncle to an alcohol-involved wreck late one night, and then her mother to heroin soon after. Age twelve, she was able to get out of foster care and live with her older half-sister, Danielle—also not her real name—who was merely twenty-two. Lily grew up fast in Danielle's house. And in a few years, she was tagging along with Danielle to the bars, country music shows, keggers, and races.

She lowered her voice. "Lily died before she turned seventeen. Heroin. They found her on the edge of some campsite near Doublin Park. There'd been an all-day, all-night party and an MDRA race. She had too much too fast. Someone, maybe several individuals, had been with her, and just...left her. Going back through PDE files that I knew had stayed on Carl's mind, Lily's was one. A year before she died, she'd made statements to friends about sexual contact with adult men. One was a teacher, and that turned out to be a lie, so our job was done at that point. But in the course of that whole deal, she'd mentioned a friend of her sister's, a Ty Kelly. Ty Kelly swore up and down he'd never known her. That always bothered Carl, because how did this kid get his name, but he's saying he doesn't even know her a little bit?

"A year later, she turns up dead at Doublin. One of the men questioned by PSP was Ty Kelly. Again, he doesn't know her. Now, that was Ty Kelly out of Hazleton. When I start looking into Carl's death, who do I see but Terry Ceallaigh out of Wild Thyme on one of the investigation reports? I run his name like I do everyone's and come up with 'Ty Kelly,' and there it is. Turns out, the Brays and Ceallaighs have a connection."

"So Carl, what, ran into Terry somewhere as he's shadowing Bray, recognizes him, maybe Bray recognizes Carl..." DeCosta gestured for me to lower my voice. I did. "You here waiting for him alone?"

"He's not coming back. He left a note for Carrianne and the kids, had Carrianne burn it, unfortunately. He doesn't make any admissions, but his meaning was clear. I've been trying to figure out where he might have gone, who he runs around with."

The pieces still were not fitting in my mind. "So what does this have to do with Shelly? Why would he kill her?"

DeCosta gave me a long, questioning look. "I don't know

that he did. Let me give you some names, see what they mean to you. There's Joseph Jonathan Blaine. Alan Stiobhard. Nathan Hancock."

John Blaine I'd never expected to see again—a petty trafficker with dreams who got burned and had to run. "What's the connection?"

"All those guys were at Tiernan's Gap together as boys. So was Bray."

Carrianne spoke from the doorway. "Terry used to work for Nate Hancock a few years back. Nate had money and a boat and that, more than he should have. Terry liked working for him. Nate stopped by a couple times this month. It wasn't a social call. They talked; I didn't hear anything. Terry said it was business. I thought he might've been selling Nate something?"

"Thank you, hon," DeCosta said.

"But was Terry ever in the system?" I said.

"No," said Carrianne.

I looked at DeCosta for an answer. "No."

"If you find him," Carrianne said, "tell him his family wants him around. Tell him we'll try to understand."

I heard gravel popping on the driveway.

"Don't run," said DeCosta. "You'll get yourself killed."

"I've been here too long," I said. "I need a car."

"Don't." DeCosta's right arm tensed and her hand hovered.

I ran out the back door—no kids this time—and halfway around the house. There was the black Crown Vic, with Collyer just getting out of the passenger side. I turned back around and sprinted for the garage. It had been some years since I rode a dirt bike. The Ceallaighs kept theirs in good condition and I got one to start right away. As I tore through the yard, I caught a flash of Collyer and Garcia standing at the back door, drawing their weapons, and then I was around the house and down the driveway.

The Crown Vic was turned onto Red Pine Road behind me. I opened the bike up but the PSP vehicle kept on. I rounded a bend and saw a county patrol car turning diagonal across the road. The bike wobbled as I braked, I pivoted on a foot and stood a moment as the unmarked Crown Vic lurched to a halt, blocking the way I'd come. I bounced up into a gap in the trees, the bike bucking and my legs seizing. Half on the bike, half on my legs, I scrambled up the slope. Ahead, a trail opened and I spilled onto the Moores' lawn, getting thrown off the bike in the process. Below, the state detectives' car had turned onto the driveway. I wrestled the bike up and tore across the lawn to the trees.

Not many men knew the trails like I did. I breathed a bit easier and my vision widened out as I picked my way down a series of switchbacks that led to a meadow full of blueberries, pinks, and the last wild thyme of summer. From there, I had three different directions I could take. I sped across the field to a trail ribbed with tree roots; it took me south to a small house, a plot of land, and a half-mile stretch of Route 189. I stopped at the edge of the road, shut off the engine, and listened; hearing nothing, I blazed over to a power line cut and climbed the ridge in sunlight. At the top, I laid the bike down, then myself, and watched as the unmarked car cruised past. Some time later, a county patrol car came from the other direction. I had time to think.

Carl Dentry hadn't been killed in a rage; he'd been killed in desperation, and his body had been torn apart to make him disappear. It was not that Terry Ceallaigh had killed that poor underage kid. But he'd used her, and abandoned her, and Carl Dentry had caught up with him about it. It wasn't what he was in Wild Thyme to do, and he hadn't expected it. I pictured Carl spending his nights at the High-Thyme, not much else going on, and one night, in walks the man he knew as Ty Kelly. Or following the Brays over to the Ceallaighs' place, looking into backgrounds, and there it is.

I had stayed in one place too long. I heard a careful, too-loud footstep on dry leaves. There at a trailhead not thirty feet from me stood County Deputy Jackson, his face swollen and angry.

"Time to come in," he said.

I stood. "My nephew home?" I looked closer. "How are your eyes?"

He blinked, then sprinted across the clearing at me, faltering over a group of sapling stumps. I tried to get the bike up and started, couldn't, left it, and only just slipped out of his grasp. We were in the woods again. He chased me to the edge of an outcropping, thirty feet down. As I slowed, I pushed moss and leaves over the edge with my feet. Then I leapt out and down for a tree branch, caught it, dropped into briar patch, and ran until I was sure he'd given up.

The day was disappearing. I ran and hid the few miles over to the woods surrounding Aunt Medbh's place. My clothesline was empty; some clothes hanging there would have signaled that Ryan had been found and was home. I saw Ed Brennan's truck in the driveway. There were voices coming from the next hill, so I followed the trail in the direction of where Ryan's tent had been found, and nearly ran in to County Deputy Hanluain and Shaun Loughlin coming down from the clearing. I headed back the way I came until I got to where a narrow stream passed through a shintag. I went down the stream from stone to stone as silently and far as I could get, and ducked down until the men had passed. I watched my house until the daylight began to fail. Nobody ever hung out the wash.

I made myself be still. At one point I saw Miss Julie walk out to the middle of the field and turn around in a circle, looking. I had one last hope of understanding things, but I could not get where I needed to get until nightfall. As the sun fell, I crept away again, walking the edge of the roads and disappearing into the shadows when headlights passed.

Where I was going in the end, the place I'd told Julie to tell the Stiobhards about, I'd once taken her to pick apples: a little abandoned farmstead off a little abandoned road that the beavers of the township had sunk and claimed as their territory. The road itself was swamp. Because the township couldn't allow the road to be used, they had recently planted lines of trees in the intersection to leave no doubt: the way was closed to automobiles. Once onto it, I risked stepping out of the trees, and then onto a deer path that ran parallel to where the road had been. As I got close, I could smell the apples I crushed underfoot.

There was enough of a clearing to where anyone watching the perimeter would see me coming. I raised my hands and stepped slowly into the moonlight. Nobody stopped me. Porch steps wasting away like cardboard. Fiddleheads grew in pale sprays out of holes in the wood, dying back for fall. The pink paint on the front door had long since flaked away, leaving only seams blended with the grain of the wood. A hint of light came from somewhere inside. The door rattled as I knocked and announced.

A moment. Footsteps, and then a boy's voice trying to sound manful: "It's me opening the door."

My nephew Ryan Conkins stood in the gloom, my .270 on his shoulder and pointed at the ceiling. I pulled him to me and onto the porch, and wrapped him in a hug, searched him and his eyes for hurts and wounds, and I have to say I did cry a bit and thanked God for his safety. There was a thin red mark all the way around his neck. The kid cried too, trying not to. But when I put my hand on the stock of the .270 to take it, he clamped a hand to it, refusing me with hard eyes.

A soft voice drifted out of the ruined house. "Tell him."

Ryan tipped his head in the direction of the voice. "You know him, right? He helped me."

Inside, pools of light from candles and oil lamps pulsed against the darkness. There was not a window left, and we were indoors and outdoors at once, the sound of rattling leaves and the Morse code of crickets and the smell of wild animals filling the house. I kept Ryan behind me. The floors had been swept clean, and empties had been removed, and at a kitchen table surrounded by mismatched chairs sat Alan Stiobhard, looking comfortable and at home. Sitting on a countertop with dangling legs was a woman not twenty, with greasy hair, wearing a long parka with a hood fringed with coyote fur. With chewed fingers she held an old flip phone.

"I hope you weren't followed," Alan said, soft as moths' wings.

"You helped him," I said.

"I can be helpful when I want. He's a good boy. Cautious. We've been at a stalemate." Moving only his eyes, Alan gestured to the tabletop, where an automatic handgun lay. "He won't put down the rifle."

I tilted my head down, showing him where my hand was in my jacket pocket, holding the handgun.

"Let's not get carried away, now," Alan said. "I'm with you."

I looked over to Ryan. He took a breath and began to speak.

IN THE DARK of the night before, Ryan had found his backpack still sitting at the far edge of the woods near Aunt Medbh's house. Nobody'd seen or heard him. With his tent, the .270, and some money, he was invincible and free. The cold quiet seemed to sing a long note that pulled him into it. No mosquitoes in this chill. He moved to a different part of the woods and a trail that led beyond. Anyone coming, he'd hear it. He sat for a while, looking into the world and into his own mind.

He felt trouble coming, but before he'd take any punishment, he'd make them see. They'd have to put him back at the center of things, and maybe he'd find some way to stay there. If not, he'd hike his way down to Dad and Brit.

From the middle of the big field, between him and the house, a shape moved and made a sharp snuff. Ryan was halfway down the trail and into the woods before he knew what he was doing. Because I'd shown him, he knew the place I liked to camp—a flat, dry hilltop with second-growth maples coming in, where the moss carpeted shale slabs and made natural mattresses. From the hilltop he could look down onto two deer trails—one leading back to the ravine the way he'd come, the other off to the east, where overgrown logging trails went in all directions. It was quiet. He didn't go far; he wanted to be found.

The tent smelled wet as he shook it out and bent the poles through the sleeves. The rifle lay nearby. He didn't hear the footsteps behind him until a man's arm closed around his neck. Henry or Grandfather? By smell, no. He fought, turned his head to the side, and pulled free. He ran and almost made it to the woods, where he'd have a chance to dodge and hide, but another man, unmasked, stepped into his path. He'd seen the man the day before. Ryan stopped and was knocked down. A rope went over his head and was pulled tight around his neck. Terror, then darkness.

The boy awoke in a different darkness, with a fuzzy, sick feeling that told him not to move. It was this feeling that convinced him he was alive. There was little to see, and what there was clicked along in his vision like freeze-frames. His neck felt raw and wet but was not bleeding. Someone had laid him out on his sleeping bag.

When he awoke again, he was stronger. He propped himself up on his elbows and focused on the narrow lines of light at the far end of the room, and the faint smears of light along one edge of the ceiling where it looked like rust had eaten through. He sat up, and his head swam. Taking his time, he drew his legs under him, raised himself to his knees, and then his feet. The noises he made echoed too loud, too long. Standing felt better. His things were gone. At the far end of the room, the light drew him, but he feared it, too. Fear, regret: this was it. Guilt at the pain it would cause his mother and sister. That was the worst thing, and in the end it was not fear of his own pain and death that got him moving and searching for a weapon, but thoughts of his family.

He crept the length of the room to the dark at the back. The floor was slightly slanted in some way he didn't understand, and the walls were metal. Turning the corner, he took just three steps before hitting the next wall. This space, he knew. A freight trailer. He walked halfway to the light at the front, then turned back again, scanning for a blade or a club. Then, again. Each time, he forced himself a little closer to the light.

On the ten thousandth turn, there was a knock on the door. Ryan froze, then crept back to the darkness at the far end. He waited what felt like a few minutes, and there was no second knock. In the darkness, he started to hear voices. Then, a second knock on the outside of the trailer.

A man's voice: "Come on, kid. Time to go home." Then, "Come on, bud. How long have you been in there?" Then, "I'm going to open the door."

One door swung open, letting light in, not quite enough to reach him where he crouched in the dark. He heard whispering.

I can only guess how he felt. He stood and walked the length of the trailer to the door. His eyes adjusted to the light. In a quick glance he counted three men standing in a line. Between him and them was a silver tarp laid out on the ground. Forest surrounded them.

"Come out, now," said a new voice, soft and high for a man's. "It won't hurt."

Ryan lowered himself from the trailer and looked from one man to the next. All were unmasked. The middle one had glasses and a very long beard, and held his uncle's .270. Ryan stepped left, and the left man moved with him. He stepped right, and the right man moved. Ryan said, "Leave me where they can find me."

A change came over the center man's face. He pulled out a handgun, lightning-quick, and pointed it at the left man's head, and held the right man in place with the .270.

"Can you use the rifle?" the bearded man said to Ryan.

"Yes."

"Stand up straight, come here, and take it."

Ryan's eyes flickered left and right, looking for escape.

The voice turned hard. "Don't you run, or I can't help. I know your uncle. Come here!"

Nobody spoke or moved, and then the stronger, shorter, left-hand man looked straight at Ryan and said, "If you go with him, I will make it hurt. And they will never, never find you."

"Come here," said the man holding the guns. Then the boy stepped forward, across the tarp. "Take this," said the man, handing Ryan the .270 while keeping the taller, right-hand man pinned with it. "My name is Mr. Alan. If he moves, shoot him until he stops," nodding toward the taller one, who, though strong, had long braids and showed weakness. He wouldn't meet Ryan's eyes.

Ryan pressed the rifle to his shoulder. He was once again aware of the world beyond the four of them there. The freight trailer was old, very old, to where trees had grown up around it and there was no way to get it out. Its wheels were hidden by brambles. A large firepit was off to the side. There was no road or trail he could see. Like everywhere up here, they were on a hill among other hills.

"We're going to walk," said Mr. Alan. "If I see either of you, I'll kill you. If you follow us on the road, I'll stop, and I'll kill you."

"You got it wrong," said the left-hand man. "I'll shoot you like a dog."

"Keep steady," said Mr. Alan to Ryan, whose gaze had strayed. "If either one moves, shoot your man where he stands. It's you or him." Ryan pressed the rifle's stock into his shoulder and got ready to pull the trigger. They all stood there. The wind picked up. "All right, then."

Ryan and Mr. Alan backed away from the trailer, slow. Once they were down the slope and out of sight, Mr. Alan turned Ryan around with a rough hand, pointed in a direction, and whispered, "Run till you see a little green car."

Ryan ran, still gripping the .270 tight, whipped and torn by branches. The woods were a blur until a dirt road took shape beneath him, and there was the green car. A black king-cab pickup was parked nearby. He approached the car from behind, tapped on the driver's window, the soul of politeness. As he did so, several gunshots snapped in the distance behind him. He yanked open the rear door, got in, and put his head down with the trash and empties back there. A young woman with a hard, pocked face turned to him from the front seat, then looked uneasily to the hill where he'd come from.

"What am I supposed to do with you if he doesn't make it?" said the woman, a girl, closer to Ryan's age than Mr. Alan's. She started the car.

Two shots, up close.

"There he is," the girl said. "Shooting their tires."

Mr. Alan got in. "Go," he said. The girl drove away.

The girl's name was Nicky. Ryan never got her last name. It was silent in the car but for Mr. Alan's commands—turn right here, faster—and Ryan had no idea where they were going. At a crossroads in the middle of nowhere, Nicky parked and they traded the green car for a blue hatchback with rust on its doors. As Nicky pulled out, Ryan noticed the road ran parallel to a set of train tracks. Something like sapphires glinted among the trees—little glass globes in rows on falling-down electric poles.

Silence, then Nicky said to Mr. Alan, "How does it feel sitting up front for once?" To Ryan, who had only just allowed himself to peer out of the window, she said, "Usually he's like you, lying down in the backseat. He never drives."

Mr. Alan lowered himself and seemed to hide beneath his hat. "Quiet," he said.

"You taking me home?" said Ryan.

"Quiet."

They drove into the hills, into the woods, and left the car a short way up a logging trail. There were no houses anywhere. Mr. Alan held a hand out for the rifle. Ryan took a couple steps back.

"Bud, it's over. You give it to me."

"It's not yours, though."

"I'm not going to keep it."

Ryan stayed quiet. They stood there, looking at each other. "If you point that at me or her . . ." Alan said, shaking his head.

"No," said Ryan. "But I don't know you."

Mr. Alan laughed softly. "If you don't know me by now." He pointed down the road and said, "You first, Farrell."

"It's Conkins."

"After you, Conkins."

NICKY HAD GONE OUT the back door and up the hill to the ladies', as there was no working plumbing in the house. Ryan stayed quiet as Alan explained his version of events, skirting certain truths. The boy broke in to say something here and there. Alan claimed that the other two men had asked him up to the freight trailer to put the fear of God in an upstart dealer from north of the border. Not to kill anyone, least of all a boy. If

I was going to accept Alan's help, there would be other lies, and meanings that changed in the light.

"Who was it asked you there?" I said to Alan.

Alan said nothing. Then, "Conkins, go stand guard on the porch." Once Ryan had left the house, Alan said, "It's not me you've got to worry about now. They can't run me, and they know it. I might have done a thing or two for them in years past, but never a kid. And not one of our own," he said, looking at me with meaning. "You're close. They're panicking, and people are getting killed. They wouldn't have taken the boy in the first place if they'd been thinking straight." He shook his head. "They finally caught on that I'm safer dead. Evidently that's what they think about you, too. Time to disappear."

"Who is 'they'?" I said, knowing very well.

"You know."

"They'll kill you if they can. Why protect them?"

"Oh, I'll not protect them. I'll kill them. If they come for me, it won't be me to blame." Alan's voice rose above a murmur, and his words came a little faster. "I don't pay no taxes. I don't have a driver license. I don't know what my social number is. I live a certain way. If I start doing things different, who knows what kind of shit I'll get into. I trust my way. You think I trust you?" He shook his head. "The men looking for the boy and me now, them I trust to do as expected." Alan began rolling a cigarette.

"We need to get the boy to safety. Then I can help."

"What're you waiting for?" he said.

"The state police think I killed somebody. I didn't like the way it looked, and I ran. I can't go back until I sort it out. I don't know who to trust myself."

He nodded. "I'm sorry about Shelly. She had spirit."

"Uh-huh."

Alan peered at me over the top of his glasses. "She didn't mean anything to you?"

The question slipped in like a needle. "She did."

"She never meant much to that husband of hers."

"Clearly." I watched Alan perfect his cigarette and light it. I said, "Did you do the work?"

"No."

"Do you know who did?"

"Not specifically."

"Can you take the boy to my father?"

Alan laughed.

"Can the girl?" I said.

"She's my ride out of here. How about your wife?"

"No."

"I understand. She'd be followed anyway. Your old man knows the place, and he can handle himself. Give him a call. Better: call my old man, have him meet yours. The cops may be listening to your phones."

By this time, Nicky had returned and was standing by the kitchen door. Like always, her cell phone was in her hand to fidget with. I asked her to borrow it, and she looked alarmed.

"I'm not going to look through it."

"Hand it over," Alan said, and she did. Alan gave the landline number for his parents, and I made the call. Bobbie picked up.

I said who I was, and asked that if Mike was free, could he call over to Aunt Medbh's place where my family was, and, using their old names for hunting spots, tell Father where we were?

"The boy, too?"

"He's with me."

"Blessings."

"If you could get word to my wife that I'm all right . . ."

As we spoke, the phone lit up and came alive in my hand like a fish. I nearly dropped it, finished the call, and handed it back to Nicky.

"They should be on their way," I said. "We have some time."

As we waited, Alan looked up at the ceiling and smoked. "I came to Tiernan's Gap in a gray van," he said. "The home was a couple gray boxes on a gray hill. At that time I still thought they could get me out. That's the only way I had of getting by. It wasn't going to be any long time, it was a mistake and I'd be home. They processed me in and threw away my shoes.

"The first day I don't think I said one word. I just watched. The nail-biters, the loons, they had their own hallway at night. Nobody was trying to teach them, nobody was trying to correct them. They were just there. Sometimes they'd get wild, but usually not in hate. It wasn't personal. You just had to watch for it.

"The everyday kids were . . . some, you wondered why. You could see their real lives—the kids they really were at home— cowering inside them. I've come to think that the more you showed your real self in that place, the sooner somebody'd beat it out of you. Some were violent, like it was a thing they did. Some kids in there were violence itself. It was what they were. Black, white, brown, whatever. All in there together, separated out by tribe, oil and water.

"What do you do when you're scared all the time and catching beatings? I mean there were kids who'd probably killed over a corner to sell crack-rock from. You catch a beating, and if you talk, the next time maybe your arm is broke, maybe worse. You don't bring it to some caseworker who can't get a job teaching gym. How many beatings can you take before the kid you were is gone? You go back to your tribe, to safety in numbers. But I was raised that my only tribe was my family. Don't trust nobody else. So I got in with the loons during the day and tried to ride it out. That was one way to do it.

"By the end of the first week I'd had enough. I just walked out the front door; it wasn't hard. How I was going to get all the way back home in my slippers, I didn't know. It was coming on winter. What I was going to do at night to stay warm, I didn't know. I had no food. I just . . . saw the door and went. Around back to the trees and gone. The cops caught me hitchhiking that same afternoon.

"I tried it a couple more times. By then they had a guard to grab me by the ear if I put a toe out of line. Sometimes I'd make them chase me, shut the whole fuckin place down. I was fast too. They started adding weeks onto my placement. Punishing the whole crew for shit I did alone. My folks came to beg me, just stay put and finish up. Danny and Jennie came. The boys had things to say about my family. I swallowed it.

"What really ended all that was, they had a small gym with a couple basketball hoops. It had one of those dividers that folded like an accordion, you know? I hid inside the housing. There was a place where I could stand straight. By nighttime, they had the whole building turned out, they had the cops out looking, all the kids had to stay in their rooms. My plan was, there was a bay door in the back of the home, where the kitchen and storeroom was. If I could get there, I'd just press the green button and go. It started to quiet down just when I thought I couldn't stand no more. They probably thought I'd made it out by then. So out I go, my legs are dead. I get to the bay door, didn't think I would, press the green button, door goes up, alarm goes off, I run, but I get tackled.

"The next day, they call us all in and say because of what I did, nobody can use the gym for a month. That didn't put me in good with anyone. A little later I get caught in my room and beat. The staff was nowhere. I thought I might die. Kids was standing around. When I say beat, I mean stomped. I could feel the head shots knocking the light out of me. I started drifting off somewhere new.

"The first boy who stepped in and threw a punch for me was a kid who'd gotten sent there for . . . I think fighting, assault. John Blaine. In comes Nate Hancock, some others. One of those kids surprised me, one who I thought brought his home with him. Joshua Bray. Not the likeliest kid. It took all the staff and real cops to sort that one out. But I fought, and after that, I survived."

"So you owe them?"

"For that, and for something down the line, something out in the world I had to do for the family. At first I owed them, then it was something they had on me. Not no more." He let silence fill the room, then, "I don't feel good about what happened today."

"My nephew's alive because of you."

"That's what I mean. We got away too easy. We ought to be dead."

Ryan stepped into the kitchen. "Quiet out," he said.

"What kind of quiet?" Alan asked.

Nicky lurked by the door, flipping her cell phone open and shut.

"Honey, what you standing there for?" Alan said. "Step in."

She stood there trembling, said, "I'm sorry," and ran.

Alan dropped to the floor. A shot knocked through the empty window where he had been and puffed into the opposite wall. I dove to the floor, and so did Ryan.

"Let's get upstairs," said Alan, crawling past me to the living room. "Henry, you go," he said. "Let's see if they've got a view in."

For an instant I thought of sending Ryan up first, then saw reason and went myself, scrambling around rotten places to the landing. No shots followed me.

"Go, boy."

Ryan was slower, and a line of semiautomatic fire tapped into the wall above him. He moved quicker then, and reached the landing.

"Alan," I said.

"I don't think I'll make that trip," he said. "You two set up front and back. If you miss them, I got them." Then, to himself, "I wish they would come in."

From what I'd been told, there were two men after us. The shooter with the semiauto had been trained. I took a post in a front room where I could see from the empty window frames. Ryan, I set up in a back room with two windows looking out over the tangle of apple trees and multiflora rose below. I told him not to take a shot unless he was sure of himself. Better to leave them guessing.

I tilted my head out of the window and felt a group of bullets pass all around me. It was so precise in the dark that I had to think night scopes were in use. If they had thermal, we'd be dead before long. I fell to the floor as another six or seven shots thudded into the rotting wall that had been my cover.

"Ryan, down!" I said. "Don't move."

I crawled down the hallway toward him, and signaled for

him to join me where there was more than one wall between us and the guns outside. The floorboards creaked beneath us. There was silence below, then two careful pistol shots in quick succession from different rooms in the house. Alan was still with us. Above my head, a cord hung down from an attic trapdoor. Slowly I stood, and slowly I pulled the cord, which broke off in my hand, leaving a foot of length. I jumped, took what was left, and yanked, and with my other hand gripped the edge of the door and pulled it down, along with a ladder and a rain of dust and droppings. When that cleared, I saw night sky through the house's rafters. I took the .270, sent the boy up with the borrowed revolver, and closed the trapdoor after him.

The shots were coming from the woods, from a distance. I could see only one muzzle as it came alive. Below, gunfire rattled into the house in neat semiauto bursts; first through the front door, then through a window. I emptied myself of thought and life, and when I saw the flash again, I sent a shot after it. There was quiet, and then the gunfire started again from a new position. I had gotten close. Maybe four shots left in the .270. I needed closer targets.

Downstairs, Alan was being driven back. He never complained, but his pistol shots were moving steadily toward the kitchen at the rear of the house. There would be someone out there too, lying in wait. I smelled what I thought at first was gun smoke. I looked down, and saw that Alan had tipped at least one lamp onto the rotting floor and lit the oil. Lines of fire flickered, creating screens of heat and smoke around his position.

"I've had as much of this as I can stand," he said to me. "Get the boy. We'll head down to the basement and take them close in."

"We got to run."

"They can see us in here," Alan said. "They'll see us out there. Get the boy."

I climbed the ladder. It took only an instant to realize that Ryan had left the attic, and a moment more to see he was nowhere on the roof. As I pulled my head back inside the house and fell to the attic floor, shots landed above me.

I hoped the boy was running. I didn't go thinking about it; I fell out of the attic onto the landing, took the stairs four at a time with splinters kicking up all around me from the rounds punching in. The downstairs rooms flickered orange. A door leading to the basement was open. Through the kitchen and out the back door I went, rolling to a stop in the overgrown yard. No shots. Ryan may have drawn the second man away. I stood and ran to where the trees grew thickest, up away from the swamp that hemmed the farmstead in, away from the gunfire. There were two shots ahead and I changed course, screaming out something I can't remember now.

A man launched at me and I hit the dirt, already grappling for a way to end his life. The coat I wore slowed his knife down, but the blade still opened me up, dragging over several of my ribs. The knife flicked out of my chest and into my cheek, just below my eye. My face poured blood. The rifle lay useless. But I got a hand on his knife arm, at the wrist. No handgun or anything bigger I could see, so he'd probably shot all his ammunition. He got on top of me and I saw what I already knew, that it was Terry Ceallaigh. He landed one good punch to the side of my head. He wound up for another and I turned my head flat as it hit, his fist skidding across my face and dimming my eyes and ears. He fell forward, his weight to his shoulder, his arm across my face, and I got my arm around his throat. I wrenched a leg out from under him and hooked it around one of his, and held him tight to me. Gravity was on my side. My strength was failing, but so was his breath. I held on. He thrashed, then slowed, and stopped. I held on. He seized once or twice more, like a dying fly, his knife hand opened, and I threw the blade somewhere into the woods. I shoved him off of me and quickly went through his person. Two small knives and a multi-tool. I felt his pulse at the neck. I circled my hands around his throat to cut him off.

Before Miss Julie came along, I had lost the feeling of life as an open, changing thing. It was just gone, black, like a hammer. It had been years since I knew what it was to be young, with your senses blazing in harmony with everything. And this man found a girl who had almost none of that left, and then took what little she had for himself. He took Carl Dentry away from his wife, and maybe Shelly from her kids. He wanted to take me away from my people and my light. But, for his children, and for my own child waiting, I let go of his throat, and watched the blood in his face seep back into the rest of him.

I reached for my handcuffs; they weren't there.

When I stood, the slash in my side pulled open. I called out to Ryan, and heard silence. No movement in the trees around me, no gunfire from the house. I called Ryan's name again, and he answered me from up the slope.

"You hurt?" I said.

"No."

"Come here, then."

At my direction, Ryan removed Ceallaigh's shoelaces and tied his wrists back. We found a slab of shale to sit on and I took a hard look at my wound and the blood coming out of it.

"You need to wrap that up," Ryan said.

"Cut away his shirt. Something soft."

Ryan did so, and helped me tie the cloth around my midsection. He put the .38 into my bloody hand. "Can you walk?" he said.

"Let's listen."

We sat and took in the quiet that had overtaken the guns. There was a hint of smoke on the wind, but no fire I could see. The next hill over, a whistle like part of a bobolink's call. Then footsteps coming toward us from below.

It was only at the last instant that I didn't fire on Mike Stiobhard, who shambled up the hill, revealing a limp that I had not noticed before.

"We made it," he said. His clothes were smeared with blood.

"Help me take him down," I said, nodding in the direction of Terry Ceallaigh.

"I'm not doing that," Mike said. "I'm old. Get off your ass and come help your father." As we walked down the hill, I felt Ryan and the old man babying me, holding me back. I pulled against them. Mike said, "Slow down."

I felt a bit fainter with every step. Father was not by the house, which was dark and empty with the oil fires put out. No sign of Nicky. We found Father's path through the brush, a line of broken branches and disturbed, bloody ground.

By a small crescent of swamp lit only by stars, we found him sitting alone. His legs were soaked to the crotch and he was shivering.

"Time to go," he said. He'd been crying, which I'd never seen before. He'd stopped, but you could hear it and see it.

"Father," I said.

Slowly, in stages, he stood. As he did, he revealed a face and clothes splashed with blood from head to where the swamp had washed him. He saw my face and said, "Don't worry."

"Where is he?"

In answer, Father swung his arm out over the small piece of swamp before us, not big or wild enough to hide a body long. I imagined the corpse leaking blood into the filthy, living water, and got so tired.

"What'd you do that for?"

Father didn't answer. Mike looked at me with real confusion. "I told him to. What else is he going to do?" Mike lit a cigarette and kindly blew the smoke away from our party. "It was Nate Hancock, if you care to know."

Terry Ceallaigh came staggering toward us, shivering. His eyes saw but did not understand. I sat him down on the ground and I kept a weapon pointed in his direction.

Mike said, "Where's Alan?" When nobody answered, he walked toward the house.

LIZ BRENNAN stitched up my chest as I lay there in a hospital bed, mooning at her in a light opioid stupor, telling her I loved her and trying to explain. She ignored me. I ignored myself. I sang "Roll in My Sweet Baby's Arms" to distract from the pull of the needle through my skin—didn't hurt, just strange, I was drugged—and fell silent once again until Julie showed up, first taking a glance at Liz's work to clean and sew the six-inch scar across my ribs, then flipping up the gauze taped to my cheek to see the gouge there.

"I love you, too!" I said to Julie.

"All right, buddy."

"I love you," I said to Julie again. "From now on, I'm just going to sit home."

"Quiet, you," said Liz. "Be still." To Julie she said, "He's going to be fine."

Sewing up the hole beneath my eye was less pleasant. Even though I told her I didn't care, Liz was determined to make many small stitches and leave me as light a scar as possible. I could see a lot more of it, with the needle wiggling under my eye. I cursed her and her family, but then it was over and I slept.

SHERIFF DALLY'S PEOPLE took Terry Ceallaigh into custody and combed the swamp in waders until they found Nate Hancock there, weighed down by his rifle, the ammunition on his person, and a piece of shale stuffed into his pants. Alan, they didn't find.

The morning after, commonwealth techs swarmed the abandoned house, prying evidence out of its walls. Elsewhere, PSP techs, detectives, and Sheriff Dally gathered with a warrant to search the places where Hancock had lived and worked. Probably they'd sent a social worker out to Ryan, and if so, I wished them luck. Me, I had been sent home to the cottage on Walker Lake, where I let the pain pills fade away, leaving a sensation on my midriff that was all things at once—itching to burning, a dull ache along my ribs, a feeling of coming apart at the seams.

In the afternoon, Lee Hillendale showed up in a German SUV to take me to the State Police barracks in Dunmore. I was not turning myself in, exactly.

Miss Julie had been by my side; I doubted she'd slept at all, and now that Lee stood in the door and I was headed out into the world again, she had opinions.

"Don't go. You don't have to. Wait until you're stronger."

"I don't need to be strong to sit in a chair and answer questions," I said. "I just need to be awake."

"These things do go wrong for innocent people," she said.

"I know," I said.

"I'll be there," Lee said.

"I'm coming too," Julie said. "It's not safe. You may need help."

"They'll help me if I need it," I said. I looked in Miss Julie's eyes; after everything, there was something she held back from me. I didn't blame her. Rather than seek that thing out, I draped a jacket over my shoulders and left. There would be time to fix what could be fixed.

On the road outside, I saw Sheriff Dally's patrol car parked, and approached him. He rolled down his window.

"Afternoon," I said. "You been here all day?"

"All night, too," he said. "One or the other of us. Got something for you to give to the detectives. I faxed it, but who knows if they got it. Anyway, thought you'd be interested." Dally handed me a stapled document. I flipped to the end and found Father's signature there. A sworn statement about the events of the night before.

"Is Ceallaigh talking yet?"

"Could be. I wouldn't know. PSP took him this morning. Given everything, just as well."

As we pulled away from the cottage, I said to Lee, "I need to see some things first."

On the quiet bend of Red Pine Road between the Moores and the Ceallaighs, the hieroglyphics of melted rubber were fading day by day. I can't tell you what exactly happened to Carl, and neither can he. But I could guess certain things: When he died, Carl had been on his motorcycle, an aging vigilante following an empty young man with a lot of toys and a wicked secret. And I could guess that Terry knew what Carl was about. Carl probably confronted him again. I read those black marks on the road as a sign of death.

I had Lee drive us up the hill to the Ceallaighs' place, where a lonely state trooper was parked to preserve evidence and discourage the press. Carrianne's vehicle was nowhere to be found, but Terry's truck was there. Before the trooper could object, I was out of Lee's car and lowering myself to the ground. There were scrapes on the bottom of the rear bumper of Terry Ceallaigh's truck, scrapes that had been scrubbed down to bare steel except for one that Terry had missed. A streak of blue paint on a bumper and some black lines on a country road, and you almost have a sentence. I took a photo. What I believe is, Carl and Carl's machine had rounded a bend, struck Terry's stopped-dead pickup, and gone under. That almost comports with what Terry has always maintained from his prison cell: that he was drunk, got into an accident, and lost his mind. He had no idea who Carl Dentry even was. Except that can't be all.

From there, Terry goes up the driveway to his home, whistling Dixie, waiting for Carl to die. Except he can't take the wait. But by the time Terry gets back to the road on foot, Carl is gone, crawled up the Moores' driveway for help that never comes. This part is borne out by bloodwork done on the Moores' front door; it was Carl Dentry's. Terry and some other beasts of the forest did the rest of the work down at the Freefall. The trouble Terry must've gone to—hauling up Carl's dead weight on a line over a tree growing out of the ravine's slope, dropping him to make it look like a fall, then deciding after all that to cut him up and make him disappear. The butchery had not been as simple as that. In the desperate half-light of a coming dawn, Terry would have placed a call to a guy he thought could help him make all of this disappear. Knowing what we do now, I guessed Terry had had a foot in the drug trade, working for Nate Hancock. Easy enough for Terry to give Nate his movements throughout the night, so Nate could help with a cover story. But Nate had demanded a price. In the end, Terry could not pay it other than in kind.

I laid this out for Lee on the drive south. Some of it turned out true. Terry Ceallaigh denies some of it to this day. Some of it I can never know, but still think it true enough.

"Yeah, you may be right," he said. "But it's not your concern anymore. Don't do their jobs for them. Stick to your truths and I'm pretty sure you won't go to prison." Lee clued me in to some of the discussions he'd been having with the AG's office, to wit, my obstruction of justice, obstruction of governmental operations, perversion of the administration of law, and so forth. I was more concerned about the deaths. We spent most of the car ride down defining and reinforcing my truths.

I didn't kill Shelly Bray. I had no reason to hurt her. They knew that now. I was frantic over my nephew, and that was why I ran.

I didn't kill Nate Hancock. Father did that in self-defense, and in defense of me and Ryan. I didn't know why Nate Hancock would want to kill me or my nephew. Lee's voice in my ear: Don't guess. Don't do their jobs for them.

Terry Ceallaigh and I had fought in the woods, and I subdued and restrained him. I had been seriously injured and was light-headed. I didn't know why Terry Ceallaigh would want to kill me or my nephew.

I didn't know where Nicole Simmonds was. She'd run out the door into the night and that was the last I knew of her.

I didn't know where Alan Stiobhard was.

When the questions got tough, the theory was that I would be able to answer with one of those truths and not get lost.

Based on what PSP learned during my interview, they'd decide how to handle Father's involvement, and where to look for answers next. I read and reread the statement Father had given. It was hard not to feel anxious. As Lee and I walked through the front door and were led through the barracks, uniformed state policemen stopped what they were doing and stared. We were dropped off in a little gray conference room.

Lee had ensured that Detectives Collyer and Garcia would not be part of the conversation. We sat waiting, not knowing exactly who would be coming to nail me to the wall.

"Your truths," Lee told me. "Nothing more."

The door opened and in walked Allie DeCosta with an older cop in a brown tweed jacket. They took seats opposite us at the table.

The man eyed me sternly, then his face softened, and he said, "Buddy, you stepped in some shit."

I liked him right away.

"Section Commander Bernard Gill. You know DeCosta, AG's office, OCS."

"OCS," I said. "Organized Crime?"

"That's right," she said.

I felt Lee Hillendale relax beside me, and saw a faint smile pass across his face. "Okay," I said. "What can I tell you?"

"Where is Alan Stiobhard, how about that?"

"I don't know."

"Can you find out?"

"Why do you want him?" I asked. Bernie Gill chuckled at this, and Allie DeCosta rolled her eyes. "I mean," I said, "what can he tell you that I can't?"

Lee shifted in his seat. "Do you have anything further for Officer Farrell?"

DeCosta spoke. "What do you know about Ton L?"

As I thought about that, Lee said, "If I may: It's a limited liability company registered in Pennsylvania. Its members, I believe, include an attorney named Andrew Swales out of

Scranton. Locally, a retired attorney named Casey Noonan has done some work here and there on their behalf, but that may have been unwitting. Neither of them will return my calls."

"Can I ask that you not contact them further?" DeCosta said. "What do you mean by 'unwitting'?"

"I mean Noonan may not have known the true business of the company."

She raised an eyebrow. "And what do you believe that business was?"

By this time, I had turned completely in my chair to watch my lawyer. Lee continued, "At first, real estate. They bought up land in Holebrook County and elsewhere in northeast Pennsylvania at the dawn of the Marcellus shale boom, diverting signing bonuses and royalty payments from leases to other endeavors, including ownership interest in gas station franchises, residential rental properties, and—I won't say fronts— horse farms and the like."

"At first," DeCosta said.

"They were in drug trafficking, with some random criminality thrown into the mix. Murder for hire, mostly as needed by the drug trade. That could have been their most, ah, profitable piece of the business." I thought of Alan. Lee left a pause, and DeCosta gave an eloquent silence. "Other members or associates, I believe but do not know for certain, include Nathan Hancock and Joshua Bray, possibly Michelle Bray. Ordinary people in plain sight. Unlikely though possible, Terrence Ceallaigh." Lee paused, then added with reluctance, "And Alan Stiobhard."

"Wait a minute," I said. "Shelly? She's a fuckin victim. If you think otherwise, you're wrong. She didn't know the half."

DeCosta said, "Do you really think that?"

"She came up here to tell me something, and it got her killed. May have gotten Dentry killed. What that was . . ." I looked to DeCosta. "You followed Shelly up here, didn't you?"

She didn't answer.

"You thought she was dirty," I said. "Maybe you thought I was. Where were you when she died? A man was killed, and you didn't lift a finger to keep her safe."

"Henry," Lee said.

DeCosta spoke. "You know the commonwealth has been fighting opioids tooth and nail. It's never enough. A lot of what's done is sensitive. What Shelly told me suggested we ought to work into Holebrook County. We didn't want to come thundering in until we got the lay of the land."

I pushed all that aside. "What is Ceallaigh saying?"

"We're not answering that."

"Josh Bray can answer for it, then," I said, furious. I could feel Lee looking at me, and didn't care.

Gill said soothingly, "You're no longer a suspect. We could shout it to the hills, but think what that gets you, Henry."

"So what's your theory now?" I said.

Gill shook his head. "You don't need to know."

Lee cleared his throat. "We'll be investigating these deaths, if you won't share."

"You won't get anywhere," said DeCosta. "You know that."

Lee knocked on the tabletop with his knuckle. "Officer Farrell has served his community for years. His own nephew barely escaped with his life. If there's a threat, Henry has earned the right to know everything. For his own peace of mind, and—"

"You can tell me what you know or not," I told them.

"Ceallaigh can hold his tongue or not. I know it was Bray. I'll make him answer."

DeCosta held up a hand. "You'll never see him again."

We all fell silent.

"If you must know," said Gill with a sigh, "the man who we believe actually killed Ms. Bray is gone. I can't tell you more than that." That meant Hancock had done it, likely a self-protective move as the walls closed in on the Ton L crew. He hadn't been at the High-Thyme that night, as far as I know. So who among the friendly faces there had seen Shelly Bray and known to call one of these boys about it? Yet, Gill had said the man was 'gone,' and Hancock wasn't the only one. There was also Alan; the thought made me low.

"Let's change the subject," said DeCosta. "How's your father, Farrell?"

I had read and reread the statement Father had provided to the Holebrook County Sheriff's Department the night of the incident. He'd also answered their questions, never changing his story once. I handed over a copy of the affidavit, which I was sure they already had. "He doesn't have any involvement in this, other than he shows up to collect his grandson and there's two men shooting into the house where his grandson's supposed to be."

"And then . . ." said Gill, reading, not looking up from the page.

"And then Hancock turns on him," I said. This was a truth Lee and I had worked on; the soul of Father's action was in defense of his family. "He saved his own life and all of ours," I said.

"If all that's true, and I'm not saying it's not, why sink the guy in the swamp?"

"He had some bad advice. He was in shock."

"Your father doesn't own an AR-15-style rifle, does he?"

"What? No."

"Does Michael Stiobhard? To the best of your knowledge."

"I wouldn't know. I don't think so."

"And neither of those men brought such a weapon to the encounter that night?"

"An AR-15. No. Nate Hancock had one."

"Not exactly. What he had was a Remington R-15 set up to fire .223. You're absolutely certain you fought only two men that night?"

I had not thought about a third attacker. There had been a lot of gunfire. "No, I'm not certain."

"Well," said Gill, "such a thing I have not seen in my many years. You've got to tell your father to stay put for the time being."

With Lee behind the wheel and my car door closed, I told him to get me to the abandoned farmstead as fast as he could. While Lee drove us north, I first called Shaun Loughlin, then Dr. Mary Weaver, first on her cell, then at the lab. She picked up and asked me how I was.

"The sow that got killed up my way, you saw her, you took the cubs. What happened to her?"

"She got destroyed. Cremated."

"You sure?"

"Shaun handled it, but yeah. No reason to save the carcass."

"Nobody would've dug the bullets out and saved them?"

"She's gone, pal."

The night in question, Ryan and I had the .270 rifle and the .38 lent to me by the Stiobhards, which I had returned to Mike, who claimed afterward to have lost it. Alan had carried what looked like a cheap 9mm handgun. We took fire from what was almost certainly an AR-15-type rifle. That left whatever Terry Ceallaigh was carrying until he'd run out of ammunition—likely a handgun.

And maybe one more weapon.

No doubt PSP detectives and techs would've combed through the woods by then. They'd had about thirty-six hours to gather evidence. Still, it couldn't hurt to check.

In the hills surrounding the abandoned farmhouse, I could feel the knife wound tugging at my stitches as I lowered myself to the forest floor, casting my eyes for the glint of bronze. When I was white and sweaty to where I knew I'd have to leave soon, and had still found nothing, I met Lee by the bullet-pocked house, and he drove me back to the cottage on Walker Lake.

MISS JULIE bandaged me, wrapping my ribs snug. She cooked for us, though I wasn't hungry. She asked me was I okay. But the closeness between us had been folded up and put away somewhere. Hard knowing what to do about it, so I went back into the field.

Terry Ceallaigh never did agree to speak to me, and I tried over the years. Out of a sheaf of charges, he pled to voluntary manslaughter of Dentry. Though he claimed then and subsequently to be under duress, the first-degree felony kidnapping of Ryan is what got him the longest sentence. I'd always wondered why that had been necessary. It could have been that Ryan was in the wrong place at the wrong time, and seen the wrong face. By all accounts those boys were already wondering how much I knew, and what to do with me. As likely, Ryan was bait. Let Alan escape with the boy, I come running, they kill Alan and me at once, and the boy, I'd imagine. Blame each one on the other. With Alan and me dead, they could pin whatever they wanted on us.

I didn't watch the state police search Hancock's home, a modest split-level built into a hillside, alongside a metal barn bigger than the house, but I'm told it contained parts of Carl Dentry's blue Harley cruiser. Nor did I go and see any of the gas stations, not right away. As Hancock had transferred some legitimate assets to Ton L, my father-in-law Willard was now stuck co-owning a couple businesses with a criminal enterprise disguised as an LLC. Ton L's assets had been frozen as a result of the investigation—Willard couldn't buy or sell his shares of the business, and expected to be questioned by the AG's financial investigator at some point soon. I trusted he had nothing to hide. It helped give Willard some distance that the man robbing gas stations all throughout the area was almost conclusively identified as Nate Hancock himself, likely attempting to undercut the value of Willard's remaining shares, to wear him down and drive him out.

Nor did I concern myself further with the Ceallaighs, who were facing a very different life than what they'd counted on. Thinking of those kids broke my heart. I couldn't be everywhere.

But there was always a good spot on the ridge to set up and watch the goings-on at the Bray horse farm, where a gang of PSP techs, detectives, and possibly some feds on the opioid task force had been circulating through the house and outbuildings for days. They brought out what looked like a safe, and then a gun safe. They took apart an SUV and a late-model pickup, then put them back together. There was always a trooper stationed a little bit up the driveway. When the search edged into the pasture and the forest beyond, I moved back to where I could listen and not be seen.

Eventually the investigators left the horse farm, leaving only the trooper. Then one day, the trooper was gone. I switched over to nights. Autumn dwindled away. Always in the back of my mind, and often in the fore, were Julie and the baby. Julie had stopped objecting to my absence, and handled my presence with a cheerfulness that was troubling and false.

Kyle Mylnarz worked his late shifts at one HO Mart or another. I asked Willard to keep him on, and he gave me his schedule in advance. Nights off, Mylnarz drank at one Hallstead bar or another. Once he led me to a strip club east of Binghamton. He was not a surprising man. But one night, instead of heading home around five a.m. after a shift, he drove west. I gave him a couple turns and then caught up with him, keeping his taillights in sight until I felt safe letting him go for a minute. I took a series of dirt roads at sixty, through Wild Thyme hills, back to 189, where I found Mylnarz's car again. As he neared the Brays' place, he slowed, then pulled onto the shoulder. I passed by without looking, rounded a bend, and parked on a dark intersecting dirt road facing 189.

When it had been long enough, I headed back the way I came, cut my headlights, and crept partway up the Brays' winding, wooded driveway. Maybe I was feeling a bit cautious after the shoot-out at the farmstead, but when I got out of my truck and eased the door shut, it was with both .40s on me. One in my hand, one on my side, digging into the bandage covering my wound.

Kyle's vehicle was parked beside a black Chevy sedan. Bar code stickers in its windows showed it was a rental. I took a picture of one with my camera phone. The sedan was cool as I crouched beside it. Flashlight beams flitted on the far side of the barn that had served as stables, tack room, and garage. I crept to where I could see two men digging in the little grave-yard where Shelly's horse Wurlitzer had been buried. There'd been a frost to cover everything, and a waning moon to make it glow silver.

The world was waking up. Among the faint rustlings and dis-tant engines coming to life, I heard muffled voices, shovel blades scrabbling at frozen earth, and then they stopped. Low laughter. I waited, pressed to the side of the barn, a .40 in each hand.

Kyle came around first, followed by a tall man in a baseball hat. Each carried a shoulder bag.

I put a .40 to the second man's ear and yelled, "Police, hands behind your head, on the ground!"

Kyle ran and slid to a stop behind the parked cars.

"Kyle," the man said.

"Shut up, on the ground."

The man did as I told him, and in doing so dropped a pistol. His hat came off, revealing a bald dome. In the dim early morn-ing I saw that it was Andy Swales. The pistol on the ground was a SIG Sauer P365. I kicked it away.

"Kyle," Swales said again, as I patted him down and removed a jackknife from his pocket. "Kill him."

"Shut up," I said. "Kyle, you kill me, he kills you. The only reason you're alive now is me."

"Kill him."

"Kyle, walk out slowly with your hands up, and toss whatever you're armed with on the ground." With my knee on Swales's back and one hand pointing the .40 into the dark, I cuffed one of Swales's wrists.

"Kill him!"

Swales made a strangled growl as I fitted the other cuff next to his white gold watch. I pushed his face into the earth and lay down beside him, with his bulk between me and Kyle.

"I don't want anybody else to die," I called out. "There's been talk about you killing me," I said.

"I don't want that."

"That's good. Now show me."

"Our lives are over," said Andy Swales. "Our lives are over if you let him go."

"Your life is not over," I said. "You can talk your way out of it. Tell them what you know."

There was silence. Then, "What do I do so you don't shoot me?"

Once Kyle was in bracelets and both men lying flat where I could see them, I hauled Swales's duffel bag over behind the car where Kyle had left his. In the bags, more cash than I'd ever seen, book-sized packages of a powdered substance that turned out to be fentanyl, two handguns, and in Swales's bag, a key drive.

Andy Swales called over, "What are you doing over there, Officer?"

I put the drive on my own key chain. All that money. Just a few bundles would be enough for Mag to start over with a new house for the kids, or to fight Dennis in court if it came to that. But if I palmed a single bill, it'd be trouble to the end of my days. I'd have enough trouble explaining the five grand Swales had left in my station. I took out my phone, photographed the open bags, and then placed a call to Allie DeCosta.

She answered on the third ring, sounding awake.

"You got somebody following Andy Swales?" I said.

Silence, then, "Holy shit, he's with you?"

"Up to the Bray place. Him and Kyle Mylnarz."

"Kyle who?"

"You'll get to know him."

As the sun rose, deep browns and grays were all that was left of autumn. I sat waiting; thinking, time to go home.

ARLY ONE November morning about four, I met Father at Aunt Medbh's house, where Ma had cooked a couple thin venison steaks. We ate them standing. This was one of Father's superstitions, and it seemed to work: when going on the hunt, eat of the animal you hope to find, and make yourself one of them. We drove to state game land on the southern edge of the Heights and met Mike Stiobhard by the entrance. The morning mist was burning off, but still clung to the low places. Father set up high, under a hemlock tree, with a view down a natural crossing point into a valley. I gave him my .30-06, and he made a quick appraisal of the rifle, brought the scope to his eye, said nothing.

"Stay out of trouble," I said.

Mike and I walked farther in, one step every few seconds, puffing out white breath, alert even though we were too late to fool any deer. It was the first time I'd seen Mike, or any Stiobhard, since the abandoned farmstead.

"I can't let him disappear this time," I told Mike. "I need to know what he knows."

"Good luck," he said. We walked on.

"He can't come back here, then, Mike. Not ever."

"He won't."

We walked far enough that I no longer knew where we were and, stepping over a barbed-wire fence half sunk into the ground, we had moved beyond the game land. Mike followed a deer trail up a slope. At the top, the land flattened out beneath a high rock promontory overgrown with brambles. Through black bare trees, a view south.

"Alan had all kind of places around," Mike said. "This was his favorite. I want you to know so you'll respect it. And if you set up on the rock there and get a buck one morning, maybe you'll think of him, and how this is where he'd rather be than any other place."

He ambled off, and so did I. I took a look around. A place like many others, but level and open, with a patch of grass to attract deer. Everything was in its place, except at the foot of the bluff there was a fieldstone firepit, recently used but swept clean. Nearby, brambles were growing around and through a small pile of deadfall. The place may once have been Alan's, but the wild things of the forest would return to claim it. I clambered up to the top of the rock and looked out over a vast horizon. Hills leapt one over the next, a world that never ended.

WINTER SETTLED over us. They cleared Father to return to North Carolina, but he and Ma and Mag's family did not go. So Miss Julie and I were stuck in a home that wasn't, in a stale honeymoon, in a marriage on hold, waiting. Of all the things to be sorted out after my headlong policing of shit I didn't understand—my father-in-law's legitimate business interests threaded into a tangle of criminal enterprises and fronts, the lives of innocents ruined, the hollow faces of the Stiobhards with Alan nowhere to be found, the whereabouts of Joshua Bray and his kids—I only truly dreaded one thing. It wasn't a fight. If Julie and I could have fixed it with a fight, we would have. We discussed my affair with Shelly Bray, and time had made my lies less acute and more forgivable. She never threatened to leave and I didn't think she would. It was something quieter missing from her expression, her tone, and the very words she said. It was because I didn't know what it was that I feared it.

Every time I went out of the cottage without her, to go play a Country Slippers show at the High-Thyme Tavern, to go to work, or a township meeting, I felt that missing thing standing in my way. It was painful to push past it or through it. And yet, every time, I did because I had to. It wasn't the baby, waiting. I didn't know what it was.

Christmas was coming. We had both of our families near and planned to go back and forth between them. Still, Julie wanted a tree of our own, so one clear morning we crunched through the snow to the woods above the cottage and with an orange handsaw cut down a raggedy white pine for the cottage. The branches and needles of the tree were like noodles. We made ornaments out of paper—stars, snowflakes, Santa with a cotton-ball beard.

"Pretty good," said Julie, not satisfied.

We drove out to a vast swamp, frozen, with yellow grasses rising through snow and ice. There was one spot of color: a good hundred yards in, a red spray of wild winterberry against solid blue sky.

"That," she said.

I picked my way out to the plant and took what we needed, and made my way back to the road, breaking through the ice only once. On the shoulder, I stood there with my one leg wet to the knee, holding this dried-out branch that had already dropped some of its berries.

She said, "Who are you?"

This was the missing thing I had feared. Standing there, I searched for the answer in my past. How much more could I share and not be whittled to nothing? And where to start: the dirt road where I was raised, the mountaintop where I first met Polly Coyne, the men I'd killed and seen killed, the work, the job, the fiddle. In my future: Miss Julie, sun sparkling on water, you and your sister, but something else: a wild shadow at the edge of the woods, moving too slowly for flight. I didn't know if it was me, or the thing I was to protect you from.

"I'm a father now." As I said it, I knew it to be true.

"Good answer. Is it ever going to change?"

"No."

We floated home, and my answer has not changed from that day to this. You were born in May, purple, eyes open, with a full head of hair.

THE NIGHT BEFORE Father and Ma left, I heard Father tell you a story while you slept in your crib. It was about four Iroquois brothers and a giant white bear. The bear had slashed at tree trunks with its huge claws, threatened the villages, eaten all the game, and kept the people inside their homes. All through the night, the brothers followed the bear's trail over hill after hill, higher and higher with the lights of villages below, never stopping for rest or food until at last they killed the beast. It's the bear's blood that turns the leaves red in fall. As the brothers sat together, tired, cooking the bear, they looked around them and realized that the lights they saw everywhere were stars. They had chased the bear into the sky.

We had another new arrival that month. One early evening Shaun Loughlin came bumping up the driveway, opened up the rear door of his Game Commission SUV, and stood there looking into it, hands on his hips. I came out there with you wrapped in a blanket and pressed against me. There was Crabapple, almost big as life again, reclining in the truck with the backseats down. Julie came out, looked at the bear, then at me, then at Shaun, took you, and walked back inside.

We put Crabapple in Aunt Medbh's house in a little back room I used for thinking. Mary Weaver had stuffed him very lifelike, one arm partly crossed over his chest, his mouth open, teeth bared. Julie called me sick, but I liked him there. Over the years, remember, you and your sister dressed him up for Halloween, Christmas, and Easter, and for a time he was the first thing you girls showed new friends visiting our house. Stuffed, Crabapple was not quite the same as I remembered when we were both alive. But when we were alone, I looked into his face and sometimes caught a flash of the way his mouth had been: raw and pink and ready.

Don't miss the first two
Henry Farrell novels

DRYBONESINTHEVALLEY.COM

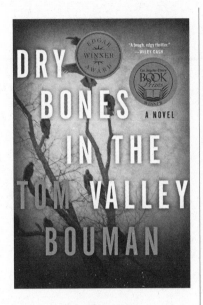

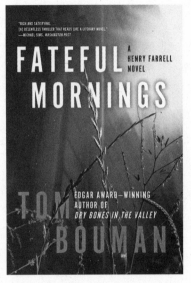

Winner of the
Los Angeles Times **Book Prize**
for Mystery/Thriller

Winner of the Edgar Award
for Best First Novel

"A tough, edgy thriller."

—Wiley Cash

"[A] relentless thriller
that reads like a
literary novel."

—Michael Sims,
Washington Post

Biography®

Jack LONDON

Tom Streissguth

Lerner Publications Company
Minneapolis

A&E and **BIOGRAPHY** are trademarks of the A&E Television
Networks, registered in the United States and other countries.

Some of the people profiled in this series have also been featured in
A&E's acclaimed BIOGRAPHY series, which is available on videocassette
from A&E Home Video. Call 1-800-423-1212 to order.

Lerner Publications Company
A division of Lerner Publishing Group
241 First Avenue North
Minneapolis, MN 55401 U.S.A.

Website address: www.lernerbooks.com

Library of Congress Cataloging-in-Publication Data

Streissguth, Thomas, 1958–
    Jack London / by Tom Streissguth.
      p.   cm. — (A&E biography)
    Includes bibliographical references and index.
    Summary: Describes the life of well-known author Jack London,
including his childhood, his writing, his belief in Socialism, and his
worldwide adventures.
    ISBN 0-8225-4987-5 (lib. bdg. : alk. paper)
    1. London, Jack, 1876–1916—Juvenile literature. 2. Authors,
American—20th century—Biography—Juvenile literature. 3. Adventure
and adventurers—United States—Biography—Juvenile literature.
[1. London, Jack, 1876–1916. 2. Authors, American.] I. Title.
II. Series.
PS3523.O46 Z9814   2001
813'.52—dc21   99-050988

Manufactured in the United States of America
1 2 3 4 5 6 – JR – 06 05 04 03 02 01

CONTENTS

Jack London, about ten years old, with his dog Rollo

Chapter ONE

HARD TIMES ON SAN FRANCISCO BAY

ON A BRIGHT, SUNNY DAY IN **1884,** EIGHT-YEAR-old Jack London was walking on a dusty road near his home in the Livermore Valley, near San Francisco, California. He was alone, and thirsty from the heat and dust. He gazed at the hills rising from the valley floor, wondering what could be seen from their slopes and peaks, and wondering if he would ever get a chance to cross them and leave this lonely place.

Jack spotted something lying by the side of the road. It was a book with its cover torn and some pages missing. The title page revealed that it was a novel called *Signa*, whose author went by the single name of Ouida. Jack took the book home and up to his room. It was the first novel he had ever seen in his life, and he read it over and over. It told the story of a young boy, born to unmarried parents, who escapes from a hard life on a small farm and becomes a famous musician. The last forty pages of the book were missing—so Jack had to imagine the ending himself.

In many ways, the book reminded Jack of his own life. It also seemed to hold a promise: that he could make something better for himself with his talent and his own two hands. But mostly, the story made him daydream of his real father, a man named William Henry Chaney, whom Jack London had never met.

AN UNWANTED CHILD

William Chaney was born into a farming family in Maine in 1821. When he was nine years old, his father died, and his family split apart. Neighbors took William in for a time, then he ran away and found work on the crew of a fishing boat. Later he joined the U.S. Navy but deserted after nine months of service. He wandered around the country, careful to avoid capture for his desertion—if caught, he would face a military trial and a long prison sentence. In 1866, in New York City, Chaney began a career as a private astrologer, telling people their future based on the position of the stars at the moment of their birth.

In 1874, after moving to San Francisco, California, Chaney met Flora Wellman. Flora came from a well-off Ohio family. She also believed in astrology, and she practiced spiritualism—communication with the

In the late 1800s, San Francisco, California, was the center of finance and industry for people in the American West.

dead. To earn money, she worked as a medium, helping her customers "speak" to their deceased friends and relatives through her. Flora claimed that an unseen Indian named Plume guided her on her mystical voyages to the afterlife.

Although they were not married, and they knew people would gossip about them, William Chaney and Flora Wellman decided to rent a room together in a boardinghouse. In the early summer of 1875, Flora discovered that she was pregnant. William did not take the news very well. He announced that he would not marry Flora and that he had no interest in taking care of a baby.

Desperate and depressed, Flora decided to commit suicide. She took a poisonous drug called laudanum and later turned a small gun on herself. She survived the suicide attempts, but William Chaney abandoned her and moved away. She never saw him again.

On January 12, 1876, Flora gave birth to Chaney's son, whom she named John Griffith Chaney. Like William Chaney, Flora had little interest in taking care

Jack London's stepfather, John London, was left permanently weakened by diseases he suffered while fighting in the Civil War (1861–1865).

of an infant. Her failure to get ahead, to find the riches promised by her dreams of California, had made her impatient and bitter.

Flora asked a wet nurse named Virginia Prentiss to care for her son. (A wet nurse takes care of and breast-feeds a baby who is not her own.) Since Flora could not afford to pay for the baby's care, she agreed to make shirts for Virginia's husband, Alonzo. Mr. Prentiss worked as a carpenter for a kind widower named John London. He was a Civil War veteran who had married and settled on a farm in Iowa, where he raised a large family. When his wife died, London had moved with two of his daughters, Eliza and Ida, to San Francisco.

John London loved Flora, and he loved her son. He married Flora in September 1876 and took the baby boy into his family. John London's nine-year-old daughter Eliza watched over Jack, as his family called the baby. Virginia Prentiss, whom everybody called Aunt Jennie, also continued to take care of Jack.

MOVING TO THE COUNTRY

The London family struggled to make ends meet. They could afford only meager furnishings and moved from one small apartment or house to the next. When Eliza and Jack got diphtheria (a serious, contagious disease), the family moved across San Francisco Bay to the city of Oakland. John London thought Oakland would be a healthier place to raise his family.

In Oakland, John managed a grocery store and raised vegetables. He had a talent for making things grow. But he was not as good at keeping track of costs, setting a fair price for his goods, and running a small business. He decided to sell his share in the store to his business partner. Feeling restless and dissatisfied with Oakland, John moved the family to Alameda, another town on the bay, where he bought a twenty-acre farm. Later he bought a larger spread of seventy-five acres in San Mateo County, south of San Francisco. The London family moved into their new home on Jack's seventh birthday.

Jack was young, but he worked hard. He helped his stepfather weed and raise crops and haul them to market in San Francisco. Other times, the two enjoyed afternoons on the shore, sailing small boats and hunting for clams and oysters. To Jack, who disliked the hard chores and drudgery of farming, the water looked like paradise, a promising route to adventure. He often told himself that when he was old enough, he would go to sea.

In 1884, the family moved to an even bigger ranch, in the Livermore Valley. John London built chicken coops and a barn and planted an orchard. But Jack felt lonely, far from familiar surroundings and the friends he had made at school in Alameda. He overcame his sadness by reading books, including *Signa*, the book by Ouida that he found on the road. Much later, Jack recalled this book in an essay:

> The story begins: "It was only a little lad." The little lad was an Italian mountain peasant. He became an artist, with all Italy at his feet. When I read it, I was a little peasant on a poor California ranch. Reading the story, my narrow hill-horizon was pushed back, and all the world made possible if I would dare it. I dared.

DUTIES

When Jack was ten, his stepsister Eliza, who was sixteen, married Captain James Shepard. Shepard had lived with the London family as a boarder. After Eliza moved out of the house, John London's chicken flock was struck with disease, and the ranch in the Livermore Valley failed. The family had to give up farming and move back to Oakland. Sick and weakened, John worked as a door-to-door salesman and then took a low-paying job as a night watchman.

Young Jack took on some of the responsibility of supporting the family. After school, he delivered newspapers. He also worked in a bowling alley as a pinsetter. When he was older, he described his working life in a letter to a friend:

> Duty! at ten years I was on the street selling newspapers. Every cent was turned over to my people, and I went in constant shame of the hats, shoes, and clothes I wore. Duty—from then on, I had no childhood. Up at three o'clock in the morning to carry papers. When that was finished I did not go home but continued on to school. School out, my evening papers. Saturday I worked on an ice wagon; Sunday I went to a bowling alley and set up pins for drunken Dutchmen. Duty—I turned over every cent and went dressed like a scarecrow.

At the age of thirteen, Jack left school for good and took a job in Hickmott's Cannery. There he worked fourteen hours a day for ten cents an hour, packing jars of pickles. He left almost every penny he earned on the kitchen table at home. When he finally did manage to save up five dollars after a full summer of hot, exhausting work, Jack got ready to buy a skiff, a small boat that he could sail on the bay. But when Flora learned of his savings, she came down to the cannery and demanded that he turn the money over to her. Her action taught Jack a lesson he would never forget: his hard labor in a factory and his long struggle to save the money he earned had brought him nothing.

As a teenager, Jack listened to the tales of hardened sailors on the Oakland waterfront.

Chapter **TWO**

PIRATE, HUNTER, WORKER, WRITER

WHEN HE WAS FIFTEEN, JACK FINALLY DID MANAGE to buy a skiff, called the *Razzle Dazzle*, with money borrowed from Aunt Jennie. He gave up his job at the cannery and spent whole days, and many nights, exploring San Francisco Bay. The winds and currents could be tricky, and the frequent fog was dangerous even during daylight. But Jack learned to handle the weather and his boat like an expert sailor.

Jack also spent much of his time down at the Oakland waterfront, learning the tricks of a very different trade. Mingling with petty criminals, he learned how to steal from drunks and how to evade the police. He enjoyed long evenings in the First and Last Chance Saloon, fighting and drinking as hard as he could to keep up with the older and tougher men he admired. Jack was not tall—he stood about five feet, seven inches—but he was strong and sturdy, with a clear, direct look in his eyes that was usually enough to ward off any troublemakers wanting to test him.

Soon after buying the *Razzle Dazzle,* Jack saw a chance to put his boat to good use. He had heard about certain oyster beds, owned by rich businessmen, that lay along the coast near the city of San Mateo. Late one night, Jack set out with a few of his mates. They sailed into the area and gathered as many of the oysters as they could. The next day, Jack brought them to the waterfront fish markets where he sold them for a good price, no questions asked.

Jack grew skilled at his new career as an oyster pirate. He liked the work—he was free and independent and living outside, breathing the brisk sea air. Among the brotherhood of oyster pirates, he enjoyed a reputation as a hard drinker, a skilled thief, and a good fighter. He held on to this reputation by not letting anybody know his best-kept secret: he was a dedicated bookworm and a regular patron at the Oakland Public Library. A librarian there named Ina Coolbrith guided him to new books and authors. Jack loved nothing more than a quiet night alone on his boat, where he read books by lamplight.

Worried that he was risking arrest and the loss of his boat by illegally harvesting oysters, Jack switched sides and joined the California Fish Patrol. As a

Johnny Miller, whom Jack's mother raised from the age of five

patrol officer, his job was to catch thieves and other lawbreakers on the water. In the fall of 1892, he decided to give up his life on the bay altogether and move back to his parents' home in Oakland. He was still expected to help Flora and John London support their household, which now included Johnny Miller, the son of Jack's stepsister Ida, who was too poor to raise the child herself. But Jack had no interest in going back to the cannery or to any other such drudgery. His adventures as a pirate and a patrolman on San Francisco Bay had given him a yearning for new sights and a journey at sea. He wanted fresh air, strong light, and salt water.

SEALING ON THE HIGH SEAS

One day in San Francisco, Jack met a young seal hunter by the name of Pete Holt. The two men traded stories and information. Holt told Jack that a three-masted schooner, the *Sophia Sutherland*, lay in port waiting for provisions. Holt was signed aboard to work on the crew, and there were a few places open for common seamen. Jack had no experience on the high seas, but he was strong and healthy and eager to learn. Holt agreed to bring him down to the ship. The *Sophia Sutherland* raised anchor on January 20, 1893, a week after Jack's seventeenth birthday.

The westward journey went well until the schooner hit a heavy storm off the coast of Japan. For a full day, tall waves tossed the ship about. The crew lowered all sails to keep the masts from being torn from the deck by the high winds. Early one morning, while the gale blew fiercely, the captain called Jack up to the deck to take an hour-long watch at the wheel.

Aboard the Sophia Sutherland, *Jack worked hard and used his fists when older crew members hassled him.*

With the rest of the crew sheltered below deck, Jack fought to keep the *Sophia Sutherland* under control. Ropes held him in place as waves swept over the decks and wind tore at his body. He had never seen anything worse than choppy water on San Francisco Bay, but now he was fighting a Pacific typhoon. Any turn to the side, he knew, and the waves would come crashing over the gunwales, swamping the ship. The lives of twenty men were in his hands.

After his watch was up, Jack went below, exhausted but exhilarated. The hour of dangerous toil at the helm of the *Sophia Sutherland* had been an important test. He had passed, and he felt ready for the worst the sea and the wide world could throw at him.

The *Sophia Sutherland* later reached the seal hunting grounds among the scattered islands of the Bering Sea. The ship's crew set to their task. They clubbed or shot hundreds of white seals, dragged the corpses on board, and skinned the valuable fur from the bodies. Jack saw the ship's deck running red with blood and entrails, while a school of sharks followed in the wake, feeding on the meat tossed overboard. He realized he was witnessing a slaughter—one species destroying another for the sake of fashion. Later, in his book *The Sea-Wolf,* Jack wrote:

> We ran to the north and west till we raised the coast of Japan and picked up with the great seal herd. Coming from no man knew where in the

illimitable Pacific, it was traveling north on its annual migration to the rookeries of Bering Sea. And north we traveled with it, ravaging and destroying, flinging the naked carcasses to the shark, and salting down the skins, so that they might later adorn the fair shoulders of the women of the cities.

With its hold full of sealskins, the *Sophia Sutherland* returned to San Francisco, making port on August 26, 1893. Jack had been at sea for eight months. He collected his pay, bought a new suit of clothes, and crossed the bay back to his home. For now, he had seen quite enough of the sea. He wanted to settle down and do his duty. He knew that his frail, poor parents needed his support.

Jack and his crewmates aboard the Sophia Sutherland *killed seals for their valuable pelts.*

WORKING AND WRITING

Back in Oakland, Jack learned that a job was open at a local jute mill, where rough plant fibers were spun into rope. He applied and was accepted. For ten cents an hour, he labored ten hours a day, winding twine around bobbins (large cylinders or spindles). The hot, dull, tiring work quickly made Jack angry and impatient. It seemed to him that work like this had only one purpose—to keep the workers hungry and desperate, willing to waste their lives and ruin their health for the sake of enriching their bosses. After three months in the mill, Jack quit.

But the family still needed money. Jack's ailing stepfather could barely hold down his poorly paid night watchman job. Although his mother had given up on her dream of being wealthy, she saw a spark of talent in her son—and a possible way for him to make some money. Reading about a writing contest in a local newspaper, the *San Francisco Morning Call*, she urged him to enter. Jack accepted the challenge.

He wrote two thousand words describing his experiences aboard the *Sophia Sutherland* and titled the essay "Story of a Typhoon off the Coast of Japan." On November 12, 1893, the *Call* printed the story with the announcement that Jack London had won the twenty-five-dollar first prize.

When the prize money arrived in the mail a few days later, Jack realized that he had earned almost one month's salary in just a few days of writing. Jack started writing more stories, dashing off more than twenty and sending them to the *Call*. The editors rejected all of them, sending them back with coldly polite notes. Jack again began looking for work.

ESCAPING THE TRAP

This time, Jack decided, he would learn a trade. Skilled workers earned higher wages, and the most skilled among them could live comfortably. He applied at the electrical power plant of the Oakland, San Leandro, and Haywards Electric Railway. The boss hired him with one condition: he must start at the bottom, as a coal hauler. Jack thought he might be able to work his way up to electrician and earn a good raise over his starting wage of thirty dollars a month.

Jack spent several weeks throwing heavy shovelfuls of coal into hot boilers. Then one day, the other workers at the plant took him aside and told him the truth: he had been hired to replace two men who had both quit after nearly breaking their backs for a measly forty dollars a month. Instead of promoting Jack, the boss would keep him in this lowly job and save money—paying Jack less than half what the previous two workers had earned together! Angry at the deception, Jack worked until the end of the day and then walked away from the Oakland, San Leandro, and Haywards Electric Railway for good.

Jack thought long and hard about his working experience. It seemed to him that there was something wrong with the capitalist economic system in which business owners set the wages they paid with no consideration for the health and welfare of their workers. Jack concluded that capitalists thought only of the profits they made, while the men and women who actually produced the goods with their hands and their sweat earned barely enough money to buy food.

A New Idea

Well before Jack London was born, the Industrial Revolution had changed the way goods were produced in the United States. Before the early 1800s, small workshops had produced goods for local markets. After the Industrial Revolution, large factories turned out mass-produced goods that were sold all over the country. Most people worked as skilled laborers, while factory owners paid the workers as little as possible. When business was slow, owners simply laid off workers. Most unemployed factor laborers had no other way of earning money.

The problems of unemployment, low wages, and industrialization led to the development of Socialism, a new economic system. According to Socialist theory, the workers should own the factories as well as the "means of production"—natural resources, machinery, mines, and land. Business owners would not profit from private property or from the labor of others. Everyone would produce what they were best able to, and unemployment and poverty would end.

Jack paid close attention to Socialist writers such as Karl Marx and began to accept the idea that Socialism was the economic system of the future. A revolution would be necessary, Jack realized. To bring about this new vision, he must join the workers to protest, strike, march in the streets, and make his voice heard.

MARCHING WITH COXEY'S ARMY

In the spring of 1894, Jack heard about a group of Oakland tramps who were heading to Washington, D.C., to join Coxey's Army, a group protesting unemployment, hunger, and the exploitation of workers. The protest was organized by Jacob Coxey, a quarry owner from Ohio. Coxey was demanding that the government spend $500 million to put unemployed laborers to work on a new network of roads in the country.

Jack had no interest in building roads—he wanted to take part in the protest and support his fellow workers. He left Oakland with nothing more than the clothes on his back and a ten-dollar gold piece that his stepsister Eliza had given him for good luck.

One night, Jack sneaked into Oakland's big railroad yard. Looking out for guards, he quietly climbed into an empty boxcar. The train took him across the peaks of the Sierra Nevada Mountains. In April 1894, in Nevada, Jack caught up with the protesters from the Bay Area. The group made its way across the Rocky Mountains, walking and riding beneath train cars by hanging on to the iron struts and supports.

From Council Bluffs, Iowa, Jack and the others walked to Des Moines. There the "army" boarded flatboats and sailed downstream on the Mississippi River as far as Hannibal, Missouri. Hannibal was famous as the setting for author Mark Twain's tales of Huckleberry Finn and Tom Sawyer. In Hannibal, Huckleberry Finn had run away from home to light out for unknown territory. For Jack London, Hannibal signified the bitter end of his journey with Coxey's Army. Jack's feet and body were tired, and he decided not to continue with the marchers. He hopped a train to Chicago, where his sister Eliza had sent him some

When Coxey's Army reached the lawn of the U.S. Capitol, Jacob Coxey, right, *was arrested for trespassing.*

Jack watched the famous waterfalls the day before he was arrested in Niagara Falls, New York.

money. After resting a few days, he took a boat across Lake Michigan, then wandered across Ohio. In a few weeks, he reached Niagara Falls, New York.

A PRISONER IN NIAGARA

Jack arrived in Niagara Falls on a slow-moving freight train. He spent an afternoon watching the waterfalls tumble into the Niagara gorge, then spent the night in an open field. The next morning, he wandered through town, feeling poor and hungry. On a downtown street, he was arrested by a police officer. Jack was brought down to the station house and thrown into a prison cell.

Sixteen prisoners were crowded in the cell, all arrested on the same charge—vagrancy, or wandering around town without a clear purpose or job. The bailiffs led the prisoners upstairs to a courtroom. Jack knew that, given a chance, he could explain himself to the judge. Surely there was no law against walking peacefully down a city street. Later, he described what happened in the courtroom:

> My name . . . was called, and I stood up. The bailiff said, 'Vagrancy, your Honor,' and I began to talk. But the judge began talking at the same time, and he said, 'Thirty days.' I started to protest, but at that moment his Honor was calling the name of the next hobo on the list. His Honor paused long enough to say to me, 'Shut up!' The bailiff forced me to sit down. And the next moment that next hobo had received thirty days and the succeeding hobo was just in the process of getting his.

Neither Jack nor any of the other "vagrants" had much of a chance to make explanations. There was no jury to hear the case, and no lawyer present to defend the accused. Jack and the others received swift justice: a sentence of thirty days' confinement in the Erie County Penitentiary.

By the time he was eighteen years old, Jack had experienced more of life than most young men his age.

Chapter **THREE**

FROM PRISON
TO THE
KLONDIKE

IN ERIE COUNTY, NEW YORK, A DINGY TRAIN CAR carried Jack London and his fellow prisoners to a gloomy brick jailhouse. Inside, Jack walked through the cell block—three stories of iron-barred cells looming above a narrow courtyard. He was searched and stripped of his clothes. His head and face were shaved. He was handed a striped shirt and trousers. The next day, he began his term of hard labor, breaking rocks with a sledgehammer in the prison yard.

Jack found that law and order carried a different meaning in prison. The most vicious, lifelong criminals were mixed with petty thieves and vagrants. The guards ruthlessly beat inmates, and the inmates themselves formed gangs that fought over their meager food and property. Prisoners who became ill were not treated, and many died of pneumonia and tuberculosis.

Jack managed to survive. The guards made him a prison trustee, appointed to keep watch over the other prisoners. By taking and handing out small bribes of tobacco or food, he occasionally managed to get a book to read or a piece of stringy meat to add to the watery soup and hard bread that he and the other prisoners ate for breakfast, lunch, and dinner.

On July 29, 1894, Jack was released from prison. Even though he had witnessed harsh, brutal scenes in jail, he wasn't ready to quit the road and return home. He wandered to New York, to Boston, and to Philadelphia. Several times, police approached him, but he always managed to talk himself out of an arrest.

While he traveled, Jack had time to think about what had happened to him in Niagara Falls. He felt he had endured an injustice, one that seemed to be reserved for the country's poorest citizens. Freedom and democracy, the Constitution, and the Declaration of Independence hadn't done him much good in jail or in court. From what he could tell, his country's justice system was owned and operated by rich capitalists to keep everybody else in their place.

Jack traveled north to Canada, riding freight trains to Vancouver, British Columbia. He then worked his way down to San Francisco aboard the steamer *Umatilla*. To achieve anything, he realized, he would have to study, read, and write. When he reached home, Jack decided to return to school to get an education. He started at Oakland High School in January 1895.

School Days

Jack was almost nineteen, an age when most high school students had already graduated. His shabby clothes, his sun-lined face, and his work-roughened hands made him stand out even more among his classmates. In class he kept quiet, feeling too self-conscious to talk much or even respond to his teachers. His main interest was writing. He wrote several stories and articles for a school magazine, the *Aegis*.

When he did speak up, Jack took every chance he could to discuss politics. He joined a debating club and stood on top of soapboxes in City Hall Park in Oakland to declare his Socialist beliefs. He joined the Socialist Labor Party, which promoted its own

While Jack attended Oakland High School, he read books on history, philosophy, and science in late-night study sessions.

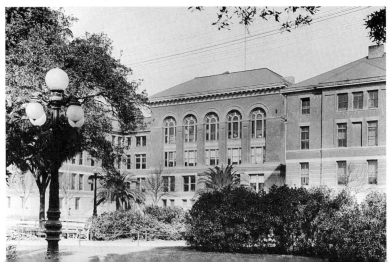

candidates for political office. He attended party meetings in Oakland and San Francisco and took part in marches through the streets.

Jack's debates and late-night studies held his attention more than his high school English or mathematics classes did. In the spring of 1896, he dropped out

THE BOY SOCIALIST

The *Call of the Wild* and his other adventure tales made Jack London a household name all over the world. But his first taste of fame came as a public speaker for the Socialist cause.

It was in February 1897 when Jack first saw his name mentioned in a newspaper. A week after quitting his university studies, he was invited to take part in a rally sponsored by Oakland's Socialist Labor Party. The group was protesting a new law that banned all public meetings within the city's "fire limits." To test the law, the Socialists planned to hold a meeting in the center of the city on Abraham Lincoln's birthday, February 12. They asked Jack London to appear as the principal speaker. Jack agreed.

On the day of the rally, he took the stand and awkwardly began one of his first public speeches. He was promptly arrested by the Oakland police and hauled off to jail. Although he was acquitted and released, the ordinance against meetings remained. The Socialists had not succeeded in changing the law, but Bay Area newspapers did take notice of Jack, referring to the twenty-one-year-old speaker as the "Boy Socialist."

of school to take on a much bigger challenge: university studies. To prepare for entrance examinations, he crammed for physics, chemistry, English, and history. In a few weeks that summer, he made up for several years of neglected schooling. On August 10, he took the three-day exams and passed them. He entered the University of California at Berkeley that fall.

In a little over a year, Jack had changed his surroundings from a dank and violent prison to the fancy halls of a college campus. But he could not adapt to this new life. He had expected more debate and study, a contest of ideas. What he found instead were lazy, self-centered students, bored professors, and a cleaner form of the drudgery he had experienced in the canneries and mills. In February 1897, fed up and as poor as ever, he left Berkeley and returned home.

NEWS FROM THE KLONDIKE

As always, Jack had to support himself and his parents. He decided he would do it with his brains, not his muscles. He borrowed one of the new typing machines that made writing by hand unnecessary. He set up the typewriter in his room and began turning out stories, essays, poetry, articles—anything a magazine might want to publish. He had no plan, no knowledge of the publishing business, nobody to turn to for help. He plowed ahead, getting up each morning to write a few thousand words.

In the meantime, he heard some exciting news. Gold

had been discovered in the Klondike, a cold, harsh territory in northern Alaska and northwestern Canada. As the newspapers told it, some lucky men were coming out of the Klondike with fortunes in gold nuggets.

Jack struck a deal with Eliza's husband, Captain Shepard. The captain, who was much older than Jack, would put up the money for the two of them to travel to the Klondike if Jack would help with the lifting and carrying on the expedition. The two men bought and packed warm clothing, food, camping equipment, mining tools, tents, and blankets: in all, one ton of goods. On July 25, 1897, they boarded the steamer *Umatilla* in San Francisco Bay and turned their hopes to the north.

DANGER IN THE NORTH

Aboard the *Umatilla,* the decks and cabins were crowded with prospectors loaded down with heavy clothing and camping gear for the expedition. Jack and Captain Shepard made friends with three other prospectors—Merritt Sloper, Jim Goodman, and Fred Thompson. The five men decided to join forces and help each other through whatever dangers lay ahead.

After a week, the *Umatilla* reached Juneau, a harbor city on the Gulf of Alaska. From there, Jack's group hired canoes and guides for the hundred-mile voyage to Dyea Beach, located at the head of a trail leading to the Chilkoot Pass. This pass led over the Rocky Mountains to the goldfields of the Klondike. On

Thousands of gold seekers headed for the Klondike. When they reached the Chilkoot Pass, they formed long lines to trek across the mountains.

August 7, Jack's group reached Dyea, unloaded their equipment, and prepared for the long trek to the goldfields, about one thousand miles north.

The group had to hurry because winter was approaching. The rivers would soon freeze solid and there would be no way to reach the Klondike before the spring thaw. Jack and his companions hiked along the rock-strewn trails that led to the Chilkoot Pass. Steep mountains covered with forests of spruce and fir trees rose on both sides of the trail, while rapid creeks flowed alongside it, the water clear and cold from melting snow and ice. Jack carried hundred-pound loads one at a time for one mile, then came back down to retrieve another load. He marched this way, back and forth, along fifteen miles of trails to the top of Chilkoot Pass.

Two days after starting out from Dyea Beach, Captain Shepard had a change of heart. He was over sixty years old, not as strong as Jack, and certainly not as adventurous. Rather than risk his life, Shepard decided to turn back to safety. Jack agreed to sell the captain's equipment and carry on.

From the top of the Chilkoot Pass, Jack, along with Jim, Merritt, and Fred, made his way down another series of trails to Lake Lindeman, which they reached on September 8. From here they would have to cross the lake to continue. The men built two plank boats, using the plentiful spruce trees for lumber. After christening his boat the *Yukon Belle*, Jack took it as far as Lake Bennett. There, Jack saw a sight he would never forget: the carcasses of hundreds of dead horses. Unable to feed or sell them, and too hungry or weak to press on to the town of Dawson, their owners had shot the horses and left them alongside the trail.

STAKING A CLAIM

Jack's party passed Lake Tagish and Lake Marsh, reaching the wide, deep Yukon River. The river's fast water buffeted his flimsy boat, tearing at its ropes and timber. Jack pressed on toward Dawson, exhausted from his physical and mental effort. It was autumn, and the river was starting to freeze. The group decided not to try to make it the last eighty miles to

Dawson. Instead, the men set up quarters in an abandoned cabin at the mouth of the Stewart River. They could prospect for gold here as well, they thought.

Jack staked his claim along nearby Henderson Creek. For several weeks he panned in the creek's freezing waters, sifting through pebbles, sand, and muck for small flecks of gold. All the time, he fought off cold and hunger, while the long Arctic winter nights blanketed him with darkness and depression. After weeks of hard labor and not much luck, Jack realized that the gold rush was a mirage. He was working like a beast, just as he had in Oakland, getting almost nothing in return and wearing himself out.

Jack decided to stop wasting his energy and move on to Dawson. The river was still passable. In Dawson, Jack stored his goods in a cabin belonging to Marshall and Louis Bond, whom he had met on the trail. The men owned an imposing dog named Jack, a cross between a collie and a St. Bernard, that seemed nearly human in his expressions. A dog like this, Jack decided, could be the center of a very fine tale—a story that might not need human characters to express heroism and wisdom.

After six weeks in Dawson, Jack returned to the Stewart River, a tributary of the Yukon. They thought they could prospect for gold here as well. With three other miners, he spent five months in a freezing cabin. As the winter wore on, hunger began to fray the men's nerves. Jack and his companions argued

The Bonds with their dog, Jack, who would be the model for Buck in The Call of the Wild

over everything: politics, history, gold, and food—especially food. For long stretches, they didn't speak at all. They lay on their bunks, too exhausted and cold to do even the simplest chores.

In the spring of 1898, Jack came down with scurvy, a disease caused by a lack of vitamin C and a poor diet. His gums bled and his skin grew soft and spongy. If he didn't get fresh vegetables or fruit soon, he knew, he risked death in this frozen wasteland, thousands of miles from home. Finally, in May, the ice on the Yukon River began to break apart. Jack took the cabin apart to build another plank boat and, with two companions, sailed downstream to Dawson. From Dawson, he would follow the Yukon's currents two thousand miles to the river's mouth at the town of St. Michael, in western Alaska.

The men set up a sleeping shelter on the boat, as well as a makeshift kitchen. At night, they anchored the craft along the river, where they cooked goose eggs and whatever fish they could catch. Jack still felt weak and hungry. During the day, the hot sun beat down on him. At night, clouds of mosquitoes tormented his sleep. But the Yukon was much easier going than the Klondike trails, and he had plenty of time to think and plan. Even though he had found no gold, he knew he could put his experiences in the Klondike to good use—if he made it home safely.

At the port of St. Michael, a stranger offered Jack a can of tomatoes to help him battle his scurvy. By this time, Jack was in very poor health, and the food may have saved his life. From St. Michael, he boarded a steamship to British Columbia. After reaching Vancouver, Jack had just enough money left to buy passage to San Francisco.

He arrived home in August, worn and exhausted at the age of twenty-two. His health was nearly ruined, and his pockets were empty. Gold mining in the Klondike had brought Jack London nothing more than a small bag of gold dust—but the trip had given him stories that would make him well known all over the world.

After returning from the Klondike, Jack set his mind to making a living by writing.

Chapter **FOUR**

The Writing Life

WHEN JACK ARRIVED HOME FROM THE KLONDIKE in the summer of 1898, he discovered that John London, his stepfather, had died the previous fall. His mother, Flora, was still living with her adopted son, Johnny Miller, and was barely managing to support her small household by giving piano lessons.

Jack could do little to help—he came back just as broke as the day he had left. He would have to find work. But in Oakland, as in the rest of the country, there were few jobs available, even for low wages. For weeks, Jack trudged from one shop or factory to the next without finding employment.

He made a few dollars by doing odd jobs around the neighborhood. He pawned his clothes and his bicycle in return for small loans. When he heard about another gold rush, this one in Nevada, he took his bag of Klondike gold dust to a pawnbroker, who loaned him $4.50. With the money, Jack headed east over the Sierra Nevada. In a few weeks, though, he was riding the freight trains back home, having had no more luck in Nevada than he had had in Alaska.

When Jack returned to Oakland, a friend told him of a job available at the post office. Jack decided to take the civil service test, an examination of basic reading and mathematics skills that government workers must take. If he passed, he would qualify for the job.

While he waited for his test results, Jack turned back to writing. For material, he had a full year of hard living and adventure in the Klondike. He knew about suffering through the long, cold Alaska winter, about climbing the rugged Chilkoot Pass, about journeying two thousand miles down the Yukon River. In September 1898, he finished a four-thousand-word article, "From Dawson to the Sea." He mailed the story to the *San Francisco Bulletin*. In a few days, the story came back, with a short note from the editor: "Interest in Alaska has subsided in an amazing degree. Then again so much has been written that we do not think it would pay us to buy your story."

MAGAZINE WORDS

Jack kept writing. He produced more stories, as well as jokes, essays, magazine articles, and serials—novels meant to be published in installments over a long period of time. Despite the rejection from the *Bulletin*, he continued to draw on his experiences in the Klondike. In his story "To the Men on Trail," he introduced the Malemute Kid, an adventurer and born storyteller:

> Malemute Kid's frightful concoction did its work; the men of the camps and trails unbent in its genial glow, and jest and song and tales of past adventure went around the board . . . . Then Malemute Kid arose, cup in hand, and glanced at the greased-paper window, where the frost stood full three inches thick. 'A health to the man on trail this night; may his grub hold out; may his dogs keep their legs; may his matches never miss fire.'

With or without the Malemute Kid, all—or almost all—of Jack's stories were rejected. (Jack did not know that a magazine called the *Owl* had already published one of his stories, called "Two Gold Bricks," in September 1897. He never received notice, or payment, from the magazine.) He wasn't quite sure what editors were looking for, but he quickly realized that they weren't looking for him. He had no reputation—nobody knew who he was, where he was from, or what he had done.

Yet Jack persevered. When his stories were returned, he simply mailed them out again to a different editor.

He soon had dozens of articles and stories circulating around the country, either going to or coming back from publishers and editors.

Finally, in December 1898, Jack received some good news from the *Overland Monthly,* a magazine that published western writers. The editor would publish Jack's story "To the Men on Trail" and pay him five dollars for it. The *Overland Monthly* would then buy seven more stories from him, for $7.50 each.

Jack desperately needed the money. Although he had passed the civil service test and could have the job of postal worker for a salary of sixty-five dollars a month, he had turned it down, determined to make a living from writing. He accepted the offer from the *Overland Monthly* and kept on writing. After a few weeks, another letter of acceptance came from a magazine called the *Black Cat.* The editor of the *Black Cat* would pay forty dollars for Jack's story "A Thousand Deaths"—if he would cut it in half. Jack immediately wrote back to accept the offer. The magazine published "A Thousand Deaths" in May 1899.

Jack was happy to see his words in print, but he could also see plenty of room for improvement in his writing. "A Thousand Deaths" is about a man who is tortured by his own father. To Jack, the story seemed silly and false. He realized that he would have to work even harder to give his stories the feeling of real life.

Jack continued to study philosophy, science, and history. Reading Charles Darwin's work, Jack came to

THE *OVERLAND MONTHLY*

With his first story for the *Overland Monthly,* Jack London was joining the company of the best writers west of the Mississippi. The magazine had been founded in 1868 by Bret Harte, a California author who first gained fame for his story "The Luck of Roaring Camp." Harte intended to showcase new voices—poets and novelists of the frontier and California who wrote in a different style than the established writers of the East.

In the first issue, dated July 1868, the *Overland Monthly* published Harte's own "San Francisco From the Sea," as well as "The Diamond Maker of Sacramento" by Noah Brooks and "By Rail Through France" by Mark Twain. The first issue also presented a poem by a young woman named Ina Coolbrith—the future Oakland librarian who would introduce Jack London to the books of historians, poets, and philosophers. Coolbrith's poem, "Longing," expressed the sentiments of a writer turning away from bookish civilization to nature for her inspiration:

O foolish wisdom sought in books!
 O aimless fret of household tasks!
O chains that bind the hand and mind—
 A fuller life my spirit asks,

For there the grand hills, summer-crown'd,
 Slope greenly downward to the seas;
One hour of rest upon their breast
 Were worth a year of days like these.

Their cool, soft green to ease the pain
 Of eyes that ache o'er printed words;
This weary noise—the city's voice,
 Lulled in the sound of bees and birds.

Jack was both excited and disappointed when he sold "To the Men on Trail." He thought he would make forty dollars instead of only five.

believe that the struggle between rich people and poor people reflected the idea of "survival of the fittest." The books of philosopher Herbert Spencer convinced Jack that evolution—the movement of life-forms from simple to complex over many generations—could be understood as the engine that drove modern society and history. Reading the works of Friedrich Nietzsche, a German philosopher, Jack saw that the world belongs to the strongest and most creative individuals.

Spencer and others influenced Jack to believe that good writers had to develop a philosophy of life, a set of beliefs that would be expressed through their plots and characters. Jack's own philosophy stemmed from his experiences sailing and pirating on San Francisco Bay, hoboing across the continent, and prospecting in the mountains of the Klondike.

Jack did not accept religion, and he didn't believe in the supernatural. Instead, he thought that science could explain everything that occurred, even the mysterious emotions of human beings. The world was a big machine, he believed, and all of its parts were interconnected and acted according to certain laws. Most people couldn't understand those laws or didn't even know they existed. In his stories, Jack tried to reveal and explain these universal principles—especially the law of survival, the idea that the fittest and cleverest individuals survive by devouring the others.

Even though Jack felt it was important to have ideas and beliefs, he also knew that too much philosophy could get in the way of a good story. In a letter he wrote in 1900, he gave some advice to Cloudesley Johns, a young writer he had recently met:

> Get the atmosphere. Get the breadth and thickness to your stories, and not only the length . . . The reader, since it is fiction, doesn't want your dissertations on the subject, your observations, your knowledge as your knowledge, your

thoughts about it, your ideas—BUT PUT ALL THOSE THINGS WHICH ARE YOURS INTO THE STORIES, INTO THE TALES, ELIMINATING YOURSELF... And for this, and for this only, will the critics praise you, and the public appreciate you. . . .

As Jack continued to write, more editors began to accept his stories. His work appeared in the *Illustrated Buffalo Express*, the *American Agriculturist*, and other monthly publications. In October 1899, Jack's story

Edgar Allan Poe interested Jack with his short stories, which often illuminated the darker side of human nature.

"An Odyssey of the North" was accepted by the *Atlantic Monthly,* one of the most popular magazines in the country. For the first time, Jack would have a national audience. The magazine would pay him $120, more money than he had ever earned from a story. When "An Odyssey of the North" appeared in the January 1900 issue of the magazine—the first issue of the new century—the country discovered Jack London.

In Jack, the editors and readers of the *Atlantic Monthly* found a refreshing new voice. Throughout the 1890s, magazines had published many polite stories about high society. These stories described the upper classes and dealt with manners and morals in the exclusive, indoors world of the rich. In this new century, however, magazines wanted to attract a new, bigger audience. They could reach this audience with adventure stories. Jack London would lead the way with the first lines of "An Odyssey of the North":

> The sleds were singing their eternal lament to the creaking of harnesses and the tinkling bells of the leaders; but the men and dogs were tired and made no sound. The trail was heavy with new-fallen snow, and they had come far, and the runners, burdened with flint-like quarters of frozen moose, clung tenaciously to the unpacked surface and held back with a stubbornness almost human. Darkness was coming on, but there was no camp to pitch that night. . . .

WRITING WITH ANNA STRUNSKY

Jack always had to work as hard as possible just to survive, and he put the same effort into writing. He slept only four or five hours a night, then woke up early, while Flora and Johnny were still asleep, and sat down to write one thousand words—his daily stint. He worked all morning to create complete, polished sentences and paragraphs on the first try. He didn't allow himself any pauses that might break his concentration. To get up from his desk before he finished his thousand words would be like leaving a job before quitting time.

In the evenings, Jack read books, magazines, and newspapers. In addition to volumes of history, philosophy, and science, he also read fiction. He enjoyed *Typee* and *Moby Dick,* the high seas adventures of Herman Melville. He read *Kidnapped,* a famous work by Robert Louis Stevenson, and the short stories of Rudyard Kipling and Edgar Allan Poe. Jack admired these authors for showing how unexpected and dangerous events could bring out both the good and the bad in people. If Jack found a story or a chapter that he especially liked, he learned from it by copying it on paper, word for word. In this way, he shared what the author might have experienced in imagining and writing the story.

On Wednesday evenings, Jack invited his friends to his home in Oakland. The "Crowd," as he called the group, listened to each other read stories and poems, played cards, and enjoyed picnics outdoors. They argued about politics, especially socialism, and about writers they knew. Among his friends, Jack had a new nickname: Wolf. He saw himself akin to a creature in the wild, following his instincts, fighting and working to become the leader of his pack.

Jack liked to have people around him, especially people who admired him and listened to his opinions. A poet named George Sterling often came to the house. Jack also made friends with Anna Strunsky, a writer from San Francisco, and Charmian Kittredge.

Anna Strunsky

Charmian worked on her own as a stenographer (a person who transcribes dictation, or spoken words). She was an independent woman who enjoyed the company of writers and poets. Jack met Charmian through her aunt, Ninetta Eames, whose husband, Roscoe, worked as an editor at the *Overland Monthly*.

With Anna Strunsky and Charmian Kittredge, Jack often talked about love. He was convinced that love was just a trick of nature, a device to get men and women together for the purpose of having children. In April 1900, Jack tried to prove his ideas. Convinced that he could make a "scientific" marriage, he married a friend named Bess Maddern, a woman whose fiancé had recently died. Bess worked as a tutor for high school students, and she was strong, handsome, and very practical. Although the two were not in love, they seemed to get along well enough, and in Jack's mind, she would make a perfect mother for his children.

Jack had moved into a new home on East Fifteenth Street in Oakland with his mother and Johnny, and Bess now joined the family. On January 15, 1901, she gave birth to a baby daughter they named Joan. Jack had been right about Bess—she was a loving mother who wanted nothing more than to care for her baby. She had no interest in Jack's crowd, in their political debates or in their games and picnics. Soon she began to drift away from her husband.

Jack began to understand that there was more to love than just finding a useful mate. He decided to

Jack's wife, Bess, admired Jack, but she didn't like socializing with his loud and eccentric friends who came to the house.

explore these ideas in another book, which he would write with Anna Strunsky. The book, called *The Kempton-Wace Letters,* took the form of letters between two characters. Anna wrote as Dane Kempton. Jack's character was Professor Herbert Wace. Dane Kempton believes in romantic love, while the logical Herbert Wace believes that marriage is a scientific matter of finding an ideal mate and creating children.

Jack and Anna published *The Kempton-Wace Letters* anonymously. But soon enough, everyone knew who

Publisher S. S. McClure paid Jack a monthly fee so he could stop worrying about money and just write.

had written the book. Rumors began to fly about Jack and Anna. Many people believed they were having a real-life love affair. The scandal helped increase sales of the book, but it deeply hurt Bess. She began to think about ending her marriage to Jack.

INTO THE ABYSS

To pay his many bills, Jack needed to take on a bigger project: a full-length novel. The book would be about life in the Klondike. He discussed the idea with S. S. McClure, a publisher in New York. McClure agreed to pay him $125 a month until the book was finished.

Jack set to work on *A Daughter of the Snows.* The story described a strong woman, Frona Welse, fighting to survive in the North while men around her struggled, failed, and died. Jack put his own ideas into his heroine's mouth. But although the character managed to conquer her surroundings, she came off as artifical, an idealized image of a woman created by a writer's overheated imagination. Even before Jack finished the book, he realized that Frona Welse came off as false, and even he stopped believing in her.

S. S. McClure was also disappointed with *A Daughter of the Snows* and decided not to publish it. In October 1901, he stopped sending Jack the monthly advance. In December, Jack heard from another publisher, George Brett of Macmillan & Company. Brett wanted to buy the best work that Jack could produce. Jack accepted Brett's challenge and prepared a new manuscript, *Children of the Frost,* which took place among the Indians of the Klondike. Brett promised to publish the book in October 1902 and gave Jack an advance of $500. From that time on, Macmillan published nearly all of Jack's books.

Despite his growing fame, Jack was afraid of running out of ideas for stories. What more could he say about the Klondike? He asked his friends for story ideas, sometimes even offering to pay for them.

Jack was also growing bored. He felt he had to get out in the world again, experience something harsh, pit himself against danger. In July 1902, his chance

On August 9, 1902, hundreds of thousands of Londoners watched the coronation of King Edward VII.

came. The American Press Association offered him an assignment as a correspondent in South Africa, where the Boer War had just ended. Jack would write newspaper articles about life in South Africa in which the armies of two South African republics had fought Great Britain for control of the area.

Jack eagerly accepted the assignment and set out from Oakland. But when he reached New York, he found that the Boer War had been over for too long, and that there wouldn't be much to write about. Determined not to return to California, Jack came up with another idea. In London, England, a new king, Edward VII, was being crowned. Many journalists would be there to cover the parades, the ceremonies, and the great pomp and spectacle of the coronation.

Jack took little interest in kings and pageants. Instead, he would go to the East End, the poorest section of London. He would talk to the people there and describe their lives in a book. He described his idea to George Brett, who encouraged this new adventure.

On July 30, Jack left New York on the steamship *Majestic.* When he reached London, he bought a ragged suit of clothes and rented a small room.

For two months, Jack posed as an unlucky American sailor who had missed his ship and could not return home. He lived as an East Ender, worked in sweatshops, and ate in soup kitchens, places where poor people could get a free meal. He often spent long nights walking through the neighborhood. During the

Jack in the East End of London. Many critics in England were upset that his exposé of this poor area of the city was written by a middle-class American.

day, he idled in parks and dozed on benches. In his room, he noted everything that happened to him and read books and pamphlets about the problems of poverty.

In the East End, Jack saw the underside of life. The people of the East End had no work, no money, and no hope. Here, in the capital of one of the richest empires in the history of the world, people were going hungry and dying young. They lived in dark, dirty rooming houses and suffered through illnesses without doctors. Jack saw desperate men lining up for food at a charity house. He watched as they picked through garbage looking for coins, clothes, or a crust of bread.

The East End confirmed Jack's belief that modern societies were built on the suffering of the poor and that the wealthiest societies, such as Great Britain and the United States, were the least just and humane. He recorded his impressions and took photographs for his book, which he called *The People of the Abyss*. In the first paragraphs of the book, Jack described how he felt when he saw a London slum for the first time:

> The region my hansom [horse-drawn carriage] was now penetrating was one unending slum. The streets were filled with a new and different race of people, short of stature, and of wretched or beer-sodden appearance. We rolled along through miles of bricks and squalor, and from each cross

street and alley flashed long vistas of bricks and misery. Here and there lurched a drunken man or woman, and the air was obscene with sounds of jangling and squabbling.

After finishing *The People of the Abyss,* Jack left England and spent a few weeks tramping through Europe. On November 4, 1902, he returned to New York. George Brett read *The People of the Abyss* and enthusiastically prepared to publish it. When Jack got home to California a few days later, he found that his family and his responsibilities had grown. His second daughter, Bess, had been born on October 20.

Jack's daughters, Joan, left, *and Bess, around 1906*

The outdoorsman at work

Chapter **FIVE**

NEW STORIES

IN FEBRUARY 1902, JACK AND BESS MOVED TO A new house in Piedmont, a rural area east of Oakland. Jack, now twenty-six years old, settled down to his daily writing stint. Every morning, he set down one thousand words for a new short novel. This story took place far from the poor and crowded East End of London. It was set where there were no people at all, in the cold forests of the north, where Nature carried out her great design: a fight to the death for survival.

On January 26, 1903, Jack sent his new short novel, *The Call of the Wild*, to the *Saturday Evening Post*, a popular weekly magazine. The story was inspired by the dog Jack had admired at the Bonds' cabin in Dawson. *The Call of the Wild* describes a city dog who is harshly treated and sent to work in the Klondike. The dog learns to fight, kill, and take his place as the leader of a pack of wolves. He soon forgets the comfort of the "Sunland," as Jack London calls it, and adopts the very different ways of the "Northland":

> Buck was merciless. He had learned well the law of club and fang, and he never forewent an advantage or drew back from a foe he had started on the way to death. . . . He must master or be mastered; while to show mercy was a weakness. Mercy did not exist in the primordial life. It was understood for fear, and such misunderstandings made for death. Kill or be killed, eat or be eaten, was the law; and this mandate, down out of the depths of Time, he obeyed.

The editor of the *Saturday Evening Post* read the story and accepted it. Then, in March, Macmillan offered to buy the story and bring it out as a book. The company would pay Jack two thousand dollars.

Jack agreed to the terms, happy to receive more money than his writing had ever earned before. To his surprise, on the day *The Call of the Wild* was published, every single copy—ten thousand in all—sold.

Jack had not realized how famous he had become. Not only was he well known for his stories, but he was also creating a sensation with his private life. To the public, he represented a new kind of writer—

someone who lived through danger and hardship, who dared to experience the world. *The Call of the Wild* became a best-seller and made Jack London famous all over the world.

AN ESCAPE TO JAPAN

In 1903 Jack prepared again for adventure. Another war was brewing far away, this time between Russia and Japan. The two countries were rivals for power in Korea and Manchuria, a region in the far northeast of China. Four news agencies asked Jack to go overseas and cover the war. Jack accepted the offer from the Hearst news organization. In early 1904, he sailed across the Pacific Ocean to Yokohama, Japan.

Jack had seen the busy port of Yokohama once before, as a sixteen-year-old novice seaman aboard the *Sophia Sutherland.* Now, at age twenty-eight, he was a world-famous writer. Yet military officials in Japan paid him no more respect than they did any other foreigner. They told Jack to remain in Japan while the Japanese and Russian armies fought in Korea. Like the other reporters, he must wait for information from Japanese officials and report what they chose to tell him about the war.

Jack was determined to get to the fighting, no matter what the expense or danger and no matter what the officials said. From Yokohama, he hired a junk, a small ship used by traders and fishers in eastern Asia. With a small crew of Japanese sailors, Jack skippered the junk through rough seas and cold winds to the coast of Korea.

When the boat landed, Jack hired a horse and a small team of packhorses to carry his equipment. He also hired a Korean man named Manyoungi to cook and interpret for him. Traveling through Korea, Jack nearly made it to the Yalu River, the front line of the war, where the Japanese soldiers were driving back the Russian army.

Jack's progress toward the front line didn't make Japanese officials—or rival reporters—very happy. The foreign reporters who were still in Tokyo complained about him, and the Japanese government ordered Jack to leave Korea. Although Jack had sent a few reports and photographs to the Hearst newspapers, he felt

Jack wanted an active role as a reporter in Japan. He sneaked into Korea, where he camped in freezing temperatures to write about the war.

that he hadn't accomplished the job he came to do. Angry and frustrated, he lashed out at a Japanese servant whom he had caught trying to steal. He was arrested by Japanese military police, who threatened

ONE WRITER'S OPINION

Jack London's dispatches from the Russo-Japanese War provided good copy—and strong opinion—for the Hearst newspaper chain, the most powerful media company of the time. Jack made no attempt to stay impartial in his writing, since the Hearst chain never claimed to be an unbiased source of information for its readers. Instead, it proudly reflected the nationalistic, sometimes racist, patriotism of its owner, William Randolph Hearst.

To the disappointment of many of his friends, Jack's articles from Asia fit Hearst's agenda well. In one story, Jack praised a group of Russian prisoners, whom he saw as men of his own kind. He harshly belittled their Japanese captors, on whom he looked down as an inferior "yellow" race. And when Jack hired an Asian servant during his journey through Korea, he angered his Socialist comrades, who saw the action as typical of a wealthy, corrupt capitalist.

Jack's books and articles reveal that he did not believe in the equality of all races and nationalities. Instead, he praised the accomplishments of "Anglo-Saxons" like himself and warned of the threat posed by immigration and "interbreeding" of the races. Some of London's biographers believe that these racist opinions stem from shame over his own origins as the illegitimate son of William Chaney, the shiftless and irresponsible father whom he never met.

Charmian Kittredge

to execute him for striking a Japanese citizen.

Another American reporter, Richard Harding Davis, heard about Jack's trouble and telegraphed the news to the United States. President Theodore Roosevelt sent a strong message to the Japanese government on Jack's behalf. Roosevelt's intervention saved Jack from a military trial, but the Japanese government expelled him from Korea.

Soon after reaching Japan, Jack took a steamer back to the United States. But he found trouble waiting for him at home, too. Bess was asking for a divorce. She claimed that Jack was spending time with Anna Strunsky and neglecting his family. She suspected that Jack was in love with Anna.

Jack was in love—but not with the woman Bess suspected. He had begun a relationship with Charmian Kittredge, whom he had met before he married Bess. Charmian had helped Jack type and revise many of his stories. When Jack returned from Japan, she was working on his new book, *The Sea-Wolf*, typing the manuscript while his friend George Sterling edited it.

As much as they could, Charmian and Jack kept their love affair a secret. If word got around that she was dating a married man, Charmian would be shamed in the eyes of her friends and family. But the couple took every opportunity they could to be together. On November 18, 1905, Jack and Bess's divorce became official. The very next day, in Chicago, Illinois, Jack and Charmian were married.

SETTING OFF THE REVOLUTION

At the time of his marriage, Jack was traveling across the country on a lecture tour. He told audiences in many cities about his Socialist beliefs. He blamed capitalism for the poverty and injustice he had seen in the United States and England. He took special pleasure in accusing well-to-do audiences of exploiting the poor. On one occasion, he declared, "We want all that you possess. We will be content with nothing less than all that you possess. We want in our hands the reins of power and the destiny of mankind."

To many Americans, Jack's support of socialism and his predictions of revolution sounded like threats. His instant marriage to Charmian after his divorce also made him notorious. Many people saw him as a dangerous radical, and immoral to boot. His reputation also suffered from his occasional heavy drinking at his Wednesday-night parties. Some newspapers and magazines refused to print his stories. Some public libraries banned his books.

Other people agreed with Jack's political opinions and cheered him on. "Progressive" writers and politicians wanted to make radical changes in the way business was conducted in the United States. They wanted to improve conditions for workers, many of whom labored twelve or fourteen hours a day in dangerous conditions for low wages. The Progressive movement stood against business monopolies, in which powerful companies controlled the production of commodities such as sugar or oil. Not all people who called themselves Progressive wanted a Socialist revolution. But most Progressives favored a more just system in which the wealthy would not always benefit at the expense of the poor.

Jack also understood the potential dangers of a revolution. In 1906 his fears inspired him to write a book that predicted a violent future for the United States. In *The Iron Heel,* the United States becomes a dictatorship controlling all of North America. Socialists are killed or put in prison. In the end, the workers revolt, and a war between the classes destroys everything. Jack modeled *The Iron Heel* on the works of English writer H. G. Wells, who wrote *The War of the Worlds* and other futuristic books.

What would finally set off the revolution? Jack thought it might be some kind of devastating natural

After the San Francisco earthquake, Jack rushed down to the devastated city and took pictures, including this one.

disaster. On April 18, 1906, while he was working on *The Iron Heel*, he witnessed such a disaster. That morning, Jack felt the walls and floor of his house begin to tremble. Suddenly, there was a great shaking, lasting nearly a minute. Jack ran outside. Cracks opened in the stone foundation of his house, and a small barn on his property collapsed. He looked across the hills to San Francisco Bay and realized what had happened. A powerful earthquake had struck San Francisco and the surrounding area. Gas explosions had started hundreds of fires all over San Francisco.

The destruction Jack saw in San Francisco made him stop and think about what he was doing with his life. He decided he would try something new: He set himself to the task of becoming a successful farmer. The year before, he had bought a small ranch in the hills above Oakland, near the town of Glen Ellen. He would raise horses and perhaps some cattle. He would tend to his orchards, buy more property when he could, conserve the land and make it bloom.

The Snark took shape slowly. Materials arrived late, and the earthquake caused a rise in the cost of materials and workers.

BUILDING THE *SNARK*

Jack and Charmian also had plans for another great adventure: a sailing trip around the world. They would cross the Pacific Ocean, see Australia and India, explore the tropical coasts of Africa, and navigate the canals of Europe. After crossing the Atlantic Ocean, they would head to Niagara Falls and sail the Great Lakes. To fulfill this dream, Jack planned to build a strong, seaworthy vessel—a forty-five-foot ketch (a ship with one tall forward mast and a smaller mast at the stern, or rear).

He hired boatbuilders and carpenters from all over the Bay Area, bought costly timber from Washington State for the decking, and shipped a seventy-horsepower engine from New York City. When the boat was finished, in April 1907, it had cost more than $30,000.

Jack named his new boat the *Snark,* after an imaginary animal invented by Lewis Carroll, the author of
Alice in Wonderland.

After many months of work and planning, the *Snark*
was finally ready to sail. Jack hired a small crew for
the trip. Roscoe Eames would be the navigator. Herbert
Stoltz, a college student, would tend to the engine.
Another student, Martin Johnson, would serve as cook.

On April 12, 1907, the *Snark* headed out of San
Francisco Bay. The voyage around the world would pit
Jack against the most dangerous enemy he had ever
faced: the wide, empty ocean. Even better, he was
again setting himself apart from the workaday world,
living the way he wanted, independent and free.

*Jack and Charmian posed
for a photograph as they
planned the* Snark *trip.
This was one of their
favorite photos.*

The crew of the Snark, with Jack at the wheel, Charmian,
seated, right, *and Roscoe Eames, Charmian's uncle,* far right

Chapter **SIX**

LIFE IN THE PACIFIC

As they set out across the Pacific Ocean, the crew of the *Snark* soon discovered that the boat was not as strong and seaworthy as Jack had thought. The hull planks leaked, allowing water into the hold and the engine compartment. The engine itself was not operating properly. And seawater and leaking gasoline dripped into the ship's storage compartments, spoiling the supply of fresh fruit and vegetables.

Come what may, Jack still found time every morning to produce his thousand words. While the *Snark* made its way across the Pacific, Jack worked on a novel about a young, poor sailor who vows to become a famous writer. He finally achieves his goal but finds that fame is not what he expected. In many ways, this book, titled *Martin Eden,* was the story of Jack's own life.

After six weeks, the *Snark* reached the Hawaiian Islands. The crew stayed in Hawaii for five months, taking advantage of many offers to stay with planters and ranchers who were eager to spend time with the famous Jack London. When they weren't visiting a private home, Jack and Charmian lived in a cottage in Pearl Harbor, on the island of Oahu. On horseback, Jack and Charmian took riding tours through lush tropical valleys and around the volcanic craters of Kilauea and Haleakala.

Jack, right, *found out that Roscoe Eames did not know how to navigate. So Jack gave himself a crash course and soon mastered the art of navigation.*

In the early 1900s, surfing, the traditional sport of Hawaii, was still unknown in the mainland United States. Jack caught on fast.

Jack also learned how to surf from Alexander Hume Ford, a promoter who was determined to make Hawaii a vacation spot for tourists from the U.S. mainland. After Jack left Hawaii, he and Ford wrote articles about surfing that helped draw visitors to the islands. The articles also inspired people in California to try surfing there for the first time.

Before leaving Hawaii, Jack told Roscoe Eames and Herbert Stoltz that he would pay for their passage back to California. He hired a new skipper and crew for the *Snark*. Only Martin Johnson stayed on, since he seemed capable of handling the hardships of a long ocean voyage. In October 1907, the *Snark* weighed anchor and left Hawaii.

A Tour of Polynesia

The *Snark* headed for the Marquesas Islands, two thousand miles south of Hawaii. Each morning, Jack carefully measured his position with a sextant (a navigation device used to determine position at sea) and marked his course on charts of the Pacific. The crew then ate breakfast from their stores of fresh fruit and vegetables and repaired any damage to the ship from wind or water.

The *Snark* spent several weeks weathering storms, contrary winds, and engine problems. At one point, the wind dropped entirely—the boat was in the doldrums, a part of the ocean near the equator where the winds might shift or stay dead calm for weeks. No shipping lanes crossed this region, and for weeks the crew of the *Snark* did not spot a single vessel.

After two months, the *Snark* finally reached the Marquesas safely. Here, two generations earlier, the writer Herman Melville had lived among a tribe of cannibals, an experience he described in the adventure tale *Typee*. Jack traveled on horseback to the village of Typee but found only a small, pitiful group of people, sick from tuberculosis, leprosy, and other diseases brought by missionaries, sailors, and other outsiders.

On December 26, the *Snark* called at the port of Papeete, on the island of Tahiti, where a large package of mail had arrived for the crew. Letters from Charmian's aunt, Ninetta Eames, and others gave Jack some bad news. Rumors were circulating that the

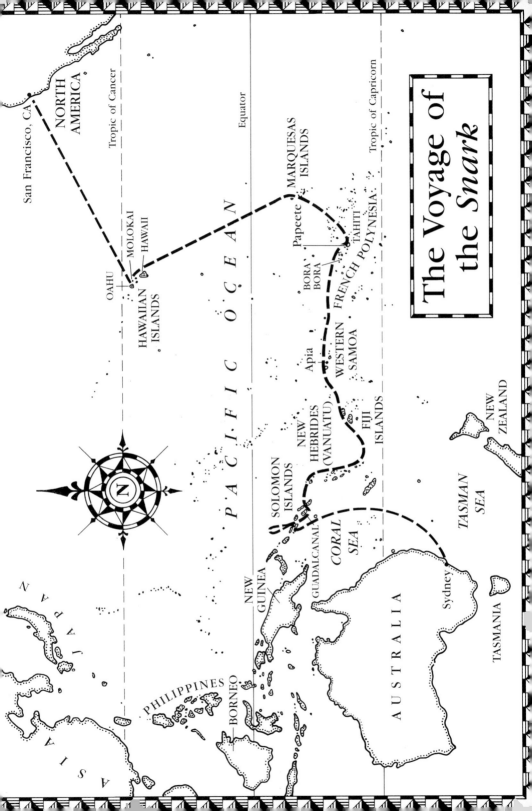

The cabin where Jack and Charmian stayed on Papeete

Snark had gone down and Jack was dead. Believing the story, a bank had taken possession of the house where Jack's mother, Flora, was living. Jack also learned that Ninetta Eames was mismanaging his business affairs—he was nearly out of money. He knew he must return home to straighten things out.

On January 13, 1908, Jack and Charmian left Papeete on the *Mariposa*, a steamship that ran between Tahiti and California. Jack felt depressed and frustrated about having to leave the *Snark* and interrupt his trip. In the book he was writing, *Martin Eden,* he supplied a dark, unhappy ending for the hero, who kills himself by jumping off the *Mariposa:*

> Down, down he swam till his arms and legs grew
> tired and hardly moved. He knew that he was
> deep. . . . His endurance was faltering, but he
> compelled his arms and legs to drive him deeper
> until his will snapped and the air drove from his
> lungs in a great explosive rush. . . . There was a

long rumble of sound, and it seemed to him that he was falling down a vast and interminable stairway. And somewhere at the bottom he fell into darkness.

JACK LONDON EXPLAINS

By 1907 Jack London had reached the status of a nationwide celebrity. This meant recognition, which he had always craved, but it also meant that his every action was reported, analyzed, and criticized. The voyage of the *Snark* was one undertaking that received a large share of the criticism. To many, it seemed like nothing more than the useless whim of an idle, rich man. Seeing himself described this way, Jack felt he had to explain. Charmian London, in her memoir, *The Book of Jack London*, quotes him:

Our friends cannot understand why we make this voyage. . . . They shudder, and moan, and raise their hands. No amount of explanation can make them understand that we are taking the line of least resistance; that it is easier for them to remain on dry land than it is to go down to the sea in a small ship. . . .

Personal achievement, with me, must be concrete. I'd rather win a water-fight in a swimming pool, or remain astride a horse that is trying to get out from under me, than write the great American novel. . . . That is why I am building the *Snark*. I am so made. I like it, that is all.

In real life, Jack and the *Mariposa* arrived in California at the end of January. Jack spent a week trying to put his affairs in order. He secured a loan from George Brett, to be paid off by the money earned from sales of *Martin Eden*. He spent a few days with his ex-wife, Bess, and his daughters Joan, who was now seven, and little Bess, called Becky, who was five. Then he and Charmian sailed away again.

Back in Tahiti, the *Snark* set out for the islands of Bora Bora and Western Samoa. In Samoa, the crew lived in the town of Apia, the largest in Polynesia. Jack and Charmian stayed in a fine old house called Vailima, which had once belonged to Robert Louis Stevenson, the author of *Treasure Island*. Stevenson had died there in 1894 and was buried on a mountainside, 1,300 feet above the house.

When the *Snark* reached the Fiji Islands, Jack fired the new captain, James Warren, who had proved to be bad tempered and a poor navigator. Instead of hiring another skipper, Jack decided to pilot the boat himself. He sailed farther east to the New Hebrides Islands and then to the Solomon Islands, northeast of Australia. On the island of Guadalcanal, the owner of a plantation called Pendruffyn invited Jack and the crew of the *Snark* to stay. The guests were treated to a grand party celebrating the great author's arrival.

Life in the Solomons was not always so festive. In this region, white plantation owners kidnapped island people and worked them as slaves. The owners broke up families and ignored the native people's suffering. In turn, the native islanders raided sailing vessels such as the *Snark,* killing the crews and looting the cargo. Cannibal tribes also lived in these islands and were eager to capture white heads, which they displayed as trophies.

Among the crew members of the *Snark,* the relentless tropical heat and the poor food were causing

Jack and Charmian lived at Robert Louis Stevenson's former home, Vailima, above, while in Apia, Polynesia.

When Jack was too weak or sick to pilot the Snark, *Charmian took the wheel.*

illnesses and short tempers. The crew suffered dangerous fevers and tropical diseases. Charmian came down with malaria, while Jack had yaws, a painful skin disease. There were no doctors available, so he treated himself by applying mercury, a metallic element, to his skin. At the time, many people considered mercury an effective treatment for skin diseases. What Jack and most doctors did not know is that mercury is a deadly poison. By using it, he was slowly but surely killing himself.

THE LAST DAYS OF THE *SNARK*

Although he was ill and exhausted, Jack still sought out new adventures. When Captain Jansen of the sailing vessel *Minota* invited Jack and Charmian aboard for a hunting expedition, they agreed. The *Minota's* quarry was not fish or big game. Instead, its crew hunted humans—islanders to sell as laborers to plantation owners in Australia. Since the islanders lived as headhunters, Jack and Charmian could find themselves in trouble if anything should happen to the *Minota.*

The *Minota* approached the island of Malu on August 19, 1908. Changing winds and tricky currents drove the boat onto an underwater reef. As Jack and Charmian watched from behind the barbed wire that had been rigged up on the sides of the deck, a group of canoes set out from the shore of the island and began circling them. The people of Malu waited patiently for the *Minota* to break up on the sharp reef. If Captain Jansen could not free the boat from the reef, the islanders would attack and loot the boat. The captain ordered the ship's guns taken out of storage, and the crew prepared to defend themselves.

Seeing the *Minota* in distress, a local missionary, St. George Caulfield, came out to help. Using Caulfield as an interpreter, Jack offered a bribe of tobacco to any islander who would go to a nearby ship, the *Eugenie,* for help. One man agreed, and in a short time the *Eugenie* appeared. For hours, the crews of the two boats struggled to free the *Minota* from the reef. The next day, Jack and Charmian boarded the *Eugenie,* which brought them back to the *Snark.* Not until August 21, two days after arriving at Malu, did the *Minota* finally clear the reef and head for home.

Once again, Jack had escaped danger. But poor health was now endangering him as well as his wife and Martin Johnson. Jack suffered an attack of

Before leaving the Minota, below, *Charmian packed Jack's manuscripts and their clothing.*

malaria. And when his skin began peeling away from his hands, he feared that he had caught leprosy while visiting a leper colony on the Hawaiian island of Molo-kai. He applied more mercury compounds to his skin.

Back at Pendruffyn, Jack decided to sail for Sydney, Australia, where he, Charmian, and Martin Johnson could get professional treatment for their health problems. Finally under the care of a doctor, Jack was treated with arsenic, another poison, to cure his yaws. Much to his relief, the doctors told him that he did not have leprosy.

Still feeling weak and depressed, and unwilling to face a long voyage to Africa and Europe, Jack decided to end the trip. He was still young, only thirty-two years old, but his body was beginning to break down. He and Charmian would return to the United States. Meanwhile, Martin Johnson returned to the Solomon Islands, retrieved the *Snark*, and sailed it to Australia. There, the boat—the symbol of Jack's dreams of freedom and adventure—was sold for three thousand dollars, one-tenth of what it had cost to build. It began a new career as an island raider, used by plundering plantation owners to entrap the native people of the South Seas for forced labor.

Jack loved facing new challenges. Establishing his ranch fed his need for another adventure.

Chapter SEVEN

BACK HOME

IN AUSTRALIA, JACK AND CHARMIAN SIGNED ON TO work their way home aboard a collier (coal-hauling) ship, the *Tymeric*. Jack worked as a purser, keeping track of passenger tickets, money, and valuables, while Charmian was a stewardess. After sailing to Ecuador, South America, they boarded other ships for passage to Panama and then to New Orleans. Finally, they returned to their ranch near Oakland in July 1909.

Jack settled down and tried to recover from the long, hard-luck voyage of the *Snark*. Instead of occupying himself with ocean currents, navigation, and the Pacific islands, he would concentrate on writing. One of his new stories, "A Piece of Steak," turned out to be one of his best. In "A Piece of Steak," an aging boxer must win a fight against a much younger man—not to gain glory and acclaim but simply to feed himself and his family. Jack could have been describing himself:

> He tired easily now. No longer could he do a fast twenty rounds, hammer and tongs, fierce rally, beaten to the ropes and in turn beating his opponent to the ropes, and rallying fiercest and fastest of all in that last, twentieth round, with the house on its feet and yelling, himself rushing, striking, ducking, raining showers of blows in return, and all the time the heart faithfully pumping the surging blood.

Jack sold "A Piece of Steak" to the *Saturday Evening Post*, which had already printed many of his stories. He knew that he could still sell whatever he wrote and that he could depend on editors to choose him over unknown writers. He was the most popular and best-paid writer in the United States, and he was winning a reputation abroad with translations of his work into many foreign languages. He was a favorite in France, Germany, and Russia.

THE DEATH OF JOY

Sure of his future, Jack bought more land and livestock. He planted thousands of eucalyptus trees and hired workers to tend his livestock and orchards. He made plans to build a new house, a fabulous mansion of stone and redwood that he would call Wolf House after his old nickname, Wolf.

Jack and Charmian also planned for a family. Just before Christmas, 1909, Charmian discovered that she was pregnant. On June 19, she gave birth to a daughter, named Joy. But the difficult delivery hurt the baby. After a single day, Joy London died.

On that day, Jack was preparing to cover a championship boxing match for the New York *Herald*. The loss of his daughter left him feeling depressed, bitter, and regretful. After walking into a bar on the Oakland waterfront, he got into a fierce argument with the bartender, Timothy Muldowney. Thinking that Jack was some kind of peddler or quack doctor, Muldowney shouted at him to leave. The two men came to blows, punching each other and wrestling as other people watched and cheered. Police arrived to break up the fight and threw Jack and Muldowney in jail. They were released soon afterward, and a local judge dismissed the case. But getting into a fight on the day of his baby daughter's death earned Jack more harsh criticism in newspapers all over the country.

The death of Joy and the fight with Muldowney marked low points in Jack London's life. To ease his physical pain and depression, he began drinking heavily, which gave him headaches and insomnia. He also began giving himself injections of Salvarsan, a new drug that contained arsenic. Medical journals

Shortly after Joy's death, Jack joined other reporters in covering the Jackson-Jeffries boxing match. Jack is fifth from the right in the second row, facing forward.

claimed that Salvarsan was a miracle cure for many ailments. In fact, it attacked the bladder and kidneys and caused depression and weight gain. Jack's self-administered cure weakened him even further.

Jack began to see himself and his illnesses as the

real cause of his daughter's death. Feeling guilty and angry at his misfortune, he argued with guests, flew into rages, and endured many sleepless nights. He felt ashamed about his failing health, knowing that his body had once been strong and healthy enough to withstand any climate, illness, or rough handling. The many injuries he had suffered over a lifetime of outdoor living caught up with him, and often he could barely stand or walk. To help ease his guilt, he wrote a book called *John Barleycorn*, a description of his struggle to overcome alcoholism.

A Last Voyage around the Horn

In the winter of 1911, Jack and Charmian planned another adventure. This time they would sail around Cape Horn, at the southern tip of South America, on a large ship, the *Dirigo*. The Panama Canal was almost finished. When it opened, seagoing vessels would be able to cut across Central America instead of making the hazardous trip around the Horn. In the future, few ships or sailors would sail that route.

The *Dirigo* was leaving from Baltimore, Maryland. Charmian and Jack traveled by train to the East Coast. In March 1912, the voyage began. The trip lasted five months, during which Jack stopped drinking and stopped using Salvarsan. By the time they were back in California, he was feeling better. But shortly after she returned home, Charmian suffered a miscarriage and lost the baby she was expecting. Jack realized that he would never have the son he had always wanted.

Even though Jack often received bad press, he was still in demand by the editors of national magazines and the public. In November 1912, he signed a contract with *Cosmopolitan,* a magazine that published news reports, travel pieces, essays, and fiction. He would be paid two thousand dollars a month, and the magazine would have the right to run his novels as serials—in installments. The contract allowed Jack to work on novels instead of short stories. In the next year or so, he wrote three novels, *The Mutiny of the Elsinore, The Little Lady of the Big House,* and *The Star Rover.* But when he read his words in print, he felt disappointed. He realized that he was losing his imagination—his power to create great stories and characters out of his own experiences. For the first time in his life, he felt afraid of the future and of death. To one of his readers, he wrote, "I am all in. The fires of my youth are out. I lie on a mattress grave, in a hospital, spitting out the entrails of my youth night and day. The one last adventure remains to me—the making of my will."

In August 1913, a fire broke out at Wolf House. The house was almost completed, but Jack and Charmian were not living there yet. Jack suspected that a worker or perhaps a jealous Socialist had set the fire, although he couldn't prove it. The redwood beams of the house burned easily, and the turpentine coating on

Jack never discovered how the fire started at Wolf House.

the beams spread the flames so fast that nothing could stop the fire. Before it was even finished, Wolf House burned to the ground, leaving nothing behind but stone walls, chimneys, and the ashes of a dream.

Jack aboard his sailboat, the Roamer

Chapter **EIGHT**

FINAL ADVENTURES

FOR MANY PEOPLE IN THE UNITED STATES, JACK London still symbolized youthful courage and vigor. And when important and dangerous events happened in foreign countries, many magazine and newspaper editors thought of Jack London. They were sure that the nation's most famous author covering a risky foreign assignment would guarantee good sales.

In April 1914, *Collier's* magazine asked Jack to go to Mexico and report on the revolution against the dictatorship of Porfirio Díaz. Jack agreed, but the assignment worried Charmian. She knew that Jack's health was failing and that he might not survive the trip. She thought of Ambrose Bierce, one of California's best-known authors. Early in 1914, while traveling on his

Jack met up in Mexico with reporters he had known from the war in Japan. From left to right: *Jack, Frederick Palmer, Richard Harding Davis, and Jimmy Hare.*

own in northern Mexico, Bierce had disappeared— murdered, probably—and had not been seen since. Charmian insisted on accompanying Jack.

With Charmian and his valet, Yoshimatsu Nakata, Jack rode the Sunset Limited train as far as Galveston, Texas. In Galveston, the three intended to board a military transport boat for a short trip across the Gulf of Mexico to Veracruz, a Mexican port. But a serious obstacle came up: Jack's reputation as a Socialist angered the local military commander, General Funston, who would not give him permission to travel. The general believed that Jack had slandered the United States Army in a short essay, "The Good Soldier." In part, the essay read:

> Young men: the lowest aim in your life is to become a soldier. The good soldier never tries to distinguish right from wrong. He never thinks; never reasons; he only obeys. . . . If he is ordered

off as a firing squad to execute a hero or bene-
factor, he fires without hesitation, though he
knows the bullet will pierce the noblest heart that
ever beat in a human breast. . . .

No man can fall lower than a soldier—it is a
depth beneath which we cannot go.

"The Good Soldier" was first published by the *Inter-
national Socialist Review* in October 1913. Socialists in
the United States used "The Good Soldier" to protest
against the military and against U.S. intervention in
foreign countries such as Mexico. The essay appeared
in magazines, newspapers, and even on posters, some
of which credited Jack as the author. In Galveston,
Jack met with General Funston and told him that he
did not write "The Good Soldier." After hearing Jack's
denial, the general allowed Jack and Charmian to
board the transport *Kilpatrick* for Mexico.

Jack may not have written "The Good Soldier," but
in 1911 he *had* written an article supporting the Mexican revolutionaries and criticizing Mexico's landowners and politicians, whom he blamed for the country's
poverty. In 1914 most people believed Jack would
side with the rebels in his reports from Mexico. In
comfortable living rooms across the United States,
Collier's readers waited for a series of daring adventures and narrow escapes, told by the country's most
famous novelist and Socialist firebrand. But they
would be disappointed.

In Mexico, Jack reported that rebels such as Pancho Villa, center left, *and Emiliano Zapata,* center right, *were "half-breeds" who were stirring up trouble for their own advantage.*

In the seven articles he wrote from Mexico, Jack expressed no sympathy for the Mexican revolution. Instead, he cheered on the U.S. military, which was occupying Veracruz to protect American companies doing business there. Jack claimed that most Mexicans opposed the revolution and that Veracruz under American occupation was better off than the rest of Mexico ever would be under rule by the Mexicans themselves.

Jack's articles from Mexico sold many copies of *Collier's*, but they also surprised and angered his friends in the Socialist party. His support of U.S. military intervention confirmed their suspicions: he was spoiled by success and had joined the wealthy, privileged class he had once sworn to overthrow.

A RETURN TO HAWAII

Jack realized that although his career as a roaming reporter might be over, he still had the energy to write one thousand words a day. His daily quota was absolutely necessary, because he had many debts to pay and would need the royalty money from the books he hadn't finished. He was one of the best-known authors in the country, and one of the first to earn money by selling the rights to one of his stories—*The Sea-Wolf*—for use as a motion picture. But he often felt the need to escape on the *Roamer,* his sailboat. He left for the sake of privacy, and sometimes to avoid being taken to court to pay his debts.

The *Roamer* could not take him far enough. In a letter to a friend, Jack reported:

> Instead of winning big at the moving picture game, I am at the present time many thousands of dollars [the] loser, and am doing the most frenzied finance to keep my head above water. I am afraid to go home for fear of having summons served on me. I have been and am being sued right and left. What complicated my serious situation is that, unlike most of you fellows who have only yourselves to care for, I am taking care of many people and running a number of households, all of which people and households are entirely and absolutely dependent upon me for food and shelter.

In early 1915, Jack and Charmian returned to Hawaii, where they had been treated so well while cruising on the *Snark*. They set out in January and stayed for five months, then returned in early 1916.

In Hawaii, Jack tried to rest and recover. But in March, he suffered an attack of nephritis, an inflammation of the kidneys. His body could no longer get rid of poisons, and the pain was so bad that Jack felt sure he was dying. He suffered more bad luck on October 22, when one of his favorite horses died at night in a pasture. Jack grew depressed and silent, sensing that his own death was drawing near. Most of his friends, fearing his rages, no longer came to the house. Jack lived a mostly solitary life, reading quietly in bed and listening to phonograph records. He outlined a last novel that would describe the deaths of five different men. The book was to be called *How We Die*.

Early on the morning of November 22, 1916, Jack gave himself a strong injection of morphine, an addictive, painkilling drug made from opium. He then slipped into a coma. Charmian called a local doctor. With the doctor's advice, Charmian and several of the ranch hands walked Jack back and forth across the room, trying to keep him awake. The doctor pumped his stomach and gave him medications to counteract the morphine. But the morphine Jack had injected was the final blow to a body already weakened by tropical diseases, arsenic treatments, and an un-

Jack a few days before his death, with Charmian

healthy diet. In the evening of November 22, at the age of forty, Jack died on the porch of his house.

Many people, including the doctor who first arrived at the house, believed that Jack London had committed suicide. Most of his friends, knowing that Jack was sick and depressed, also believed that he had deliberately taken a morphine overdose. Others, including Charmian, were sure that he hadn't intended to do himself harm, only to find relief from the terrible pain he suffered. Charmian followed her husband's wishes by having his body cremated. In this way, she prevented an autopsy (medical examination) that might have determined the exact cause of his death. Jack's ashes were placed in an urn, which was buried on a hillside half a mile from his house.

EPILOGUE

JACK LONDON IS FAMILIAR TO MANY READERS AS THE author of short novels such as *White Fang, The Call of the Wild,* and *The Sea-Wolf.* Several of his stories have never gone out of print and they have sold millions of copies around the world. Long after his death, Jack remains the most popular American author in many countries, including Russia.

Many readers don't realize that only some of the fifty books that Jack London wrote are adventure tales. The popular image of Jack as an adventure writer came partly from a myth he told about himself: that he wrote only for money, that adventure tales sold best, and that he was a simple, working-class man with no interest in writing anything profound.

The Roamer was a haven for Jack toward the end of his life.

Much of his work contradicts this myth by expressing a deeply held philosophy of life. Jack carefully developed his philosophy by reading thousands of books and experiencing as much of the world as he possibly could. Jack wrote about an imaginary future in *The Iron Heel*. He wrote an autobiographical novel, *Martin Eden*, and an account of alcoholism, *John Barleycorn*. He wrote an epistolary novel (a novel told through letters) about love, *The Kempton-Wace Letters*. He collected his essays on society in *Revolution*.

Of his own writing, Jack most admired the books that expressed his belief in socialism and the revolution of the working class. He once said that *The People of the Abyss*, his report of conditions in London's East End, was his personal favorite among all his books. Although few of his speeches were recorded, he wrote many essays and articles for Socialist magazines and newspapers. These works reveal a heartfelt commitment to a cause he believed in throughout his life.

SOURCES

12 Clarice Stasz, *American Dreamers: Charmian and Jack London* (New York: St. Martin's Press, 1988), 39.

13 Robert Barltrop, *Jack London: The Man, the Writer, the Rebel* (London: Pluto Press, 1976), 20.

20 Jack London, *The Sea-Wolf* (New York: Chatham River Press, 1980), 642.

27 Russ Kingman, *A Pictorial Life of Jack London* (New York: Crown Publishers, Inc., 1979), 53.

42 Ibid., 83.

43 Jack London, "To the Man on Trail," Greenwich Unabridged Library Classics (New York: Chatham River Press distributed by Crown Publishers, 1980), 244.

48 King Hendricks and Irving Shepard, eds., *Letters from Jack London: Containing an Unpublished Correspondence Between London and Sinclair Lewis* (New York: Odyssey Press, 1965), 108.

49 Jack London, *To Build a Fire and Other Stories,* selected by Donald Pizer (New York: Bantam Books, 1986), 44.

58–59 Jack London, *The People of the Abyss* (London: The Journeyman Press, 1977), 13.

62 Jack London, *The Call of the Wild and Other Works,* Greenwich Unabridged Library Classics (New York: Chatham River Press distributed by Crown Publishers, 1980), 56–58.

67 Andrew Sinclair, *Jack: A Biography of Jack London* (New York: Harper & Row, 1977), 127.

78–79 Jack London, *Martin Eden* (New York: Penguin Books, 1984), 482.

88 London, *To Build a Fire,* 253.

92 Sinclair, 192.

96–97 Barltrop, 156.

99 Hendricks and Shepard, 443.

BIBLIOGRAPHY

Barltrop, Robert. *Jack London: The Man, the Writer, the Rebel.* London: Pluto Press, 1976.

Dyer, Daniel. *Jack London: A Biography.* New York: Scholastic Press, 1997.

Hendricks, King, and Irving Shepard, eds. *Letters from Jack London.* New York: Odyssey Press, 1965.

Kershaw, Alex. *Jack London: A Life.* New York: St. Martin's Press, 1998.

Kingman, Russ. *A Pictorial Life of Jack London.* New York: Crown Publishers, Inc., 1979.

Labor, Earle. *Jack London.* New York: Twayne, 1974.

London, Jack. *The Call of the Wild and Other Works.* New York: Chatham River Press, 1980.

London, Jack. *To Build a Fire and Other Stories.* Selected by Donald Pizer. New York: Bantam Books, 1986.

O'Connor, Richard. *Jack London: A Biography.* Boston: Little Brown & Co., 1964.

Sinclair, Andrew. *Jack: A Biography of Jack London.* New York: Harper & Row, 1977.

Stasz, Clarice. *American Dreamers: Charmian and Jack London.* New York: St. Martin's Press, 1988.

Stone, Irving. *Irving Stone's Jack London: His Life, Sailor on Horseback (A Biography) and Twenty-Eight Selected Jack London Stories.* Garden City, NY: Doubleday, 1977.

Stone, Irving. *Sailor on Horseback: The Biography of Jack London.* Boston: Houghton Mifflin, 1938.

SELECTED WORKS OF JACK LONDON

NOVELS

The Call of the Wild (1903)
The Sea-Wolf (1904)
The Game (1905)
White Fang (1906)
The Iron Heel (1907)
Martin Eden (1909)
The Valley of the Moon (1913)

ESSAYS AND JOURNALISM

The People of the Abyss (1903)
Revolution and Other Essays (1910)
The Cruise of the "Snark" (1911)
John Barleycorn (1913)

SHORT STORIES AND SHORT STORY COLLECTIONS

To the Men on Trail (1899)
The White Silence (1899)
In a Far Country (1900)
An Odyssey of the North (1900)
The Son of the Wolf (1900)
The God of His Fathers (1901)
Batard (1902)
Children of the Frost (1902)
The Faith of Men (1904)
Tales of the Fish Patrol (1905)
Moon-Face and Other Stories (1906)
To Build a Fire (1910)
The Gold Hunters of the North (1912)

INDEX

OTHER TITLES FROM LERNER AND A&E®:

Arthur Ashe
Bill Gates
Bruce Lee
Carl Sagan
Chief Crazy Horse
Christopher Reeve
Eleanor Roosevelt
George Lucas
Gloria Estefan
Jacques Cousteau
Jesse Owens
Jesse Ventura
John Glenn
Legends of Dracula
Legends of Santa Claus

Louisa May Alcott
Madeleine Albright
Maya Angelou
Mohandas Gandhi
Mother Teresa
Nelson Mandela
Princess Diana
Queen Cleopatra
Queen Latifah
Rosie O'Donnell
Saint Joan of Arc
Wilma Rudolph
Women in Space
Women of the Wild West

ABOUT THE AUTHOR

Tom Streissguth lives in Florida and works as a writer and editor. He has written more than twenty-five nonfiction books for young people, including biographies and books on history. His volumes in the BIOGRAPHY® series include *Legends of Dracula, Jesse Owens, Queen Cleopatra,* and *John Glenn.* Tom has also written scripts for television.

PHOTO ACKNOWLEDGMENTS

Library of Congress, 2, 26; © California State Parks, Jack London Collection, 6, 10, 53, 66, 71, 74, 82, 104; Archive Photos, 9, 40, 94, 98; The Oakland History Room, Oakland Public Library, 14, 31; The Huntington Library, San Marino, CA, 17, 38, 51, 57, 59, 64, 69, 70, 72, 78, 84, 90, 93, 102; San Francisco Maritime National Historical Park, L. Weule, 18; © CORBIS-Bettman, 20; © CORBIS/Bettman-UPI, 25, 54; Jack London Collection, Special Collections and Archives, Utah State University, 28, 46, 60, 86, 101; National Archives and Records Administration-Pacific Alaska Region (Anchorage), 35; Independent Picture Service, 48; © Hulton-Deutsch Collection/CORBIS, 56; Bishop Museum, 75; The Writers' Museum, Edinburgh, 81; © Baldwin H. Ward & Kathryn C. Ward/CORBIS, 96.

Front cover: Jack London Collection, Special Collections and Archives, Utah State University
Back cover: Jack London Collection, Special Collections and Archives, Utah State University

jB
LONDON

Streissguth, Thomas.

Jack London.

$25.26